THE TIME OF
JACOB'S
TROUBLE

DONNA VANLIERE

HARVEST HOUSE PUBLISHERS
EUGENE, OREGON

Cover design by Faceout Studio

Cover photo © photosforlive, aspen rock, caesart, Marilyn Volan, Volodymyr Burdiak, Songquan Deng, Matej Kastelic, Mrs.Moon, studioalef / Shutterstock

The Time of Jacob's Trouble
Copyright © 2020 by Donna VanLiere
Published by Harvest House Publishers
Eugene, Oregon 97408
www.harvesthousepublishers.com

ISBN 978-0-7369-7875-0 (pbk)
ISBN 978-0-7369-7876-7 (eBook)

Library of Congress Cataloging-in-Publication Data

Names: VanLiere, Donna, author.
Title: The time of Jacob's trouble / Donna VanLiere.
Description: Eugene, Oregon : Harvest House Publishers, [2020].
Identifiers: LCCN 2019020314 (print) | LCCN 2019021531 (ebook) | ISBN 9780736978767 (ebook) | ISBN 9780736978750 (softcover)
Subjects: LCSH: Rapture (Christian eschatology)--Fiction. | GSAFD: Christian fiction.
Classification: LCC PS3622.A66 (ebook) | LCC PS3622.A66 T56 2019 (print) | DDC 813/.6--dc23
LC record available at https://lccn.loc.gov/2019020314

Printed in the United States of America

20 21 22 23 24 25 26 27 28 / BP-SK / 10 9 8 7 6 5 4 3 2 1

For Terrie Carswell,
my longtime friend, who is looking up!

THE TIME OF
JACOB'S
TROUBLE

I make known the end from the beginning,
    from ancient times, what is still to come.
I say, "My purpose will stand,
    and I will do all that I please"…
What I have said, that I will bring about;
    what I have planned, that I will do.

ISAIAH 46:10-11

"I am the LORD. That is my name…
The things I said would happen have happened,
    and now I tell you about new things.
Before those things happen,
    I tell you about them."

ISAIAH 42:8-9 (NCV)

CHAPTER 1

Queens, NY

W e have to get out of the city!" twenty-five-year-old Emma Grady shouts, watching images of destruction on the TV.

Her boyfriend Matt grabs her arm, yelling as he pulls her to the door. "No time! Get to the basement!"

They scream and yell through the hallway, warning people in the other six apartments. Emma stops at the apartment at the end of the hall, banging on the door. A young Indian woman opens it when she sees Emma through the peephole. "Piya! Get your family to the basement."

The young mother is frightened and shaking. She has been up all night. "We have to evacuate," Piya says, her words quivering from terror.

Emma grabs her hands. "Please! You won't make it out of the city!"

Matt runs ahead, banging on doors and shouting a warning as they speed down the stairs. The sound of glass shatters above them and the building quakes, shattering their nerves. The air is pierced with indescribable fear as the apartment building basement fills with eighteen residents, each clinging to loved ones and the stranger next to them. The explosion is deafening, crumbling the ceiling above and shaking the walls. The lights flicker for several seconds before thrusting the room into darkness, shrieks and screams slicing through the black.

CHAPTER 2

Queens, NY—one week earlier

E mma tiptoes out of the bathroom, passing Matt, still sleeping, before pulling the bedroom door closed. She's careful not to make noise in the hall as she steps to the kitchen for a cup of coffee. Matt has been working the late shift at Demarco's, a restaurant in Midtown, while he finishes his law degree during the day. Their schedules rarely afford them the time to see much of each other. Emma leaves the apartment each day at 7:00 a.m., arriving at work thirty minutes early to help prep the physical therapy room. She's worked as a physical therapist at Thrive Rehabilitation in Brooklyn for two years, and while Matt and several friends groan at the prospect of going to their jobs, she loves her work and looks forward to seeing her patients.

She puts a K-Cup into the single-cup coffeemaker, closes the lid, and presses *brew* on the machine. The coffee begins to stream into her travel mug as her phone buzzes. She reaches for it and reads a text from her sister, Sarah. *Call me later. Mom and I are sampling reception food after work today!!!*

Emma texts, *K. Will call on my break. Have fun!*

Sarah is three years younger and getting married. Emma is happy for her; Jason seems great, but there's some part of her, somewhere deep and hidden away, that wonders why she isn't the one planning a wedding. She tosses the nagging thought aside, ashamed again to be jealous of her sister for getting married. Growing up in Indiana, Emma was a track and field star at her local high school. She would pull her light brown hair into a high ponytail and race around the track, dreaming of running in college, but too many injuries on the university team cut all those dreams short. Between that and a failed relationship with her college sweetheart, Emma couldn't get out of Indiana fast enough. She met Matt at a bar with some friends her second week in New York, and they seemed destined for one another.

"Are you headed out already?"

She jumps at Matt's voice and turns to see him at the end of the hall, squinting into the light of the kitchen. He's standing in his boxer shorts and his dark brown hair is standing straight up on his head and flat on one side, as if it's been ironed. They dated for six months before deciding to move in together two years ago. Her dad liked Matt but didn't approve of them living together. Her parents were old-fashioned, but she loved them anyway. She had hoped that Matt would get to know her dad better, but he died four months after they moved in together, after a short battle with cancer. She sees his mom often; she lives just over the New York state line in New Jersey, where Matt grew up with an older sister. Matt's mom and dad divorced when he was fourteen, and his relationship with his dad is fragile at best. She's never met him, and Matt rarely speaks of him.

"You scared me!" She reaches for cream out of the refrigerator. "Did I wake you up?"

He walks behind her and reaches his arms around her, kissing her cheek. "Couldn't sleep. Need to study for the exam."

She turns and kisses him. "You'll do great!" She slides an elastic hair tie off her wrist and pulls her hair into a ponytail, then reaches for a banana out of a bowl on the counter. "Don't forget that Rick and Brandon are coming over for drinks tonight."

Matt throws away her used K-Cup, groaning. "After a day of exams and a night at the restaurant, I doubt I'm going to be up for Rick and Brandon."

"You're the one who invited them!" she says, laughing. "I found a new appetizer recipe." He looks at her, bored. "It has bacon in it," she says, her voice tingling with excitement.

"All right," he says, brewing a cup of coffee. "I'm in."

She laughs and waves. "See you later. Love you!"

"Later!" he yells toward her. He didn't say, "I love you." Sometimes he did. Sometimes he didn't. Although she knew he loved her, his love just didn't seem to be "all-in" all the time. Maybe Jason's love for Sarah was all-in all the time. Maybe that's why they were getting married and she and Matt weren't.

Emma is thankful their apartment is so close to the subway, and in just a few minutes, she's headed that way. On many days she walks there with Brandon, who lives upstairs, but he had to be at work earlier than usual today. She uses the time on the subway to read some news on her phone and eat the banana. Neither of her parents would like her hurried routine of grab and go. Her dad had especially liked sitting around the breakfast and dinner table just talking. Her eyes mist over thinking about him, and she scrolls through the news: some red-carpet event has brought out several stars, two new online shows debut tonight, a construction accident will have traffic in knots on the East Side today, people are opposing the mayor's new regulations on small businesses, and President Thomas Banes will meet with the president of China at the Oval Office.

Linda and Carrie are both at the front desk when Emma arrives at Thrive. Linda must be in her fifties; both of her children have recently graduated from college. Carrie is in her thirties with three children in elementary school. She has beautiful dark almond skin, long cornrows, and typically wears a bright scarf tied around her head.

"Hi, Emma," Carrie says, looking over her computer. "It's gonna be a great day!"

Carrie grew up in the foster care system but has somehow managed to turn the pain and hardship of her early life into eternal optimism. She's famous for saying, "God's got this" to employees at the office when their car has broken down, or they are struggling financially, or they need another job. She and Roderick have been married twelve years, and Emma can always tell when she's talking to him on the phone because her laugh, a high-pitched cackle, can be heard throughout the therapy room.

Aliyah, Reggie, and Mateo are busy looking over their patient lists for today. Aliyah has short black hair and skin the color of smooth milk chocolate. She's somewhere in her late twenties and expecting her first child with her boyfriend, Keenan. Reggie is in his forties, from Honduras, and the divorced father of two. He sees his girls every other weekend. He's been a physical therapist for more than twenty years and the one Emma turns to when she needs help with a patient. Mateo is from a large Hispanic family, looks like he's in his late twenties or early thirties, and has a smile as big as his personality.

Emma's first patient will be Art Gleason, a cranky man in his late sixties who makes an hour feel like a day. She is thankful when she sees that Mariana Ramos is coming later in the morning; she always looks forward to seeing her.

Midtown, NY

Elliott Hirsch bounds up the stairs from the subway platform and heads toward the brokerage firm where he's been employed the last two years. Two blocks before the building, he enters a market with the daily specials written on a sidewalk chalkboard. His cell phone begins to ring as he walks through the entrance.

"Hi, Mom!"

"Elliott! You didn't get back with me yesterday about Saba's birthday party."

He pushes his glasses up to the bridge of his nose and makes his way to the back of the market. "Super busy day at work."

"I assumed that's why you didn't call, but Saba's party is coming up, and we need to give a head count of who's coming."

Elliott chuckles, shaking his head. In the twenty-four years he's been on this earth, his mother has never been known for flexibility, and as she's getting older, she's becoming even less so. "His birthday is nine days away. Even if I got back with you three days from now, that would give them six days' notice that I'm coming."

"Well, it would be nice if they knew ahead of time."

"And they will. I promise you. I will look at my calendar and let you know. I need to go. I forgot to grab something for a party at work today. I'm at the market just blocks from the firm, so I'm trying to rush through here." He reaches for a prepackaged cheese platter.

"How about now?"

"What?"

"You're in a market. You're not working at the moment. How about looking at your calendar now?"

He laughs out loud. "Of course! Right here next to the Gorgonzola is perfect." Elliott checks the calendar on his phone, types the information into it, then puts the phone back to his ear. "I'm wide open. So please, on my behalf, would you RSVP *Hirsch party of one* for Saba's birthday?"

"Oh! I'm just thrilled that you can come! Thanks so much for getting back to me."

"You called me, Mom," he says, rushing to the cashier to pay.

"I know! But it was in your heart to call me yesterday." He can hear her on the other end, shuffling papers around, probably figuring out who she needs to call next. "Your father and Ben and I will be heading back to Ohio two days after the party, but hopefully we can all get together with you while we're there."

"You're flying to New York. Of course we'll get together."

"Only if you're not too busy. I mean, it was hard for you to make a phone call yesterday."

He slaps his palm on his forehead. "Mom, you're killing me."

She gasps. "That is not my intention. I just wanted you to know our schedule. Do you need to write it down?"

"I got it." He pushes up his glasses again and places the cheese platter in front of the cashier.

"Wonderful! How's your day, my love?"

"At the moment? A bit hectic. How about yours?" He reaches for his wallet in his back pocket.

"Your father's complaining about some sort of foot condition. What do you think it could be?"

Elliott laughs. "I have no idea!"

"I just wonder if it might be something like you had in high school. Remember?"

He pauses for a moment, remembering. "When I broke my toe playing hockey?"

"Remember how painful that was?"

"Yeah! I broke my toe! Playing hockey! Has dad broken his toe?"

"No."

"Has he been playing hockey?"

She laughs on the other end. "Of course not!"

"Then how is this anything like what happened to me in high school?"

"Because it's a foot problem. *And* it's painful."

He pays the cashier and reaches for the bag. "I don't think I'd make that your lead-in when you visit a doctor with Dad. Love you, Mom."

"I love you, Elliott."

He prepares to hang up when he hears her voice rising. "Oh! Oh! Do you need to write down the date for Saba's party?"

"I already put it on my calendar. Remember?"

"You're sure?"

"I'm sure."

"I'm just asking because Saba's rabbi is going to be there."

"He's my rabbi, too, Mom."

"Oh, that's right. He is! I wondered if you had forgotten."

Elliott sighs, smiling. "I remember the rabbi." Most mothers would be asking about his interest in girls, with the goal of grandchildren in mind, but his mother has always been more concerned about the condition of his soul rather than his love life.

"You know what? I'll call you the day before, in case your computer or phone crashes or there's some sort of cyberattack."

"Love you, Mom." He hangs up before she can take another breath.

Elliott and his brother, Ben, were born in Cleveland and lived there until his dad was transferred to New York, where they settled in Long Island, and Elliott and Ben played hockey in the winter and baseball in the spring. They lived there until their dad was transferred back to Cleveland during Elliott's sophomore year in college, but he stayed in

New York, claiming it as his permanent home. He sees his parents several times a year and talks to them on the phone at least once a week, more if his mother is calling. For the last year he's worked as a purchase and sales clerk at a brokerage firm, hoping that one day he'll become a financial advisor. At twenty-four he's single and lives alone, while Ben, who's two years younger, has traveled Europe and has yet to take a career seriously. The fact is that Ben has always been the outgoing and charismatic one, while Elliott has always been shy, content to bury himself with work. This isn't the life he envisioned in college, but then again, it's not terrible. At least that's what he tells himself.

Mr. Gleason must have been having a better-than-average day because he grumbled only once to Emma about the cost of the therapy and the hassle of dealing with his insurance company and Medicare. When Mariana Ramos arrives for rehab at eleven, Emma is ready for the woman's sweet conversation. Mrs. Ramos and her husband, Miguel, are both in their mid-sixties and own 316 Deli in Brooklyn, known for their Cuban sandwiches, soups, sweet-potato cake, and coconut flan. Emma will often leave the apartment early so she can stop by the deli and pick up one of Mariana's Puerto Rican sweet rolls for breakfast. "No sugar. The secret is honey," Mrs. Ramos said when she brought a sweet roll for her first therapy session.

Mrs. Ramos is reading when Emma opens the door to the waiting room. "Mrs. Ramos?" Emma smiles, noticing a bag in her hand. "I'm pretty sure I smell something delicious in that bag," she says, holding open the door to the therapy room.

"Just a Cuban sweet roll," Mrs. Ramos says, handing the bag to her. "You haven't been by in a while."

Mrs. Ramos's once pepper-black hair is now heavy with salt and resting on the back of her head in a soft bun. Wrinkles edge her mouth and eyes, but Emma thinks she's beautiful and looks much younger than her age. She gives her a quick hug. "It seems I'm running late every morning," Emma says. "Thank you so much!" She leads Mrs. Ramos into the therapy room and sets the bag on the window ledge behind them. Mrs. Ramos sits at the end of the therapy table; Emma puts her hands on her shoulders. "I can say this with all honesty…you are my favorite patient ever!"

Mrs. Ramos throws her head back, chuckling. "I love to feed people, and I love it when they love my food!"

Emma puts a hand on her hip and looks at her. "How's the knee?"

"It's good," Mrs. Ramos says in the soft Puerto Rican accent that Emma so enjoys. A torn meniscus put Mrs. Ramos into surgery and brought her here nearly two months ago for therapy.

"Are you being careful at work?"

"Yes!"

"Honest?"

The petite woman laughs. "Yes, honest! I sit on a stool when I'm rolling out the dough, and I sit on a chair when I work the cash register."

"And you're doing your exercises?"

She nods. "Yes, yes. I'm doing so many exercises I could go to the Olympics." Mrs. Ramos extends her leg as Emma keeps her hands on the knee, feeling the motion.

"What's the latest in the wedding plans?" Mrs. Ramos asks.

Emma tries to smile and makes her voice sound happy. "Sarah and Mom will be trying out caterers today. Can you do ten extensions for me?"

Mrs. Ramos does as she's instructed and smiles. "And how is that cute boyfriend of yours?"

Emma shrugs. "The same. Working hard and going to law school."

"Wedding bells in the future?"

"None that I'm aware of." Emma leans in, whispering, "I'm not sure he's the marrying type. Or maybe I'm not the type he wants to marry."

Mrs. Ramos pats her arm. "That is impossible to believe. God has wonderful plans for you. Sometimes we're just hard-of-hearing."

Emma smiles. Mrs. Ramos reminds her so much of her own mom that she never gets angry or irritated when she brings up God. Somehow, God is a friend to both her mom and Mrs. Ramos, and somewhere deep inside she wishes she could be more like them.

CHAPTER 3

Israel

Twenty-seven-year-old Dr. Zerah Adler gets into his car in the physicians' parking lot at Hadassah Medical Center in Jerusalem and begins the drive to Modiin, eighteen miles west of Jerusalem. He grew up there and thought he would eventually leave, but the parks, countryside, wineries, easy access to the airport, and his family have kept him rooted in the suburbs while other young professionals choose Tel Aviv, Petah Tikva, or some other city boasting high-tech industries. He lives in a small apartment just five miles from his parents.

He drives straight to their home, a small single-story house with a basement, in the neighborhood where Zerah rode his bike on the streets and played basketball and soccer at the park around the corner. When Zerah opens the door, the smell of chicken schnitzel makes him smile. "My favorite!" he says, closing the door.

"Zerah!" His mother Ada walks into the living room, drying her hands on the kitchen towel, the one with the apples printed on it. She grabs his face, kissing his cheek. "So glad you could join us! How was your work today? Come, come," she says, leading him into the kitchen.

He pops a couple of spiced cracked olives into his mouth, nodding. "Good."

His mother opens the oven door, looking inside at her noodle kugel. "Making progress in your research?"

Zerah has been part of a team researching what they hope will be a breakthrough in Parkinson's disease. "I hope." He reaches for some pita

18

bread, tearing off a piece before dipping it into another of his favorites, his mother's famous baba ganoush, careful to get a few slices of Kalamata olives sitting on top of the dip. "Mm! The best," he says. "My whole meal could be this." He scoops another piece of pita into the dip.

"Why do they keep you there so late each evening?"

"*They* don't keep me there. I choose to be there and finish what I've started. Besides, seven-thirty isn't that late," he says, sliding another bite into his mouth.

She taps the face of her watch. "It's eight-o'clock and it's too late if you want to have a family. Little ones go to bed at this time."

Zerah smiles, reaching for a few more spiced olives. "Well, the good thing is I don't have a family right now."

His mother puts the platter of chicken schnitzel on the table. "And you'll never find a woman working these crazy hours."

He sighs in exasperation and changes the subject. "Where's Dad?"

"Downstairs watching the news. He turns it up so loud that I can't hear myself think, so I make him go down there."

Zerah removes the noodle kugel from the oven for his mom and places it on top of hot pads on the kitchen table. Whereas some cooks would take a shortcut and use applesauce in their kugel, his mom always takes the time to grate fresh apples into hers. "Mm," he says, breathing in the aroma. "I'll go get him." He shoves another large bite of the baba ganoush into his mouth before opening the door to the basement. The voice of the newscaster pronouncing doom and gloom over the entire world fills the kitchen and Ada rolls her eyes, shaking her head. Zerah closes the door behind him.

His parents bought this home over twenty years ago because one room in the basement was a bomb shelter, a place that Zerah and his sister Rada ran to many times while they were growing up. One of his earliest memories of a bomb shelter was when he was around seven or so, huddled in a neighbor's shelter playing cards with a girl two or three years older than him. His parents never let him or Rada live in fear; this was simply something that had to be done from time to time. The stark room features nothing more than a small television set, a two-decades-old couch, and a few folding chairs around a small folding table. The walls are still plain and gray, and his dad looks like he's staring at a TV in a sterile waiting room.

Zerah watches as his dad's hand shakes while pointing the remote at the TV. In a cruel twist of irony, his father Chaim was diagnosed with essential tremor, a cousin to Parkinson's disease, just six months after Zerah landed the research position at the university. He has felt helpless, as his medical degrees have done little to help alleviate his father's tremors. "Dad," he says, touching his dad's shoulder. "Dinner's ready."

"Zerah!" his father says, clicking off the TV. "I forgot you were coming! Of course you were. The only time we eat this late is when you're coming."

Zerah hugs his dad. "Not you too! I just took my first round from Mom."

His father laughs. "She's your mom. She worries. Your life is work, work, work." He shrugs. "To your mother that's unnatural. There's an order to things for her." He pats Zerah's cheek. "I've got your back. In the meantime, you keep doing what you're doing. Only wonderful things are ahead!"

Queens, NY

Emma uses earphones to talk with her mother on the phone as she makes the bacon appetizers. "So finger foods are cheaper than an actual meal for the wedding?" she asks, spreading ricotta cheese onto several toasted baguette slices.

"It ends up being about three dollars less a plate," her mom says.

"Uh-huh," Emma says, wanting to be interested. "Has Sarah asked Uncle Robert to walk her down the aisle?" Her heart hurts at the thought of having an uncle walk her sister down the aisle, and she misses her dad all over again.

"She did. He said yes. Your dad would want him to." Emma is quiet, thinking. Her mom has always known when something isn't right, and says, "Is everything all right, Em? Is it the wedding?"

Emma reaches for the slices of cooked bacon, breaking them in half to put on each baguette. "I hope it's not. I mean, I hope I'm not that shallow."

"You've never been shallow. You are my deep well."

Emma smiles. "I'm happy for Sarah. I really am."

"I know you are. And it's okay to be in a funk. That happens a lot as we go through different stages in life and we watch other people go through their stages."

Emma keeps her voice low so Matt can't hear from the bedroom. "I kind of thought that I would be the first one to go through that stage. If you know what I mean," she says, chuckling.

"I know, but this isn't your lane, remember?"

Emma nods as she mixes some honey with a teaspoon of hot sauce, sprinkling some over each slice of bacon on top of the baguette. "I know, I know. I can't run someone else's race. I have to stay in my own lane and run my own race." Ever since she and Sarah were children, her mom has told them that.

Her mom laughs. "You remember!"

"You still say it all the time!" Emma says, biting into the appetizer. "Oh…yum! I think I just made another finger food that would be perfect for the wedding!"

"I wondered what you have been doing. What did you make?"

"A bacon appetizer for Matt, Rick, and Brandon."

"The next time we chat, I'll have to get the recipe from you. I'll let you go. Hug each one of them for me. Love you!"

"Love you, Mom!" She ends the call on her cell phone and puts the other half of the bacon baguette into her mouth.

"How's your mom?" Matt says, putting on a shirt as he walks out of the bedroom.

"She's great. She and Sarah were trying to find a caterer today," she says, holding one of the bacon appetizers in front of Matt.

He takes a bite and quickly reaches for the rest of it from her hand, shoving it into his mouth. "This is amazing! These will totally be worth having Brandon and Rick over."

She smiles, cleaning up the mess she made in the kitchen. "You love Rick and Brandon."

He wraps his arms around her, kissing her. "No. I love *you*. I find *them* amusing. I'd rather be here alone with you tonight."

She's surprised that he said he loved her without her saying it first. "Then why didn't you tell me?" she says, swatting him with a kitchen towel. "I invited them only because it was your idea."

"Why do you listen to me?"

"Maybe because I think you're brilliant and I love you," she says, sticking the unused bacon inside the refrigerator.

He reaches for her arm as she closes the door and pulls her to him. "And I love you." His tone is different; and Emma looks at him, wondering if something is wrong. "Why aren't we the ones getting married?"

"Wha…?" She is stumped, looking into his eyes. "What do you…?"

He laughs. "Seriously! Why aren't we the ones planning a wedding?"

She is confused and tries to put together another sentence. "I don't… You've never said anything about…"

He pulls her tighter. "Marry me, Emma." Her eyes are full of surprise. "Tonight even. Let's just go do it!"

He kisses her, and she begins to laugh. She leans back, looking at him. "Are you serious?"

He holds out his index finger and taps it with the index finger of his other hand. "I love you." He holds out a second finger and taps it. "I want to marry you." A third finger is extended. "I want to marry you tonight."

"Oh my gosh! Matt!" she says with nervous laughter. "Was this because of the bacon?"

"No!" He thinks for a moment. "Well, maybe. Okay, no! It wasn't because of the bacon. It was because I keep hearing you talk about your sister's wedding and I think it's nuts that she's getting married before we are. I mean, we've lived together. We know we're compatible. So come on, let's go do it!" He grabs her hand and begins to pull her out of the kitchen.

"No! No! No!" she says, laughing. "I want my mom and my sister to be there. And I would like to wear a wedding dress and not a pair of jeans with a ratty shirt."

"But I love those jeans and that ratty shirt," he says, kissing her neck.

"Plus, we invited Rick and Brandon over. It would be rude to run out and get married and not even invite some of our best friends." He smiles, and she hugs him tight. She doesn't want to let go of him. Not now. Not ever.

"So when will you set the date?" Brandon says, refreshing his and Rick's drink.

"Soon," Emma says, snuggled next to Matt on the sofa. "I think we need to let Sarah get married, and then we can," she says, craning her head to look up at Matt. "Her wedding is only two months away."

"Whatever you say," Matt says. "I just hope I don't change my mind between now and then," he says, winking at Brandon and Rick.

She knows he's teasing, but for whatever reason, Emma is hurt. She thought by now that she was used to Matt's offhand remarks.

"Where will you get married?" Rick says, reaching for his drink.

"Probably in Indiana," Emma says, hoping it's okay with Matt.

"Really?" Matt asks. "Not here?"

She shrugs. "Most of the people I know are there. My family's there. My only friends in New York are in this room."

"And I will walk to Indiana if I have to!" Brandon says.

"I've never seen hay bales or chickens running through a front yard, so I'm in," Rick says, making Matt laugh.

Emma has always liked Brandon and thought he deserved someone better and kinder than Rick. Rick is white, in his thirties, and works for an IT firm. Brandon is a twenty-four-year-old black man with striking brown eyes and a wide smile. He's worked in the publicity department for a small publishing house for the last three years. He moved to New York from Louisville, where he was raised by a single mom and squeaked through high school, passing by a hair. He never met his dad, and while he has said that it doesn't bother him, he has confided in Emma that he hates the man, whoever he is, for abandoning him and his mother. Whereas Brandon is caring and thoughtful, Rick often comes across as mean-spirited and insincere, even mocking Brandon's mother's Southern accent. His boorish personality drives Emma crazy but she still cares for him as a friend, and for the sake of Brandon, she has always remained quiet.

"You guys always talk about it, so…" Emma says. "When will *you* tie the knot?"

"We'll wait and see how long you guys last before *we* take the plunge."

The three men laugh, but Emma notices that Brandon's laugh is halted and sad, as if he was wondering whether Rick would abandon him as quickly as his father had.

More drinks are poured, and they all laugh until they cry as they share stories of their college years and early days of working in the city. In spite of their individual flaws Emma loves this little group, where she feels safe and cared for, and rests her head on Matt's shoulder, grateful for their life together.

CHAPTER 4

Queens, NY

Seven days later, Emma flips through pictures in a bridal magazine as she eats a quick breakfast bar before work.

Matt looks over her shoulder as he reaches for a coffee cup. "Should I be seeing pictures of wedding dresses? Isn't there some sort of rule against that?"

She giggles, taking a bite of the bar. "There is a tradition in some circles that says you shouldn't see the bride in her wedding dress before the wedding. I haven't heard of the picture rule. I don't think that's a thing."

He begins to brew a cup of coffee and turns back to the pictures in the magazine. "You really don't need to be looking at these. I can tell you exactly what kind of dress to wear."

She closes the pages, looking at him. "I can't wait to hear this."

"You just need something with a slit up to here and a cut down to here with an open back."

"You just described lingerie."

He shrugs. "I don't care what you call it. I'm just saying it's all you need to wear."

She laughs, throwing her phone into her bag and reaches for her Yeti mug of coffee. "Let's just leave me in charge of finding the wedding dress."

"Then that leaves me in charge of finding the lingerie."

She kisses him and slings her bag over her shoulder, throwing the magazine onto the coffee table with a couple other wedding magazines she bought this week. "See you tonight. Love you." She walks to the door, waiting for it.

"Love you too."

She smiles and closes the door. Brandon is waiting at the front door of the apartment building today. "You look tired," she says.

Brandon slings his backpack over both shoulders. "Yeah."

"What's up?"

They keep up a quick pace to make it to their trains on time. "Another round."

Emma shakes her head. He and Rick sometimes act more like children than adults. "What is it this time?"

"He wants to go to some new club that's opening tonight, and I told him I was tired. I just want to stay in. He said he would go without me, and I know what that means." He looks over at her as they walk. "*You* know what that means." Rick has a hard time being faithful, and Brandon has been hurt more times than he can count. "I told him that relationships shouldn't be like this. Something is out of whack."

She sighs. "It's the craziness in the world. Everything's out of whack."

Brandon dodges an upcoming group of people and picks up his pace to catch up to Emma. "You're not helping."

"Just saying that everything is crazy. It's not just you two."

They run down the stairs to the subway and Emma's phone rings. She waves good-bye as she and Brandon go in different directions toward their trains.

"Hi, Mom!" she says, answering her phone.

"I know you're running off to work, but I'm going to send you a link for a barn nearby that has been converted into an event space. It's really cute and it books up fast for weddings."

It sounds great, but Emma can already hear Rick's snide comments about her and Matt getting married in a barn. "Sounds awesome! But you don't have to think about my wedding until Sarah is off on her honeymoon."

Her mom scoffs. "I can do both. Besides, it keeps me busy."

Since her dad died, Emma has worried about the quiet days inside her mom's home. With the exception of when Sarah has been home from college, her mom has come home from work and spent most evenings and weekends alone. "I've been looking at wedding dresses and have something in mind," Emma says.

"I can't wait to see some pictures. Love you, Em!"

"Love you, Mom. Talk to you later."

Carrie is on the phone and waves to Emma as she walks into the therapy room. Emma puts her bag in her locker and looks over her schedule. It's a busy morning, but it includes seeing Mrs. Ramos before lunch, and she can't wait to tell her about her engagement.

Elliott stands near the back of the mourners at the cemetery in Midtown, wearing a black suit, tie, and yarmulke. He's here for his longtime friend, Simon, whose mother died after a lengthy battle with leukemia.

Elliott and Simon are both twenty-four, went to the same university, and have worked together at the same brokerage firm for the last two years. Elliott is the only Jewish co-worker to take time off today to attend the funeral. There are other Jews at the office, but none of them are close to Simon. Simon's family secured this plot for his mom in the Jewish section of the cemetery when her fight against the disease took a turn for the worst.

Elliott is thinking through his day, wondering what time he'll get back to the firm and how late he'll have to work, when he notices across the drive that winds through the grounds that another burial is taking place in the Gentile section.

Emma's face stretches into a huge smile when she sees a small white bag in Mrs. Ramos's hand. "You really are spoiling me, Mrs. Ramos."

"Just a Cuban sandwich for later," Mrs. Ramos says, handing it to her.

"I didn't pack a lunch today, so this is perfect! Thank you so much!" Emma sets the bag on the window ledge behind her as Mrs. Ramos sits on the end of the therapy table. "So…how's the knee feeling since our last session? Still getting ready for the Olympics?"

Mrs. Ramos smiles. "It's good. It's coming along. Healing has a lot to do with attitude, right?"

"Absolutely!" Emma then leans over, whispering to her. "That's why you're one of my favorite patients. You come in with the right attitude." Speaking louder again, she puts her hand on Mrs. Ramos's knee. "Okay, can you do twenty extensions?"

"I'll do twenty cartwheels if you'd like," Mrs. Ramos says, extending her leg. "So how's that cute boyfriend of yours?"

Emma has been waiting for the question and here it is, as if on cue. "Well, he asked me to marry him," she says, grinning.

Mrs. Ramos stops the extensions and looks up at her. "Isn't that wonderful! What a journey you're about to go on. And your mother is thrilled?"

"She is. She likes Matt. I think she secretly wanted us to get married a long time ago."

"When's the date?"

Emma puts her hand on Mrs. Ramos's knee, indicating for her to start the extensions again. "That depends on the venue."

Mrs. Ramos chuckles. "Venue. When we got married everybody looked for a church. Neither Miguel nor I had ever stepped foot in a church except on Christmas and Easter, but for my Puerto Rican family it was a huge thing! 'You must get married inside a church and before God!'" She stops the extensions and smiles. "Weddings are so exciting, but that's the easy part, you know? It's harder *being* married."

Emma smiles. "I know. My mom and dad always said that."

Mrs. Ramos looks at her with those kind eyes and soft smile. "Miguel and I are still married because we both found the Lord." She giggles, raising her hand. "I know. He wasn't lost, but we were. We knew about God and Jesus because we went to church on Christmas and Easter, so we said we knew him, but we didn't. He saved our marriage forty years ago." She squeezes Emma's hand. "I hope that you and Matt will come to know him too. If you ever have any questions, I'm always so happy to tell people about Jesus."

This would be off-putting and angering if it wasn't coming from Mrs. Ramos. Why would she assume that Emma and Matt didn't know God? Why does Mrs. Ramos think that she has any questions about Jesus? Emma would have felt offended had this come from anyone else, but she squeezes Mrs. Ramos's hand, smiling.

The rabbi looks over the simple wooden casket to Simon, his father, and his two sisters, and reads the eulogy for Simon's mother. He is mid-sentence when sounds of explosions shake the cemetery grounds. Mourners scream and cover their heads, falling to their knees. Elliott grabs the woman standing next to him and pulls her down, but the explosions have ended as abruptly as they started. The air in the cemetery is still, with no signs of fire or smoke. Elliott, Simon, and the others begin to stand as they hear a woman's hysterical cries behind them. The woman's words send a chill down Elliott's spine.

"Where are Arthur and Lenora? They were right here!" Elliott pivots, looking for the elderly man and woman who were standing behind him a moment ago. Bloodcurdling screams from the burial taking place across the drive make Elliott's body tremble.

"Where's Mother?"

Elliott and others from among the mourners at Simon's mother's funeral run toward that burial site. A woman in her fifties is looking into an empty casket, the top off its hinges.

"Oh my God! Where's Mother?" she shrieks. "Oh my God!"

Emma puts her hand on Mrs. Ramos's shoulder, easing her to lie back on the table, but Emma's hand slips through her, as if pushing against air, and she stumbles into the table. Inexplicably, Mrs. Ramos is gone. "Mrs. Ramos!" Emma panics, grasping her head with her hands as she spins around, looking all over the room, screaming. "Mrs. Ramos! Oh my God!" She screams louder, terrified. "Mrs. Ramos!"

"Where's Carrie?" Emma turns to see Linda at the front desk, who looks stricken and is trying to sit down. Linda's voice doesn't even sound like her. "She was right here and handed me this file, and…!" Linda is making noises that Emma has never heard from another human and can hear her own heart beating in her ears.

"Reggie's gone!" Mateo yells, looking frantically.

Elliott stumbles backward as he looks across the cemetery. Many graves are wide open, revealing empty caskets, the dirt scattered atop the ground as if from bombs that had exploded from within. "What's happening?" he says, his head swiveling to take it all in.

"I don't know," Simon shouts, his voice stretched thin. "I don't know!"

They hear cries and spin around to see the same woman who had been looking into the empty casket. She is on her knees, sobbing and shrieking. "Where's Ellen? Where's my Ellen?"

"Where's Uncle Bill?" another voice howls. The small group of mourners is desperate in their search, holding each other up or covering their mouths as others slump to the ground.

Elliott and Simon run through the cemetery littered with cavernous holes and scattered earth, heading for the columbarium. Several marble plaques lay broken on the ground; Elliott's hand trembles as he reaches inside one of the openings for an urn. The lid is off, and he looks inside. "It's empty." He and Simon frantically reach for urns along the wall, their breathing frenzied and quick as they look inside each one.

A man yelling on the street outside the cemetery catches Elliott's attention as he stumbles toward the road. The man is outside his car, waving his arms. "Pulled right out in front of me, and now he's gone! Look what he did to my car!" The man is looking in all directions. "Where did he go? Did anybody see him?" Other drivers are honking as they try to pull around the accident.

Elliott and Simon look up and down the street. A couple is walking and holding hands, unaware of what's just happened inside the cemetery. Others are headed to a nearby market or to work without distraction, while some seem to be looking behind them or inside an open business as if they're searching for someone. Elliott runs toward a cable truck parked at the side of the road with the driver's side door open. A cell phone appears as if it had been left on the front seat. "What's going on, Simon?" Elliott asks, looking terrified. "How do graves burst open? How do ashes get sucked out of an urn?"

"Where did they go?" Simon asks, his voice as tense as his eyes. "Where did all these people go?"

Linda calls the police, and Emma can hear her yelling but can't make out the words; they're garbled and distorted in her ears. She feels lightheaded and reaches to steady herself on the window ledge. Her hand crushes the bag with the Cuban sandwich that Mrs. Ramos had brought her; she clutches it, leaning against the ledge, crying. Her phone rings, and she pulls it out of her pocket. It's her sister. "Sarah! Oh my God!" she says, breathless. She can't hear and covers her other ear, but Sarah is out of her mind, screaming into the phone and Emma shouts, "What? I can't understand what you're saying."

"Mom is gone!" Sarah's voice sounds like it's shredding.

Blood drains from Emma's head and she tries to take a breath. "Don't say that, Sarah! Don't tell me that! I just talked to her! Not Mom!"

"I'm freaking out, Emma! She was here! We were talking! But she's gone! She's gone!" Sarah begins to wail and moan, and Emma's legs weaken. She can't move. Shock has taken over and she can't speak. Sarah continues to scream, but then the line goes dead. Emma's entire body shakes and she feels like throwing up. How can she live in a world without her mom in it? The room turns black; she tries to catch herself but wavers, collapsing to the floor.

To discover more about the biblical facts behind the story, read Where in the Word? *on page 187, or continue reading the novel.*

CHAPTER 5

Israel

Zerah grabs a cup of coffee before taking a seat in the conference room. He and a team of researchers will be discussing recent findings in Parkinson's disease at Hadassah Medical Center. Dr. Akiva Benjamin takes a seat at the middle of the conference table and opens his computer. Zerah and four other doctors spread files and their own computers in front of them.

"Where's Dr. Haas?" asks Dr. Benjamin.

"She's coming," Zerah says. "I just saw her in the hallway."

Dr. Benjamin has never tolerated tardiness. "Dr. Adler, would you find her, please?"

Zerah rises from his seat. "She might have gotten pulled aside for a consult."

As he leaves the room, Zerah can hear Dr. Benjamin begin discussing their latest research. The hallway outside the conference room is empty; Zerah walks to the main lobby, where several hallways branch out through the department. "Have either of you seen Dr. Haas?" he asks two colleagues standing at the reception desk.

"Not since this morning," one of them says.

"Do you know where Dr. Haas is?" Zerah asks, moving to the young woman on the phone at the desk.

She shakes her head, and Zerah goes back to the conference room.

Dr. Benjamin looks up when he enters, and Zerah shrugs. "I can't find her. She was right behind me as we were headed here."

"We'll move on without her," Dr. Benjamin says, rumpling his brow.

Brooklyn, NY

"Get up, Emma! Emma…come on! Get up!" She opens her eyes to see Mateo beside her, shaking her awake. "Come on! We're getting out of here."

She turns her head to see that most people have already scrambled out of the therapy room. "Where'd they go?"

He helps her to her feet. "They're running for home!"

She stands, grabbing his arms. "No! Where did Carrie and Reggie and Mrs. Ramos go?"

Mateo shakes his head, helping her to the lockers for her purse and jacket. "I don't know!" His voice sounds as terrified as his eyes look. "Vaporized!"

Emma grabs her purse and jacket, and as they dart across the room, she remembers Mrs. Ramos's purse and turns back for it, along with the Cuban sandwich. They have the presence of mind to lock the door and close it behind them before running down the hall and stairs, and out the front doors. The sun is still shining and Emma squints, looking into it. The sky is blue and puffed up with white clouds. How can it look like an ordinary day?

She tries to dial Matt's number but can't get through. "Not Matt. Please, not Matt," she whispers under her breath, running. A few people are in the street trying to move driverless cars to the side of the road. Some people look shell-shocked and confused, but she's surprised at how many are walking along as if unaware. "Vaporized by what?" she gasps, running. Mateo isn't answering. "Mateo!" she shouts. "Vaporized by what?"

He pulls her along, screaming as he runs. "I don't know. Evil!" Emma's heart races at the thought as she and Mateo sprint toward the subway. She tugs Mateo's arm to stop him when they pass 316 Deli. "What are you doing?" he asks. "Come on!"

She looks at Mrs. Ramos's purse and back at him. "I have to tell them. They need this. Go on without me."

Mateo is irritated. "Come on! Give it to them later!"

"Go on. They need to know."

Mateo shakes his head and runs on without her. Emma steps inside 316 Deli and the smells of soups and roasted chicken and baked goods fill the space as usual, but tables and chairs have been toppled; the place is empty. She thinks of what Mateo said about everyone being vaporized by evil and hurries behind the counter and into the kitchen, shouting as she searches the restaurant. Chicken, beef, and vegetables are sizzling to a charred black on the grill, and steam rises from a pot that's boiling over. Emma turns everything off and steps to the walk-in refrigerator, where she sees a young girl crouched in the corner and trembling. She looks at her nametag. "Gina. Where is everyone? Where's Carlos and Viviana and…"

The young girl looks up at her, traumatized. Her eyes are dark, and her hands are shaking. "We were all working…and then they were gone." Emma walks to her, extending her hand, and Gina looks up. "People were screaming and running, and I hid. I had to hide before they got me too."

"Before who got you?"

"Aliens. Right?" she whispers, looking for answers from Emma. "Right?!"

Emma doesn't respond as she helps Gina to her feet and closes the door to the refrigerator. "Run home."

Gina begins to cry. "But what if my home isn't there?"

Emma looks around the restaurant. "Buildings are still here. It's people who are gone."

"Viviana was right next to me handing food to a customer in line and Carlos was talking to his wife and their two little kids, who had just come in. The food that Viviana was holding crashed to the floor, and Carlos's voice suddenly stopped. I looked up, and he and his wife and kids were gone." Gina looks at Emma. "People freaked out!"

Emma's voice is quivering. "Run home, Gina." Gina rushes for the door, and Emma grabs her arm. "Be careful."

As Gina leaves, Emma looks over the restaurant once more and feels her throat filling again as she locks and closes the door for 316 Deli.

The subway station is packed, and people shove their way past the turnstiles and onto the platform; just like Elliott, they all want to get home. Two of the lines are down and fights are quick to break out as the crowd from the street rushes toward the oncoming train, shouting about a terrorist attack on the city. Mothers grab the hands of their children in the panic and race for the subway platform; others slug it out, jockeying for position closest to the doors.

It's pandemonium, and Elliott wonders if he should find another way home. If the city were under a terrorist attack, then the subway system would be a primary target. But there's no time to leave before the doors open and he's pushed, even lifted, along with the crowd onto the train. He grabs a pole and it's impossible to move; people are packed so tightly around him that he has trouble taking a breath. In contrast to the people on the platform, everyone on the train is quiet; an eerie, unnerving quiet prevails until a boy around twelve says, "Where'd Mom go?"

"Shh," the man with him says.

"Where'd she go?"

The man's face is pale as he looks at his son. "I don't know."

"It's terrorists!" A man barks in the father's face. "Just tell him the truth, for God's sake!"

"How is it terrorists?" the father says, shaking. "How did they make her disappear?"

The man is red-faced and angry. "Chemical weapons!"

"It was Satan," an elderly woman says, her hands trembling on her purse strap. "He and his demons have been let loose." The hair stands up on the back of Elliott's neck.

People begin to panic, but there's nowhere to go. Shouts and curses fill the train before fright and anxiety strangle each passenger, and the father pulls his son closer to him. In his mind Elliott sees the empty graves again and his body begins to shiver, while the muffled cries around him continue.

Brooklyn, NY

Even if she wanted to, Emma couldn't get to the subway platform. People are overflowing into the streets and trying to get down the stairs, while another flood of them run up the stairs, stumbling and falling over each other at word of the subway's closure. Emma finds herself in the midst of them, being carried along in the wave of hysteria and chaos in the middle of the street. Her ears have not stopped ringing since Mrs. Ramos disappeared and it's hard to catch her breath. Gridlock in the street makes running difficult; people fight their way to taxicabs or nearby vehicles. Sirens, alarms, shouts, and crying fill the air, pressing down on her chest, and she tries to take a breath. She is jostled on every side and clings to her bag and Mrs. Ramos's purse.

The door to a restaurant is open ahead and she pushes her way through the crowd, heading toward it. She needs to get out of this sea of people to call Matt. She has to hear his voice and have him tell her that everything will be okay. She breaks from the crowd and stumbles toward the open door, but a few workers inside the restaurant are pushing people away from the door as they try to close it, keeping them out. "Get out!" A man in a black apron yells. "Get away from the door! Get out!" Three people fall to the sidewalk as the man inside slams the door, locking it behind him.

There's nothing left to do but continue running, and Emma reaches inside her bag for her phone. She touches Matt's phone number and presses the phone to her ear. It doesn't ring but goes directly to an automated message about being unable to connect the call at this time. Panic rises to her throat and she shoves the phone into her purse, clutching it to her chest, and running toward the next subway station, hoping it's open.

Brawls are breaking out as people try to push their way down the stairs for the subway. A growing fear sets in when word spreads that the entire subway system has been shut down. An elderly man and woman lose their footing in front of Emma and fall to the sidewalk. "Here," Emma says, helping the woman to her feet before reaching for her husband. "Get away from this crowd," she yells, grabbing the woman's arm and leading them away from the stairs. She maneuvers her way to the front of a building and looks at the old man and woman. They are shaken and stunned, and Emma wonders what in the world will happen to them.

"What's going on?" the old man asks. Emma shakes her head. The lump in her throat claims her voice. The old man's voice is trembling as he says, "How will we ever get out of here?"

Emma is knocked from behind and falls toward them. "You can't try to walk through this right now. Stay here. Tight against this wall," she says.

The old couple looks so vulnerable and afraid. She touches the woman's purse. "Tuck your wallet under your bra." She stands in front of her and the woman's wrinkled hands shake as she lifts her wallet from her purse and slips it under her shirt. Emma helps remove the woman's sweater and moves the purse so that it is behind her back instead of at her side, then pulls her sweater over the strap so it can't be seen.

"Now it's harder for someone to get your purse, and even if they did, your wallet won't be in it." The woman's eyes are wide as she looks at her. "The crowd will eventually thin out and then you get home as quickly as you can."

The old man nods and grabs her hand. "Thank you. We'll be fine."

He said that for her sake and for the sake of the old woman, and she covers her mouth to keep from screaming as she turns away from them.

As soon as the doors closed on the subway, the entire system was shut down and evacuated, forcing everyone off the trains. Elliott found himself among the stampede for the stairs leading up to the streets. It is a madness he's never seen before. Fear has gripped the entire city. Chaos and confusion have erupted in the streets; people are fighting over abandoned cars and battling for taxis. Elliott gasps for breath as he races toward the next block. If he can just keep running from one block to the next, he'll make it back to his apartment, he tells himself. The streets are sheer pandemonium, and it doesn't take long before people begin to plunder businesses and restaurants. This isn't a simple case of confusion or disorder. It isn't even rioting, but anarchy. Police are trying to control the situation, but even they don't know what the situation is or what's happening. Elliott has a hard time breathing, and he realizes he can feel his heart pounding in his ears. He stops for a moment to take a breath.

Another fight breaks out, this time as a man tries to drag a taxi driver from behind the wheel of the cab. Elliott watches and in moments seven or eight people are in the melee, extracting the driver and his passengers and waging war on one another for ownership of the taxi. One man lays crumpled and bloodied on the ground as the riot accelerates around him.

Elliott backs away but as he turns to begin his race to the end of the block, a man with the composition of a steel post runs into him, leveling him to the ground. The side of his face grinds into the asphalt, making his glasses fall off; in his mouth he can taste blood. In the charge he is kicked and stepped on, and he struggles to get to his feet. Elliott shouts into the pavement, scrambling to put his glasses back on. He feels arms swooping in from behind him, lifting him to his feet, and setting him on course to run again. There is no chance to see who helped him or to shout out a word of thanks. More and more people are trying to commandeer taxicabs and other vehicles. His left eye and mouth are bleeding and his ribs ache with every step, but he tells himself again, *Just one more block. Go one more block.*

Israel

Zerah looks up from his notes at the sound of the door opening. It's Gila, one of the administrative assistants for the department.

"Apologies for the interruption," Gila says. Her voice has lost all inflection. "Several people are missing from the building."

"What do you mean people are missing?" Dr. Benjamin asks, a tinge of annoyance in his voice at being interrupted.

Her face looks stricken. "I don't understand it myself, Dr. Benjamin," she says, her voice losing strength. "But many staff and patients are gone." The team around the table jump to their feet.

"Dr. Haas!" Zerah whispers, looking at Dr. Benjamin.

"It's on the news. It's happening all around the world," Gila says, her voice quivering now.

"What?" Dr. Benjamin says, clicking on the television. When the images on the screen are in view, each doctor stands and walks closer to the TV.

"Change the channel," Zerah says, hoping that this is nothing more than a TV publicity stunt. But the coverage on every channel is the same: a horrible, unimaginable scenario is taking place all around the world.

"All nonessential personnel have been asked to evacuate," Gila says.

Zerah has the frame of mind to grab his computer before running for the door. "Who else is missing?" he asks Gila as the others in the room scramble past them.

She shakes her head, fear filling her eyes. "I don't know."

"Dr. Haas wasn't here for the meeting. Is she one of them?"

A tear falls down one of Gila's cheeks and she swipes it away. "I don't know," she says again, her voice breaking.

He nods. "Get home, Gila. Go be with your family."

As Gila runs down the hall, Zerah can see her shoulders shaking. He makes his way down the hall that leads to his office; when he passes Dr. Haas's door he stops, pushing it open. Stepping to her desk, he scans the top of it for anything that might be out of order, but the books and files and computer are all in their usual places. He opens the drawers of the desk and of the credenza behind it. Her purse is in one of the credenza drawers. He opens it and spots her car keys inside before closing it and shutting it back inside the drawer. People hurry past the door and he walks to it, looking for any familiar faces. "Amsel," he says, waving at one of the young computer techs for his department.

"Dr. Adler," Amsel responds, crossing through people to get to him. His large brown eyes are dark with fear and his eyebrows furrowed in worry.

Zerah pulls him into the doorway. "Amsel, have you seen Dr. Haas?"

Amsel shakes his head. "Not since this morning." The realization settles on him. "Is she one of the missing?"

"I don't know. Do you know of any others who are missing from the department?"

Amsel's voice breaks. "Dr. Sokolof was testing a new patient when…" The young man gropes for the right words.

"What?" Zerah snaps, his voice tightening.

"I was working in an office down the hall when I heard the scream. Several of us rushed toward the sound. When we opened the door, the patient was standing in the middle of the room screaming. His wife was slumped in a chair next to him, looking as if she'd seen a dead man that had come back to life."

"And Dr. Sokolof?"

Amsel looks away as if trying to piece together a long-forgotten memory. "He vanished. He was there in the room with them, and then…he was gone."

CHAPTER 6

Queens, NY

Emma has run or walked the nearly thirteen miles to get back to her apartment and is exhausted when she spots a delivery truck with a Queens address on the side, making its way at a snail's pace through the street. It's the kind of truck where both the driver and passenger doors are gone. She can't see the driver's side, but the passenger side is filled with a large, beefy man who is quick to kick off anyone who tries to climb inside. She is desperate to get off the streets and before the truck makes its way past her, she breaks out into a run, pleading with the bulky man filling up the door. "Please, I live in Queens," Emma says, lifting her hand toward him.

"Get away!" he shouts, his hand gripping a box cutter.

She jogs alongside the truck, grateful for the slow pace of traffic. "Please! All I want to do is get home. I have money. I'll pay you whatever I have in my purse."

He reaches down and pulls her inside, shoving her past him to the back of the truck, packed with thirty or so people who look back at her. She reaches inside her purse and pulls out forty-two dollars, but he swats away the money, keeping his body positioned at the door. Another man is on the other side of the driver, watching that door, ready to fight off anyone who would try to hijack them. Emma tucks herself just inside the doorway, trying to make herself small in case anyone else comes aboard. The air is stifling with so many people on top of one another, but no one says a word. With the exception of crying, fear has turned each one of them mute. It's clear that they're all in this together, even the guards at the door: They just want to get home. It feels like another world inside the truck, as if for a moment these steel walls shelter them from the mayhem and horror on the streets. Emma tries to call Matt again but puts the phone away when she hears the same automated message.

Her eyes catch those of a thirteen- or fourteen-year-old boy who is looking at her. She tries to see who is with him, but there doesn't appear to be any closeness between him and any of the people crowding against him. She wonders if he's alone and trying to find his way home. The thought of being alone without her mother is terrifying and fills her with incomprehensible sadness. She convinces herself that the boy ran from school when people disappeared, and his mom or dad or both are waiting for him at home. He keeps watching her with brown eyes drenched in sorrow, and her thoughts overwhelm her; she can't imagine being a child right now.

The mile or so inside the truck gets her closer to home, but when gridlock prevents them from moving any further, Emma and many others decide to jump out through the back doors. When she's on the ground, Emma looks for the teenage boy who jumped out ahead of her, but he's gone. "Headed home," she says, trying to convince herself.

Elliott runs into his apartment and slams the door, locking it. He ran the twelve miles from Midtown back to Queens, terrified for his life. He reaches for a bottle of gin from his kitchen cabinet and opens it, drinking it straight as he turns on the TV. He has been trying to call and text his parents in Ohio for hours with no luck; cell towers are unable to keep up with the demand. Every email and text has bounced back.

As he stands in front of the TV he realizes that his body is throbbing.

He listens as a local news anchor delivers the unfathomable news of the disappearance of what seems to be millions, if not billions, of people around the world. Widespread panic has created the biggest stock market crash in history. Planes have been circling airports for hours due to the absence of air traffic controllers. All planes have been ordered grounded for fear of terrorism, leaving millions stranded at airports around the world. Buses, commuter and freight trains, taxis, semi-trailer trucks, barges, ships, and cars around the globe sit abandoned or with a skeletal crew. Many prisons are on lockdown, while several are dealing with prison breaks.

"Reports are coming in from as far away as Iceland," the anchor says. "It has been reported that in some parts of Africa, entire villages are gone. At this time there are thousands, perhaps millions, missing from New York City alone. It is impossible to track." The anchor looks weary as he reads his notes. "We have several colleagues who are no longer here," he says, clearing his throat. "And we're working with a smaller crew today. Please forgive the quality of this broadcast as we try to make sense of what…" His voice trails off and his co-anchor takes over. Her voice isn't bold and smooth as it normally is, but hesitant and small with an uncertain tone.

Elliott flips to a national news channel that features reports of world governments in turmoil, the US National Guard and military branches being mobilized but missing many among their troops, chaos in the streets, and the global stock markets crashing. The world is on the brink of disaster and his own city is in mayhem. He's never felt such terror and loneliness in his life. He takes another drink and sinks into a chair, trying again to call his parents. He receives the same message as before: "Unable to connect your call at this time"; he throws his phone, crying for the first time today.

He switches to another national news channel and is stunned by the report. "The first lady has vanished along with the president's two young children. His two college-aged children with his former wife were discovered safe at college. Vice President Sanchez and his wife, Marguerite, have vanished, and at this time it appears that nearly sixty members of Congress and at least ten governors are also missing.

Numbers are also coming in from the Justice Department, the State Department, the Pentagon, the president's cabinet, the Armed Forces, the NSA, CIA, FBI, and the Supreme Court." The anchor pauses and clears his throat. "I keep hoping this is a nightmare or a hallucination and that we'll all wake up, but the news keeps pouring in from all over the globe."

Elliott clicks the channel button on the remote because he can't listen anymore. Another network features a panel of experts who are tossing out a barrage of theories: One panelist suggests it was biological warfare that spread a virus, bacteria, or some form of germ into the water or air; the next claims entomological warfare disintegrated humans after the bite or several bites from an insect carrying an infected pathogen; another asserts that aliens abducted people from around the world and raided graves in order to populate other planets; and still another panelist believes there has been a great cleansing of the earth as Mother Gaia rids herself of the poisonous religious fanatics that have inhabited her planet for far too long.

Jumping on that thought, the final panelist hints that it was Jesus Christ himself who called his people to heaven. The panel of moderators, thankfully, jumps on his ignorance. "Maybe it was Satan," one of them says, mocking him.

"They've said it for centuries," the man says, shouting them down.

"Who is they?" asks the Mother Gaia theorist, an attractive blonde wearing a form-fitting blue dress.

"Christians," the man says. "They've been saying that one day Christ would take all his followers into heaven."

Elliott shakes his head, disgusted and angry. People needed real answers, not make-believe.

"I've never heard anybody say that," the biological warfare panelist says.

"You're just pandering," the woman says. "Preying on weakness and fear, what Christians have done for years, and exactly what people don't need right now!"

"I'm not saying it's true," the man yells. "I'm just saying it's what Christians have said for over two millennia."

"If that's true, then the world will be a far better place without millions of hatemongers and bigots," the believer in aliens concludes.

Elliott reaches for the phone on the floor and picks it up, desperate to hear his parents' voices.

CHAPTER 7

Queens, NY

Emma opens the door to her apartment and Matt grabs her, pulling her inside. "Where have you been? I've been calling for hours! I thought you were gone!"

She falls into him. "I thought you…I couldn't get through. My mom is…"

He pushes her from him. "What? What?!"

Her face is contorted and wet. "My mom is gone, and so are Carrie and Reggie and Mrs. Ramos and her family."

He puts his hands on top of his head and sways from side to side with his mouth open. "What's happening?" He mutters, running to the TV and pointing. "People are missing everywhere! It's not just here. It's all over the world."

Emma's legs feel heavy as boulders as she walks to the TV, staring at images from Oklahoma and Dubai, Charleston and Barcelona. She wipes tears from her face, covering her mouth as she watches. In one video after another security cameras from banks, malls, hospitals, businesses, government buildings, airports, schools, grocery stores, military bases, prisons, and surveillance systems from around the world reveal the disappearance of countless people who vanished right off the streets, from lobbies, waiting rooms, supermarket aisles, school playgrounds, offices, airport security lines, university campuses, and restaurants. Reporters are on the streets, in cemeteries, and in news studios, trying to piece together what has happened.

Emma's legs lose whatever strength is left and she falls to the sofa, staring at the screen. "What have they been saying?"

Matt shakes his head. "A lot of them are saying terrorism. Many are saying it's aliens."

"That's what Gina said."

"Who's Gina?"

She can't stop looking at the screen. "A girl who works at Mrs. Ramos's deli. I was running by there and went in to tell them that she was gone, but the entire place was empty." She begins to cry and Matt sits next to her, holding her head on his chest. "Carlos, Viviana, Angel, Luis, and Mrs. Ramos and her husband. All gone. Just Gina was there. Hiding in the refrigerator from aliens." She looks at him. "Aliens!"

"It could be. Or terrorists."

She presses the palms of her hands to her eyes. "How did terrorists make people disappear from the rehabilitation room?" She points to the TV screen at the reporter in a cemetery. "How did they open graves and empty them out?"

"Nobody knows, Emma."

She turns to look at him, trembling. "Where did they go? Why were they taken?"

He shakes his head. "I don't know."

Hysteria is rising in her voice. "Mateo said it was some sort of evil that vaporized people."

"What sort of…"

She screams over him. "Why is my mother gone and where is she?!"

"I don't know." He pulls her to him again. "I don't know."

Israel

Since the nation of Israel went on lockdown, Zerah, his parents, and his sister Rada's family have not left his parents' bomb shelter. The entire Israeli Defense Forces have taken their positions around the country, prepared to defend Israel and her citizens from attack. Many residents have disappeared, but with so many in bomb shelters, there's no way to get an accurate count.

"How did this happen?" his father Chaim says, rubbing his head of white hair, his hands shaking from the tremors or fear, or both. "What sort of evil did this to the world?"

"Papa, you're looking pale," Rada says. "You shouldn't get so excited."

Rada's oldest child, eight-year-old Taavi, wraps his arms around his grandfather's neck and leans against him. Rada's three-year-old daughter, Batya, sits on her father's lap, unaware of what is happening.

"I keep trying to understand," Zerah's mother says. "Who were these people who have disappeared? And why?"

"I think a colleague is one of them," Zerah says from the sofa.

Each family member turns to look at him. "Why do you think that?" Rada says.

"She was right behind me as we were headed to a meeting. We all took our places and she wasn't there. I went back into the hall and all the way to the reception desk looking for her. She wasn't anywhere. I tried calling her cell phone in the meeting, but she didn't answer, and then our meeting was interrupted with news of this," he says, pointing to the TV screen.

"She could have had an emergency," his mother says.

"That's what I thought, so I tried calling her repeatedly."

"With no answer?" his sister says. Zerah shakes his head no.

His father stands and paces the small living room. "Who was she?"

"Dr. Miriam Haas," Zerah says. "A good doctor. A wife and mom. We didn't talk beyond research. She was a messianic believer."

"That's one of the theories!" Rada says.

"It is preposterous!" Chaim yells, silencing his daughter. No one would say the name of Jesus Christ in this household. They turn their eyes to the TV and watch in silence.

CHAPTER 8

Queens, NY

Rick and Brandon sit on the sofa in Matt and Emma's apartment, drinking. It has been the only way to soothe their nerves as they have watched events unfold on TV for the last seven hours. Emma has turned her eyes from the screen many times at images of people looting buildings throughout the country. In the past, many have resorted to theft and property damage following elections or after a sports team's loss, but watching this behavior after the disappearance of millions makes Emma wince. At three in the morning they are all nauseous from fright; their eyes are bloodshot from exhaustion and swollen from crying.

"This has shaken the foundation of our global security to the core," the newscaster says to the panel of experts in front of him. "We've seen the debilitation of our government and the military. Our stock market has plummeted, and as a result we're witnessing the chaos in the international financial markets. Tokyo, Hong Kong, Paris, London, and other world markets are falling, toppling like dominoes, which will surely usher the world into a global depression. What does it mean for the housing market and loan institutions across the country? Our own banking system or business and manufacturing? What does it mean for our schools, health care, transportation, or our food supply? What about our…"

Emma can see the news anchor's mouth moving but can't process what he's saying anymore. "What happened to the old couple I picked up off the street? What happened to the teenage kid who was alone, or the people crammed into the truck with me?"

"They're home, Em," Matt says. "Just like you."

"With their families? Or are they gone?" Her eyes are heavy and dark rings have formed beneath them.

"It had to be aliens or Satan," Rick says, squeezing Brandon's hand. "Those are the only things that make sense."

Emma becomes angry. "How does Satan taking people make any more sense than Jesus taking his followers?"

"Come on, Em," Matt says. "Nobody believes that theory."

She stands, pacing in front of the TV. "How is that any more outlandish than aliens or chemical warfare or people being vaporized by some satanic force?"

Matt attempts to calm her. "Come on, sit down. You're exhausted and upset. You still miss your dad and now your mom…"

His voice is kind and Emma doesn't want to sound shrill, but she does. "My mom wasn't abducted by aliens! What kind of answer is that? It's insane!"

"We're all just trying figure it out, Em," Brandon says. "But maybe we don't have as much at stake as you do."

He smiles, and her heart softens. Throughout the night as texts confirmed where their loved ones were, she has wondered if they have all secretly sighed in relief that it was her mom that was taken and not theirs. She slumps into a chair and looks at them. "That guy on TV said that Christians believed that one day Jesus would call for his followers and take them up to where he is. My mom followed him. So did my dad. They took Sarah and me to church, but we never believed like they did."

Her voice is cracking, and Matt moves from his chair and sits on the floor in front of her, holding her hand. "You believe in God, Emma. I believe in God and Rick and Brandon believe in God."

"I don't believe in God," Rick says.

"But you do believe in Satan?" Emma snaps. "You believe in evil but not in good. Makes sense."

Rick opens his mouth, but Matt lifts his hand. "Rick doesn't believe but we do, and we all believe in Jesus."

She shakes her head. "But it's different. There's something different in just believing but I don't know what it is. My mom told me several times that even demons believe."

Matt grips her hand tighter. "What does that have to do with anything? You can't compare yourself to demons. You are a good, honest person. You are one of the kindest people I've ever known in my life. You are helpful and generous and sweet and sincere. Your mom wasn't taken because she was any better than you. We don't know why she was taken, but it wasn't because she believed in God any stronger than you did or than I did or than Brandon did." Her eyes are full looking at him. She wants to believe him.

"Mrs. Ramos was right there in front of me. My hands were on her shoulders when her eyes darted upward as if she saw or heard something."

"Like she was scared?" Matt asks.

"No. It was…" She tries to find the right word, remembering. "It was like somebody she knew had just called her name. Her eyes flicked upward and…" She begins to cry. "And she was gone. Right out of my hands." Matt squeezes her shoulder, pulling her tighter to him. "Even some of the footage on TV shows some people at malls or grocery stores, work, or wherever, and some of them glanced up." She looks at Brandon and Rick. "I think they heard Jesus." Matt and Rick exchange glances but remain quiet, not wanting to upset her more.

"How could Jesus make all those people disappear?" Brandon asks.

She looks at him. "How could aliens? How could Satan?"

Rick shakes his head. "We're just going to have to wait for some answers. Someone will figure it out."

To discover more about the biblical facts behind the story, read Where in the Word? *on page 199, or continue reading the novel.*

CHAPTER 9

Queens, NY

Elliott has barely moved from the TV during the last twelve hours. After he heard the noise of an apartment down the hall being ransacked and looted, he has been afraid to leave. He hasn't slept and has scarcely eaten; he can't tear himself away from the news coverage.

Countless numbers of people are crossing the border from Mexico into California, New Mexico, Arizona, and Texas; on the video on TV, they look like ants scurrying along the ground and over the border. North Korea has fired nuclear warheads at South Korea, inflicting incalculable loss. India and Pakistan, both powder kegs before the vanishings, are now engaged in a war that's already killed thousands. Sects in Lebanon are in battles of bloodletting; many African countries have erupted in conflicts against each other throughout the continent, resulting in gruesome images on the screen; Vietnam, Japan, and the Philippines are in a war against China over the South China Seas; and countless other conflicts are raging around the globe. In a blood-soaked attempt to take over the government of Egypt, the Muslim Brotherhood has assassinated key leaders, but their attempt against the president's life has failed. Despite the peace agreement drawn up by President Banes between Israelis and Palestinians, clashes are already raging in their lands. Unprecedented unrest saturates the globe, and thoughts reel in Elliott's mind. It's unfathomable that this nightmare is the world's new reality.

Noise from the TV jolts Elliott awake at five in the morning. He works out the kinks in his neck, unaware he fell asleep twenty minutes ago. He stands up from the chair and stares at the screen. The US Capitol, the Pentagon, the White House, and much of DC is in rubble as smoke and ash rise from bomb-cratered buildings and roads.

"An unprecedented attack against our nation's capital took place less than ten minutes ago," the breathless anchor says. "It is unclear who is behind the attack, but much of the city's main houses of power were targeted. This is complete devastation. My God! Look at those images! The president, speaking from a safe house, has issued a warning to all major cities to evacuate." The president is seen standing in front of a background that is the great seal of the United States, appearing to maintain composure in light of his own personal loss, and urging people to flee.

Elliott falls back into the chair; his ears are ringing with a deafening noise. His body feels paralyzed. The woman on the subway was right: Satan and his demons have been let loose and the world is now gripped by darkness. He tries calling his parents again; this must be the hundredth time. The call won't go through and he clicks on text messages, typing *Get out of city! Nukes r coming!* He pushes send and hopes it will go through. He cries when his phone buzzes.

Ur alive! We love u! We'l try. Pleas get out too! Meet at Harold's

His uncle's house in southern Ohio. He texts *I love u! B careful! C u in OH. I promise!*

He pushes send and holds the phone to his forehead, weeping. The sound of an explosion hurls him to his feet and he runs for the door, but falls, crippled by intense, blinding light.

"Look up, Elliott." It's an unfamiliar voice, terrifying and awful, yet good and kind, and Elliott covers his head on the floor. "Look up, Elliott." Elliott lifts his head, shielding his eyes from the light, and screams. He struggles to see but the light is too powerful, filling the room and moving in waves. He wants to stand but his body is at peace, floating, filled with indescribable warmth. It seems he's been like this for hours when the voice says, "Look at me, Elliott."

He moves his hand from his eyes and can make out the face of a man unlike any he's ever seen. His eyes are brighter than the sun and Elliott hunches over again, putting his forehead to the floor.

"Do you know who I am?"

A wind surges through the room when the figure speaks, and Elliott grips his fingers into the carpet, holding on. "I don't know!" He screams into the wind. "Hashem! Help me!" Elliott feels a touch on his shoulder, and his body fills with heat as peace flows through every cell. He lifts his head.

"I am Yeshua. Your Messiah." Elliott trembles at the name. "Don't be afraid, Elliott. You are one of my chosen servants for this time."

Elliott sees the hands of Jesus among the waves of light and his heart throbs at the sight of puncture wounds in each of his palms. "You are!" Elliott reaches for him. "You are Yeshua!"

"I am." Wind fills the room again as Jesus touches his hand.

"All those people," Elliott says into the gusts. "They were yours."

He senses Jesus's smile and the wind subsides. "They are all here with me, and now you and your Jewish brothers will be my 144,000 servants on the earth who will lead people to the truth."

Elliott stumbles for words, shielding his eyes. "How? I don't know how to do that. Truth is different for everyone."

"I am the way, the truth, and the life. I am Truth, Elliott."

The wind blows across Elliott's face and he feels it…it is Truth. For the first time in his life he believes that Jesus is the Messiah. He is Truth. Elliott is shaking as he speaks. "What do I do?"

"Stay in the city. The Holy Spirit will lead you and teach you as you spread word of my love. He will instruct you on when to leave the city. Don't be afraid to open your mouth to speak; the Holy Spirit will fill you with the words you need. The end is coming on the whole world, but I will come back again, and every eye will see me. Then I will make all things new. Great multitudes will listen to you as you lead them to me, Elliott. You will be one of my greatest witnesses throughout the earth."

A hand shimmering with waves of light touches Elliott's forehead with searing heat. "You are sealed with my protection. Nothing and no one can harm you." Elliott is jolted by the sound of a deafening explosion. The building quakes, and outside his living room window buildings crumble across the river, but he looks at Jesus. "Rest, Elliott. Lie down and rest."

As the sound of wailing inside his building grows louder, Elliott closes his eyes.

CHAPTER 10

Queens, NY

Every resident of the apartment building huddles in the basement with Matt and Emma: Rick and Brandon; Piya and Aarav and their two children; Mr. and Mrs. Gruebber, the elderly couple on the first floor—he was once a professor of classic literature; the Kramers with their son, Brody; the single mom on the second floor and her two children; and the Kleins with their two children. Emma rarely saw any of these people with the exception of Rick and Brandon. Some brought twin mattresses or sofa cushions as feeble protection. The hours of darkness in the windowless basement has made it feel like a tomb, each person struggling in the quiet after the bombing.

"What's going to happen?" Piya's daughter asks. She looks to be around nine years old, but Emma doesn't know and she regrets how little time she's taken to meet the people in her building.

"We're not sure," Piya says. "We just want to make sure we're safe."

"Will they keeping attacking us?"

Piya feels the others looking at her, but can't answer her daughter.

"I think they've stopped," Matt says.

"You don't know that," Mr. Kramer snaps. He's a man in his thirties with a receding hairline and sharp, angular features.

"It's better than the alternative," Larry Klein says.

An argument follows, and Mrs. Gruebber clings to her husband, crying. The children each hold on to a parent, burying their heads in their mom's stomach or father's chest.

"Stop it!" Emma yells over the noise. "Everybody's afraid, but none of this helps!"

"They attacked when we were weak," Mr. Gruebber says.

"Who attacked?" the single mom says.

"Iran? Russia? North Korea? Any of them are capable."

"But we're fighting back," the single mom finally says to Mr. Gruebber. "Right?"

Mr. Gruebber looks at her with small, sad eyes. "With what's left of our military, I assume, yes."

"We'll kill them," Rick says, squeezed into a corner with Brandon.

Mr. Gruebber shakes his head. "That's impossible. Don't you see what's happening? This is our end."

Nobody argues. The old man's grim prophecy has squeezed the breath from their lungs.

Israel

Zerah and his entire family have not left his parents' bomb shelter; each breath is edged with terror and desperation. Fearing attack from hostile nations at this time of global weakness, the Israeli government continues to enforce a nationwide lockdown, citizens huddled into bomb shelters with family and neighbors. Zerah has continued to try calling Dr. Haas but calls still can't go through inside the bomb shelter. He's even tried Dr. Sokolof's number without reaching anyone. Without being at work, there's no way of knowing who else is missing from his department or how many from the entire building.

Under the guise of fetching more food from the kitchen for all of them, Zerah leaves the bomb shelter and runs upstairs into the home, dialing a friend who works on the fifth floor of the medical center.

"Tavi," he says into the phone, surprised that he got through. He shuts himself in the bathroom in case someone from the family comes upstairs. "It's Zerah."

"Is everything okay, Zerah? Is your family safe?"

bullying and hype. By all military estimations, the greater threat came from Iran.

Russia had been selling arms and nuclear technology to Iran for decades, supplying components and equipment, and training Iranian technicians in the needed skills and methodology they lacked. Russia's training and the billions of US dollars given in the Iran nuclear deal were key factors in making Iran self-sufficient in nuclear missile production. Together, Russia and Iran are a formidable threat to the entire world, but the United States retaliated. America's nuclear weapons have destroyed much of Tehran and Moscow, but the United States is crippled.

In New York City alone, the United Nations, One World Trade Center, the Empire State Building, the Bank of America Tower, the New York Times Building, Rockefeller Center, Grand Central Terminal, much of Wall Street, and countless other buildings are leveled. They are completely gone from the skyline; others look as if their tops have been razored off or someone took a wrecking ball and riddled them with holes. An unnerving wail of sirens covers the grave-like city as ash and fire rise from bomb-cratered buildings and roads, and broken water mains gush a flood of water over what's left.

Terrorist sleeper cells within the United States had been waiting for this opportunity, when many of them could strike at once, hitting financial centers and houses of government in various cities. Buildings around the country were pocked from explosions or scorched from fire. The victims who could stumble away were physically disfigured and emotionally crippled. The country has been devastated.

Now that much of Israel's once-great ally the United States is shattered, the Jewish nation's enemies begin aligning. Within Palestine, members of Hamas retrieve their caches of weapons from underground bunkers. President Banes's plan for a two-state solution called for Israel to withdraw from ninety percent of Judea and Samaria (the West Bank), dividing Jerusalem so Palestinians could also claim it as their capital, and keeping the Jordan Valley to be used as a buffer zone against possible future aggression from the east. In the end, Palestine ended up with eighty percent of the West Bank and nearly one-half of Jerusalem. Israel kept the Jordan Valley.

"Yes. We are all together at my parents' home," he says, whispering. "Is your family safe?"

"We are. Frightened, but safe. It seems it's only a matter of time before our enemies strike. Everything feels so dark…" He can't find the words.

"I know." Zerah says. "I'm curious. Two colleagues that I know disappeared from our floor. Do you know of any others in the building?"

"A data specialist on our floor," Tavi says. "He was talking with a coworker. That man had to be helped out of the building. Shock, I suppose. I've heard there are between fifteen to twenty who are gone, but I don't know. Could be more."

"Did you know anything about any of them?"

"Not too much."

Zerah doesn't know how to ask the next question and pauses, thinking. "Was the man on your floor Orthodox?"

"What would that have to do with anything?"

Zerah feels a surge of panic. He can't appear interested in the messianic believer connection to the disappearances. "Just wondering how his family is doing. If they have other friends and family to count on."

"I've been told his family has also disappeared."

"His whole family!" Zerah says.

"And he wasn't…"

Zerah waits for more, but Tavi has stopped. "Wasn't what?" Zerah asks.

"Orthodox." Tavi's voice gets so low that Zerah struggles to hear. "He was messianic."

Zerah's heart races at the words. "Did you ever talk to him about it?"

"No. No one did. He was a very kind man and he often invited coworkers to a special service at the messianic church he attended so they could hear about God's plans for his chosen people, but no one ever went. Some people got very angry and insisted he stop inviting them."

"What did he say?"

Tavi is still whispering. "He said that a Jewish man named Paul called it a mystery, but that a partial hardening has happened to Israel until the fullness of the Gentiles has come in."

Zerah is quiet. "Do you know what he was talking about?"

"No. It was just babble to me. It doesn't make sense."

Questions loom between them, but there is nothing more either of them can say. Zerah hangs up and mutters curses as he sits on the lid of the toilet.

CHAPTER 11

Queens, NY

Elliott jumps awake and looks at his watch. It's 6:00 in the eveni. His eyes scan the room looking for the light of Jesus. He runs to t bathroom mirror and feels his forehead. There's nothing there to s He races to the TV. The screen is black; the power is out in New Yo but shock waves are ricocheting around the world.

Iran's and Russia's nukes had been ready for years and wasted r time in attacking the United States when millions disappeared, whic left the country exposed. The US military and government were i chaos, making them vulnerable targets. Three Kilo-class submarin from the Iranian fleet targeted two American aircraft carriers in th Strait of Hormuz, launching missiles that lifted the ships out of th water, breaking them in two, and destroying both.

Russia fired multiple Zircon hypersonic anti-ship missiles, targe ing US submarines, naval aircraft carriers, and other ships at sea. Inte continental ballistic missiles hit US military bases within the countr and abroad, leveling them and further collapsing the power of the U Armed Forces. With the military scrambling, missiles struck DC an Manhattan with little effort. Russia's hypersonic missiles, able to trav over five times the speed of sound, leveled several major cities, inclu ing Chicago, Los Angeles, San Francisco, Houston, Boston, Atlant and Seattle, devastating them. Russia had been forecasting a nuclea winter against the United States for years, but experts blew it off a

One of the stipulations of the two-state solution was that the Palestinian pay-to-slay had to be completely eradicated and their military and terrorist operations destroyed. They were also to set in motion democratic reforms that would protect the human rights of their own people. With the entirety of the land of Israel within reach, these stipulations were a small price to pay. Realizing that no one will come to the aid of Israel, leaders of Hamas, who have been quiet since the two-state solution, mobilize their forces, reach out to their allies, and begin plans for the "annihilation of the Zionist pigs."

Videos and pictures showing the Israel Defense Forces killing hundreds of Palestinians rushing across the border spread throughout the world. "Innocents are being slaughtered," news anchors are saying. But there's more to this story than the one side the news is presenting: The time is riper than ever for an Islamic caliphate to spread throughout the world, including in Europe and the United States.

Blood rushes from Elliott's head as he looks at the war zone outside his window, a product of ruthless, determined killers. "Help me! I don't know what to do!" he says.

He checks the lights. They're still out. He tries to get an Internet connection but there isn't any; the power is gone, along with the city. He bolts from the apartment into the hallway. It's dark as he knocks on the neighbor's door, and no one answers. He moves to the next apartment and knocks. No response. Then he runs to another and another before taking the stairs by two to the next floor. As he pounds on the third door, he can hear someone moving inside the apartment. "Please, are you in there? My name is Elliott, and I live downstairs."

"What do you want?" a woman responds with fear in her voice.

"Do you have a Bible?"

Elliott hears her fidgeting with the lock and the door opens a crack; a young black face peers at him through the chain. Her face is wet and her eyes bloodshot; her voice is shaking. "You want a Bible?" He nods, and she furrows her brow. "The city is destroyed."

"I know. I just saw what happened."

She looks closer. "What do you mean you just saw? Weren't you downstairs with everybody else when we were attacked?"

His face is solemn as he shakes his head. "I slept through it."

"That was thirteen hours ago." She begins to close the door. "You are wasted!"

He reaches for the door. "I'm not on drugs. It was Hashem." He notices her confusion. "God. It was God. Please. I need a Bible."

She strains her eyes to study him. "When the city was hit, we couldn't hear ourselves scream. How did you sleep through that…?" She begins to sob. "It was…It was so loud and then…" She cries, remembering. "Silence. And so dark. People were screaming that the terrorists were trying to kill us and that aliens had taken everyone." She covers her mouth, sobbing.

"No! It was Jesus Christ."

She looks at him, staring in disbelief. "Aren't you the Jewish guy downstairs?"

"I am. Again, I'm Elliott."

She squints as she looks at him through watery eyes. "Why are you talking about Jesus if you're Jewish?"

"I'll tell you all about it," he smiles. "What is your name?"

"Kennisha."

"Do you live here alone?"

Her tears fall over her cheeks. "I lived here with my sister and my niece."

"They're gone now?" he asks. She nods, closing her eyes. Elliott steps closer. "Please…could you tell me what happened?"

She closes the door and unlocks the chain, opening the door for him. He steps inside as she shuts and locks the door behind them. Kennisha steps into the living room and Elliott follows, sitting on the sofa next to her.

Her voice breaks as she begins to speak. She shakes her head and holds her hand in the air, waiting for words. "My niece was getting her appendix out. Kaala and I were in the waiting room talking. She was telling me about something she needed to do at work and then she…"

"Was gone."

She uses her hands to wipe her face and struggles to speak. "I freaked out. The others who were there started to scream; then I heard voices rising through each of the halls and I knew that something had happened. I ran as fast as I could, screaming for my niece. Some nurses tried to stop me, but I kept running and screaming for her. I finally found the operating room and the surgeon was white as a ghost. He was still holding some sort of surgical instrument in his hand and the nurses and other people were just stunned. He was operating on her, and then she just disappeared." She swipes her cheeks and looks up at the ceiling. "I don't even remember how I got home."

Elliott reaches for a box of tissues on the end table next to him, handing it to her. "Your sister and niece belonged to Jesus, didn't they?"

Kennisha uses a tissue to wipe under her eyes. "How do you know that?"

"Because all of the people who are gone are with him now. It wasn't terrorists or aliens or demons. Jesus called all of them home to be with him."

She begins to weep, groaning. "No! That's not true!"

Elliott's voice is gentle. "Jesus filled my apartment and told me." He knows he sounds insane. "I'm a Jew. I've never stepped foot in a church. I've never believed in Jesus my entire life. My family has never mentioned his name. When I heard the theory that someone thought that Jesus had returned for all of those who followed him, I was physically angry. I thought it was the most ignorant thing I'd ever heard. But then Jesus came to me."

She looks confused and full of pain. "What do you mean he filled your apartment?"

"There was this insanely bright light, and Jesus was the light. He was there. He touched me. I felt him. I talked to him. He told me that everyone who's missing is with him, and that he will come back again and this time, everyone will see him." She puts her hand over her mouth, listening to him. "I wouldn't believe it either if it hadn't happened to me. I'm the last person that you would expect to say that Jesus came and we missed him, but it's true, and your sister and niece are with him today."

Kennisha squeezes her eyes shut as tears begin to fall again. "Kaala told me over and over again that Jesus was real. She said God loved me.

But I couldn't stand it. Sometimes I felt like she was suffocating me." Her sobs are louder, shaking her shoulders. "But she tried," she whispers. "She and Keesa both tried to tell me." She looks at him through bloodshot eyes. "Jesus came."

Elliott nods. "Do you have any family besides your sister and niece?"

"No. Our mom died a few years ago and we didn't know our father. Mom believed in Jesus when she got sick and she told me and Kaala about him, but I just couldn't listen. I thought I knew enough about him. I mean, don't we all know about Jesus?" She stares at him, her face still distorted in pain. "Kaala *knew* him. My sweet Keesa *knew* him." She shuts her eyes again. "What do I do? What do I do?" she says, whispering as she rocks back and forth.

Elliott lays his hand on hers, squeezing it. "I'll be your friend, Kennisha." She looks at him. "We need each other, right?"

She nods, swiping another tear. "This building shifted when the city was hit. It felt like it was made of popsicle sticks. I thought it would crumble." Her voice rises, sounding hysterical. "I can't even look out the window. All those buildings gone...the city. How many people are dead beneath that rubble? What's going to happen to us?"

"I don't know. That's why I need a Bible. I know it has the answers."

She stands and walks into a bedroom. Upon returning to the living room, she holds out a Bible. "This was my sister's," she says, her eyes misting over as she looks at it. "She would love for you to use this." Elliott takes the Bible from her and looks at the cover. He's never held a Bible before. She sits next to him. "When is Jesus coming back?"

He shakes his head. "I don't know. I don't even know where to start in this book. Do you?"

CHAPTER 12

Israel

Israel's defense minister, deputy minister, and chiefs of staff from the Israel Defense Forces, the national security advisor, and Mossad director and deputy director stand in the middle of the room at the Ministry of Defense headquarters in Tel Aviv, staring at the wall of computers and screens lit up with satellite images from neighboring countries. Movements in Lebanon and from 213 kilometers away in Damascus have their attention. The rounds of hostilities between Israel and Palestine have emboldened Israel's enemies and they are about to move into place. The Israel Defense Forces are firing on the Palestinians and keeping them away from the border, but how long can they hold them off?

The faces of the defense minister and the men with him are shrouded with concern as images of Syria's elite Republican Guard are seen running over the Mezzeh Air Base compound. A few years ago, the Organisation for the Prohibition of Chemical Weapons found a stockpile of 1,300 tons of chemical weapons in Syria. Who knows where that number stands today? Years earlier, Israel bombed an unidentified site in Syria using Maverick missiles and 500-kilogram bombs. Intelligence revealed the site was a nuclear reactor under construction, and officials suspected North Korea (aided by Iran) of supplying a reactor to Syria for their nuclear weapons program.

According to the International Atomic Energy Agency, at the time, Syria possessed fifty-plus tons of natural uranium, enough for three to five nuclear weapons. Those numbers could only be much higher now. Israel has long suspected that many of Syria's chemical and nuclear weapons have been stored at another site, possibly close to Damascus, even beneath the city itself. Intelligence on the ground in Syria reveals that Hezbollah and units of the Iranian Revolutionary Guard that are stationed there and just over the northern border in Syria are on the move, headed toward them, and less than 100 kilometers away. Hezbollah was founded by the Iranian government, which wrote Hezbollah's manifesto in 1985 and has funded and equipped them since. The Iranian Revolutionary Guard Corps trained the terrorists themselves, and they share a common goal: destroy Israel.

The activity on the ground does not cause panic within the Ministry of Defense; they knew this day was coming. There is the grave realization that there has been no better time than now for Israel's enemies to try to wipe Israel from the map. Their greatest ally, the United States, has been devastated through the disappearance of millions and the near ruin of its military and is unable to help. At this point, the two-state solution with the Palestinians is nothing more than a flimsy piece of paper.

The defense minister, a stern-looking man with heavy jowls, regards the magnitude of the words of his chiefs of staff and generals and what this means for their country.

CHAPTER 13

Queens, NY

Emma hadn't prayed in years but found herself shouting, "God, save us! Don't let them kill us!" as an intercontinental ballistic missile hit the city. Prayers rushed out as cries and screams as the possibility of death gripped her soul. Emma's thoughts began and ended with her family. Images of her mom and dad and Sarah riding bikes, playing basketball in the driveway, and eating dinner together played like a reel of film in slow motion in her mind as the sounds of war erupted in the heart of the city. Her body felt cold, yet she was sweating; she could feel her heart pounding under her ribs. The group sat in unnerving silence hours after the explosion was heard, before finally deciding to leave the basement and slowly creep up the stairs as if to the gallows.

Their apartment building lost power during the attack and the entire building is wrapped in quiet as Matt and Emma enter their apartment. Matt rushes to the kitchen sink and turns on the faucet. "We still have water."

"For now," she says, skeptical that it will last.

"We have it. So that's something."

They walk together to the window and look out over the gutted city. A cloud of ash the pallor of death hangs over the city, and thick plumes of smoke stain the white clouds gray. The building blocks of the once-great city are now mangled heaps of stone and iron, glass and marble, gravestones for the dead who lie beneath. The brutal reality of the view sucks the breath from Emma's lungs and she gasps for air. "My God!"

she says sobbing. "I can't…" She presses her hands against the window. "I can't believe…" Matt reaches for her arm and pulls her from the window. "What do we do?" she asks as she wraps her arms around him, weeping. "What do we do?"

"I don't know, but we'll figure it out."

"We're going to die."

He pushes her from him, grabbing her arms. "We're not going to die! Look at us. We're alive!"

Her eyes are hollow and dark as she looks at him. "For how long?"

Elliott sits close to the window for sunlight, opens the Bible, and prays for help as he begins reading in Matthew, where Kennisha suggested he begin. He feels his heart flapping like a bird trying to take flight for the first time; here, he sees Abraham, Isaac, and Jacob listed in the genealogy of Jesus. "Jesus is from the line of Abraham, Isaac, Jacob, and David!" he says aloud. He continues reading as fast as he can and says, "All of these people are Jewish!"

He notices a note in the margin written by Kennisha's sister, Kaala: *Isaiah 53.* He knows who the prophet Isaiah is and flips to the table of contents at the beginning, trying to find his name. He turns to the pages for Isaiah and finds chapter 53, reading, "Who has believed our message and to whom has the arm of the LORD been revealed?" Further on he reads,

> Surely he took up our pain
>   and bore our suffering,
> yet we considered him punished by God,
>   stricken by him, and afflicted.
> But he was pierced for our transgressions,
>   he was crushed for our iniquities.

Elliott's heart beats faster as he reads and realizes this entire chapter, written hundreds of years *before* Jesus was born, is *about* Jesus. He looks again at verse one. "To whom has the arm of the LORD been revealed?"

His eyes fill at the words. "You have been revealed to me," he says. He sits in silence, grateful and humbled and desperate in a way he's never felt before.

When Elliott begins to read again from Matthew, he pauses in chapter 4 when Jesus says, "Repent, for the kingdom of heaven has come near." He looks at the words and realizes this is his mission: to bring people to repentance because the kingdom of heaven is nearer than ever before. He raises his arms, looking up. "I'm not qualified to do this. I don't know how." He waits in the stillness, hoping for an audible voice or the light of Jesus to fill the room again. He looks down at the page and reads about the calling of the apostles, following another side note written by Kaala in the margin and turns back to Isaiah. This time to chapter 43:

> "You are my witnesses," declares the LORD,
>   "and my servant whom I have chosen,
> so that you may know and believe me
>   and understand that I am he.
> Before me no god was formed,
>   nor will there be one after me.
> I, even I, am the LORD,
>   and apart from me there is no savior.
> I have revealed and saved and proclaimed—
>   I, and not some foreign god among you.
> You are my witnesses," declares the LORD,
> "that I am God.
>   Yes, and from ancient days I am he.
> No one can deliver out of my hand.
>   When I act, who can reverse it?"

Elliott's mouth falls open as he gapes at the words. God has used two hand-scribbled notes in Kaala's Bible to speak to him through this ancient text. He is God's witness, a chosen servant who would point people to the Savior, and that has left no room for argument.

"Forgive me," he whispers.

CHAPTER 14

Queens, NY

The endless wail of sirens in the streets and the whir of helicopter blades in the air have been constant noises since the city was destroyed. The sirens' high-pitched squeals would be nerve-shattering if Emma's weren't already stripped bare. "I want to know if my sister is okay," she says, her voice quivering. Wedding magazines still lay on the coffee table, but Emma hasn't noticed them. The idea of a wedding is absurd now. "What if I never get to talk to her again?"

Matt moves to her side on the sofa. "You will. They just need to get the power fixed and cell towers working."

"The electrical grid would need to be rebuilt, Matt! Cell towers are destroyed. Everything's gone."

"It'll just take some time, but…"

She screams over him. "Look at the city, Matt! Who can fix *that*?" Her eyes are bloodshot and swollen from crying as she looks out the window in disbelief. "I hate not knowing what's happened to Sarah. I'm so afraid."

"She lives in a small town. I'm sure she's safe," Matt says.

"This doesn't even feel like our city anymore. It doesn't feel like our apartment." She bolts upright on the sofa. "We need to get out of the city. We need a gun!"

Matt puts his hand on Emma's leg. "We have to try to stay calm. We'll take it a day at a time and see what we need." He looks down at her lap and notices a book. "Is that a Bible?"

She nods, picking it up. "I found it in Mrs. Ramos's bag."

He looks at her. "Were you reading it?"

"There has to be something in here, Matt. There's a reason in here that Mrs. Ramos and her family and my mom are gone."

He shakes his head. "We've been through this, and…"

She doesn't let him finish. "No. We haven't been through *this*," she says, holding the Bible closer to his face. "The only things we've been through are our own ideas and opinions. You said there's no way that it could be Jesus who came for his people, but how is that fact?"

Matt stands to his feet, irritated. "It's farfetched. That's all I'm saying."

"But aliens, Satan, or biochemical warfare aren't farfetched? How can you go throughout the day just accepting that it was one of those theories or some sort of nuclear holocaust, and not want to research to see if there's something more in here? There have to be answers in here about the end of the world, Matt. Why would God tell us about the beginning of the world but not the end? We've heard about the apocalypse and 666 and other stuff, so the end *has* to be in here somewhere!" She says, looking in the Bible.

He shrugs, standing in front of her. "I don't know. You heard some of those people on TV. Maybe the earth was cleansed from all the bigoted haters."

Emma hasn't had time yet to grieve the loss of her mom, let alone the loss of her city and possibly her country, and can't deal with this; she feels like she's losing control and finds herself screaming. "My mom wasn't a bigot! She didn't hate anybody. She loved you and Brandon and Rick! You know how much she loved you. How could you say that?" She bursts into tears, and he pulls her into him.

"I'm sorry. I'm so sorry. I know that. Your mom was awesome. I'm just so exhausted that I'm sick." She looks at him and nods as he kisses her forehead. "I'm sorry, Em. I'm just so tired."

He leaves her alone, and she feels the tears welling again.

CHAPTER 15

Israel

Zerah and his family have been in the bomb shelter for nearly two days. With five extra mouths to feed, his mother and father have only been able to serve a couple of small meals. All of Israel is still in shock after seeing the images and reports coming from the United States, their one true ally in the world. So many US cities have been decimated that it now looks like a third-world country. By all accounts, it appears that Iran and Russia targeted "the Great Satan's" major cities with nukes and activated terrorist sleeper cells that had been pre-positioned for years within the United States to carry out bombings on what was code-named "Judgment Day."

Unable to stop a chain of events that was spinning out of control within the country, the US military struck back at Iran and Russia in what limited capacity it had, but the damage had been done. As one news anchor said, "The supergiant of the world, the United States, has been slain."

Zerah feels sick to his stomach listening to the stories and watching the charred images of the once-great United States. Electrical grids and cell towers are destroyed following the attacks on several major cities, and many US citizens have yet to know if family and friends are alive. The videos and pictures that flash on the screen are incomprehensible. With the United States hobbled, what does that mean for the rest of the world? What does it mean for Israel? Though their history together had been strained at times, there is no other nation that would come to the defense of Israel like the United States. Despite a two-state solution and peace treaty that was put in place by President Banes between Israel and Palestine, it won't be long before Israel's enemies turn their greatest weapons against her.

For the last several hours, news reports have been swirling about wars that have erupted throughout the globe; the entire planet seems to be launching missiles and attacking their enemies. A group of world leaders has announced that, in response to the disappearances, wars, and chaos throughout the globe, they are planning to meet in Europe. They offer promises of "peace and protection during this time of unprecedented world upheaval."

Zerah has attempted to reach everyone on his contact list, wondering if those he knows are still here. If someone mentions that they know a person who has disappeared, he excuses himself from the bomb shelter and speaks quietly on the phone. In every instance, the person who has disappeared has been a follower of Jesus. For all his years of scientific training, he can't wrap his mind around this; nothing makes sense. And while he wants to talk this through with someone, he knows he can't utter a word inside these walls.

He hasn't stopped thinking about his conversation with Tavi. As his mother and sister begin preparations for their simple meal, and he and his father and brother-in-law, Amir, watch TV reports, he types the few words he remembers from his call with Tavi into his phone: *partial hardening of Israel.* It takes a while due to slower-than-usual Internet service, but little by little, results begin to pop up on his screen. He realizes the first result is taking him to the New Testament and he looks up at his father and brother-in-law, engrossed in the TV. He is reluctant to click on any of the results, but feels that he must. He waits a moment longer before clicking. After what feels like several minutes, Romans 11:25-26 appears on the screen:

> I do not want you to be unaware of this mystery, brothers:
> a partial hardening has come upon Israel, until the fullness
> of the Gentiles has come in. And in this way all Israel will
> be saved, as it is written,

"The Deliverer will come from Zion,
     he will banish ungodliness from Jacob."

It doesn't make sense. There's the word *mystery* that he recalls Tavi saying, but what is the hardening of Israel? He also remembers Tavi said that everything feels dark, followed by a news reporter saying it felt like "evil was in the air," and his sense of foreboding and feeling of uncertainty are stronger now. He wishes he had never dug into this. He's about to close the site when he sees the words *full chapter* and clicks, painstakingly waiting for it to load before reading from the beginning:

> I ask, then, has God rejected his people? By no means! For I myself am an Israelite, a descendant of Abraham, a member of the tribe of Benjamin. God has not rejected his people whom he foreknew. Do you not know what the Scripture says of Elijah, how he appeals to God against Israel? "Lord, they have killed your prophets, they have demolished your altars, and I alone am left, and they seek my life." But what is God's reply to him? "I have kept for myself seven thousand men who have not bowed the knee to Baal." So too at the present time there is a remnant, chosen by grace. But if it is by grace, it is no longer on the basis of works; otherwise grace would no longer be grace.

> What then? Israel failed to obtain what it was seeking. The elect obtained it, but the rest were hardened, as it is written,

> "God gave them a spirit of stupor,
>   eyes that would not see
>   and ears that would not hear,
> down to this very day."

What is this? Zerah thinks. Questions and thoughts swirl in his mind. Who is this Jew, this descendent of Abraham who wrote this? And there's that word *hardened* again. *Eyes that could not see. Ears that could not hear.* He doesn't understand any of it. His heart is pounding and he can't read anymore. He stands up to get away from the sound of the TV and moves toward the door.

"What's wrong Zerah?" Rada asks. "You look ill."

He looks at her and his mother trying to parse together a small meal for the family. "Just concerned," he says, wishing he could sit down and have a conversation with his sister. "I'm going upstairs for some air."

"You mustn't do that, Zerah," his mother says, stepping toward him.

He takes hold of her hands, smiling. "I need to breathe some fresh air, Mom. I promise you that no one will see my nose in the window." He squeezes her hands and smiles at Rada. "I will be back in a couple of minutes."

His mind is swimming as he cranks open a window in the living room. He rests his head against the screen, letting the breeze lift his hair and fill his nostrils.

"What is wrong, Zerah?"

He jumps and turns to see Rada. "I got lightheaded is all. The news. The same four walls closing in on us."

She tries to smile, but it's hard to fake anything right now. Zerah has always loved his sister. He was her fierce defender when she was a little girl, but when she turned seven or eight, he realized she could defend herself and everyone else in the household. She is funny and bright; a wonderful mother and the best friend he's ever had.

Her eyes reveal concern as she whispers, "What did you read on your phone?"

To discover more about the biblical facts behind the story, read Where in the Word? *on page 213, or continue reading the novel.*

CHAPTER 16

Queens, NY

Emma positions a chair near the window so she can see better and looks in the back of Mrs. Ramos's Bible at the concordance for any clue as to what has happened. She looks under "Jesus" and there are so many entries that she feels overwhelmed, but begins to tackle the reading. After a few hours she feels as though she's still floundering yet reads the next entry in the concordance: 1 Thessalonians 4.

> We do not want you to be uninformed, brothers, about those who are asleep, that you may not grieve as others do who have no hope. For since we believe that Jesus died and rose again, even so, through Jesus, God will bring with him those who have fallen asleep. For this we declare to you by a word from the Lord, that we who are alive, who are left until the coming of the Lord, will not precede those who have fallen asleep.

She stops, rereading the passage. Then she reads aloud, beginning in the middle of verse 15: "We who are alive, who are left until the coming of the Lord, will not precede those who have fallen asleep." Her heart begins to race and she sits upright on the chair, holding the Bible closer to her face and still reading aloud. "For the Lord himself will descend from heaven with a cry of command, with the voice of an archangel, and with the sound of the trumpet of God. And the dead in Christ will rise first." She puts her hand on her head. "Oh my God!"

She stands as she reads, "Then we who are alive, who are left, will be caught up together with them in the clouds to meet the Lord in the air, and so we will always be with the Lord. Therefore encourage one another with these words." She falls to the chair and stares at the Bible. "Does it really say this?"

She reads the words again and again, her heart thumping against her ribs.

Elliott has slept only in spurts since Kennisha gave him her sister's Bible. With the exception of nodding off for five or ten minutes here and there, he has read it almost nonstop, including by candlelight when darkness falls. Until the electricity can be fixed (if it can be), the building and the city itself sit in unnerving blackness at night. Each time he sleeps, his dreams are vivid and powerful as the Holy Spirit carries him along, teaching and instructing him. He wakens with a jolt, his neck strained from his position in the chair. He moves to the table, spreading the Bible open in front of him. For the last day he has wanted to run to the streets to help the people who have survived the bombing but lost their apartments or homes. They have taken shelter inside local missions or churches, but each time Elliott wants to leave his apartment, he senses the Holy Spirit telling him to stay and learn and prepare.

He reads the verses aloud from 1 Thessalonians 4 one more time, letting the words sink in, then begins reading chapter 5, arriving at verse 2: "For you know very well that the day of the Lord will come like a thief in the night." He stops, rereading the verse again before continuing to verse 3: "While people are saying, 'Peace and safety,' destruction will come on them suddenly…and they will not escape." He puts his finger under the next verse: "But you, brothers and sisters, are not in darkness so that this day should surprise you like a thief."

He keeps his eyes on the words "For you know" in verse 2. "Your followers knew," he says, whispering. "People were saying, 'Peace and safety.'" He remembers every president or prime minister or government leader using these very words in nearly every speech that was given regarding the condition of the world for the last several years. "Destruction came on *them*. *They* did not escape. *They* weren't prepared. *Them*. *They*. *They*," he says, studying the words. "Your followers, the *brothers and sisters*, weren't in darkness, and your coming didn't surprise them like a thief." He stares at the words on the page. "Why didn't they tell everyone this?"

He looks at the next verses: "You are all children of the light and children of the day. We do not belong to the night or to the darkness. So then, let us not be like others, who are asleep, but let us be awake and sober."

"Children of the light," he says. "Children of the day. Your children weren't stumbling around in the dark." He looks up from the page as if seeing something in his mind. "They were awake and sober, not sleeping." He shakes his head, wondering how many are still sleeping despite the evidence of Jesus's return for his followers. "Your followers weren't like *the others*, who were asleep. They were different."

He continues to read aloud verses 9 and 10: "For God did not appoint us to suffer wrath but to receive salvation through our Lord Jesus Christ. He died for us so that, whether we are awake or asleep, we may live together with him. Therefore encourage one another and build each other up, just as in fact you are doing." He rereads the words. "Your children weren't appointed to suffer wrath. All those sleeping in the ground. All your children awake on Earth at the time." He reads aloud, "Therefore encourage one another and build each other up."

"They weren't afraid," he said. "They encouraged each other about your return."

The sound of glass shattering makes Elliott jump to his feet and look out the window. Since it became obvious that the attack on the city was over, looting has been nonstop. Supermarket aisles in the city are empty, restaurants and businesses are being trashed. Malls had shut down immediately following the disappearances, locking their doors and securing their storefronts with bars, but it has proven futile. Many people have stayed locked in at home, too afraid to step beyond their own door until this madness stops.

Elliott watches as a lighting store down the block is emptied. Men, women, and even children are carrying lamps, pendant lights, and chandeliers down the street. The shoe store next door looks as if a swarm of bees has attacked it. He can't tell man from woman as they scramble on top of each other for a pair of loafers, pumps, or tennis shoes. He feels sick to his stomach watching them. It is as if all good-ness has disappeared from the earth.

"Go to them." Elliott shakes off the thought, thinking it's his own. But there it is again: "Go to them."

The voice he hears isn't from within the room or the next one, but from somewhere inside. He pushes his forehead against the window. "How? I don't know what to say to them."

"I am with you."

Elliott puts his hands on the glass and feels angry, watching a mother shove a pair of too-big shoes into the hands of her ten- or eleven-year-old son. The shoes are quickly pinched by another woman, and the mother punches her in the head. They come to blows as the boy snatches up the shoes, hitting the woman with one of them.

"Go."

Elliott grabs his keys and runs for the door.

CHAPTER 17

Israel

Rada steps toward Zerah. "What did you read on your phone?"

He shrugs. "The same chilling news stories that we've been hearing. War tearing apart the seams that are left of the world."

She shakes her head. "It wasn't the same stories, Zerah. You were visibly shaken a few minutes ago. What do you know?"

He turns to look out the window to the view of the modest street they've seen for the past twenty years in this house. How can it still look the same and yet everything be so different? He feels her hand on his shoulder.

"Please, Zerah, tell me."

He looks at her. How can he tell her? "It doesn't make any sense."

"Maybe it will make sense to me."

He glances toward the kitchen to make sure no one has come upstairs from the bomb shelter. Whispering he says, "I'm just trying to piece things together."

Her eyes are earnest. "And?"

"There is one common thread with the people who have disappeared."

She looks skeptical, leaning in. "You're not going to say that it is the messianic connection."

"So far, all of the people at the medical center…"

"How many people that you know of, Zerah? Four? Five? Maybe ten?" She is hissing at him. "Ten people out of millions around the world and you think you've figured out the connection?"

She's angry and he puts his hand on her arm. "I know. I know! But you said yourself that Jesus coming for his followers is one of the theories."

"Because that's what they said on the news! I didn't say I believed it!" She is about to turn away, but he holds her in front of him.

"I didn't say I believed it either, but I called a man I work with and he said that a coworker in his department was a messianic believer. He always invited everyone in the department to his church. Of course no one went. It made them angry to hear him speak of it. But he mentioned the words *a partial hardening of Israel.*"

She looks confused. "So? What does that mean?"

He pulls his cell phone from his back pocket and turns it on, reading, "I do not want you to be unaware of this mystery, brothers: a partial hardening has come upon Israel, until the fullness of the Gentiles has come in. And in this way all Israel will be saved, as it is written, 'The Deliverer will come from Zion, he will banish ungodliness from Jacob.'"

She bends her neck forward to look at his phone. "What are you reading?" she asks, anger in her tone.

"A Jew named Paul wrote this over two thousand years ago."

"So? Why should we care? What does that have anything to do with what's happening in the world today?"

He holds up his hand so she'll listen. "I ask, then, has God rejected his people?" He reads, looking up at her. "By no means!...So too at the present time there is a remnant, chosen by grace. But if it is by grace, it is no longer on the basis of works; otherwise grace would no longer be grace. What then? Israel failed to obtain what it was seeking. The elect obtained it, but the rest were hardened, as it is written, 'God gave them a spirit of stupor, eyes that would not see and ears that would not hear, down to this very day.'" His eyes are wide, imploring her for help in understanding.

"This means nothing, Zerah. The ramblings of a madman is all. And I don't know who is madder. This Jew," she says, jabbing his phone, and then poking him in the chest, "Or this Jew."

He has told her too much and needs to back off. Nodding, he smiles at her. "Maybe I am mad. I'm sorry, Rada. Like you said, ramblings of a madman." As she slips away, he turns off his phone and slides it into his back pocket, looking out to the street again.

"Are we hardened, Zerah? Do we have eyes that won't see and ears that won't hear?"

Her voice startles him, but he doesn't turn to look at her this time. "I don't know." He feels her hand on his shoulder.

"I'm sorry, Zerah. I don't think you're a madman. I think you're as confused and scared as the rest of us." She squeezes his shoulder, then leaves him alone.

He's unable to rejoin his family just yet; he sits on the sofa and snaps up the remote, turning on the TV in the living room. An emergency signal is blaring as Israel's defense minister steps to a podium from the Ministry of Defense headquarters. The signal ends as the defense minister begins to speak. He is brief and to the point.

"All active members of the Israel Defense Forces have been vigorously defending our country, but due to the enormous threat to our national security, all inactive members of the IDF who are forty-five or below must report for duty immediately."

It has been years since Zerah has performed his duties in the IDF, and the threat of war makes his hands tremble.

CHAPTER 18

Queens, NY

Elliott races to the street below and stops, unsure of what to do now. People are in a frenzy to clean out each business along the street, threatening one another as violence breaks out among them. When the city still had power, the mayor and chief of police were on the news, urging people to stay off the streets, to remain calm, and to think of the city's peace and individual safety, but since the attack, the city has been upended.

A year earlier, riots broke out in the streets after the mayor's victory, and that was *with* police presence, and no one can forget the rioting and looting that took place after President Banes was voted into office. What can anyone expect now that the police presence has been diminished, along with any sense of kindness and reason? Law enforcement is predominantly focused on protecting what government buildings are left and larger businesses in the city, leaving owners of smaller establishments to fend for themselves. Most restaurant, store, and business owners are too frightened and have become weary from the constant state of vigilance they've had to keep and have given up.

"Please stop this," Elliott shouts. He may as well be yelling into a hurricane. He spots a car that had crashed into a business front, one that is wrecked beyond driving or stealing, and jumps on top of it. "I know what happened! I know where everyone went!" The free-for-all continues, and Elliott feels anger stretching through his chest. He shouts louder over them. "I know what happened to the people you love!" A few on the street stop to look at him, but most ignore him. "They aren't here, are they?" he says, looking at a woman around fifty or so. She shakes her head, her eyes filled with sadness. "No matter how long you wait, they don't answer the phone or come through the door, do they?" he says to a man around thirty. The man looks at the ground as others begin to gather. Elliott looks at them, those who were asleep just like him when Jesus came; those who are left to patch together some sort of life without many of the ones they love.

"The people you lost all had one thing in common: They followed Jesus. They didn't just *say* they followed Jesus. They didn't post just the right verse on social media to make you feel good. They *followed* Jesus. They listened to him; they knew his voice because they read his word," he says, holding the Bible in the air. "They knew he meant what he said in his word, and they lived by his word. They were true followers. It wasn't a faith that they made up to suit their life, was it?" He looks at a couple in their forties who aren't responding. More are gathering, and Elliott shouts louder, trying to be heard above the ruckus of the looting.

"How do you know this?" an older woman says as she clutches two pairs of shoes to her chest.

"Jesus told me," Elliott says, noticing their reactions of confusion and anger. He knows that some faiths are represented here who don't want to hear the name of Jesus, as well as people of no religion at all. The melee around him is almost too much, but Elliott taps the Bible. "It's all in here. I've been reading it since everyone disappeared." He reads John 14:1-4 to them, emphasizing certain words: "Do not let your hearts be troubled. You believe in God; believe also in me. My Father's house has many rooms; if that were not so, would I have told you that *I am going there to prepare a place for you*? And if I go and prepare a place for you, *I will come back and take you to be with me* that you also may be where I am. *You know the way to the place where I am going.*"

Elliott looks out at the growing number of people who have stopped to listen. "After the death and resurrection of Jesus, he went back to his Father's house, to heaven, to prepare a place for all who believe in him. And he said, 'If I *go* and prepare a place for you, *I will come back and take you to be with me.*'" Excitement builds in his voice. "*I will take you to be with me.* Jesus came back and took his followers to be with him just as he said he would." People begin to shout over him, but he presses on. "He said, '*You know the way to the place where I am going.*' His followers knew the way to heaven."

Some men curse and leave the group, but Elliott begins reading from 1 Thessalonians 4: "Listen to this: 'According to the Lord's word, we tell you that we who are still alive, who are left until the coming of the Lord, will certainly not precede those who have fallen asleep. For the Lord himself will come down from heaven, with a loud command, with the voice of the archangel and with the trumpet call of God, and the dead in Christ will rise first. After that, we who are still alive and are left will be caught up together with them in the clouds to meet the Lord in the air. And so we will be with the Lord forever. Therefore encourage one another with these words.'"

Elliott's actions become animated as his arms begin to flap. "Did you hear that? It says right here that Jesus would descend from heaven, and the dead in Christ would rise first when they heard his command, and then those who are alive would be caught up together with all those people who just came out of their graves, wherever their dead body was. I was standing in a cemetery when many graves burst open and urns became empty. I've never heard of anything like that before in my life, and I've never been so scared."

The shouting continues and a young man around twenty yells, "That doesn't mean it's true."

Elliott lifts the Bible over his head. "The Bible says right here exactly what would happen, and it did happen. Graves burst open and then living, breathing souls were snatched away right in front of us. Their disappearances were captured on security cameras around the world!"

"I don't believe it!" the young man shouts.

"And I would have been the first to not believe it," Elliott says, looking at him. "I'm a Jew. Do you think for a moment I would have believed that Jesus was responsible for the disappearance of all these people? Do you think your unbelief is any greater than mine was? Jews don't talk about Jesus. Jews don't mention his name. Just like the Bible says," he says, tapping the Bible, "I was asleep. Just like you're asleep."

Elliott makes a sweeping motion with his arm over the crowd. "You are all asleep! It's time to wake up because in Revelation, the last book of the Bible, and in other books in here, we read that Jesus will be coming again, but this time he won't just step into the air for his followers. He won't be snatching them up to heaven. He will come back *with* his followers! He will come *down* from heaven on a horse and all those people who just left this Earth will come back with him on horses of their own. Did you hear that? The people you love who are now gone will come back with him. He's returning to judge the world of sin and set up his kingdom. Once he splits open that sky in judgment, you won't have time to change your mind and follow him. Now is the time!"

"He did this just so we could have another chance to follow him?" a woman mocks. "That's not love!"

"God didn't destroy our city. He didn't do this," Elliott says, motioning with his arm toward the rioting in the street. "God is loving," he says. "That's why I'm standing here today. For years I lived with emptiness inside of me. I knew that something was missing. You *know* there's an emptiness inside you. We all know it. That emptiness, that hole is because Jesus is missing in our lives. He loved me so much that he came to me revealing his salvation. He is revealing his salvation to you today so that no matter what happens over these next few years of judgment, you can live with him forever."

"Judgment?" a young man of twenty or so shouts. "Your God is judging us?" Many in the crowd become agitated, yelling abusive and foul remarks over each other.

Although they are shouting and cursing, Elliott feels strangely peaceful as the words rise up within him. "God is patient and good and longsuffering, but in his word we are told that he judges sin. He also says that all have sinned. All of us are sinners and we need him."

These words make the people angrier and many of them shout over him. "We aren't sinners!" Their voices ring out. "The sinners are gone—just like everyone is saying. The universe took them."

Elliott raises the Bible higher. "We are *all* sinners. Our sin has created a world full of evil and wickedness, and God is judging the world of that sin. It says in Romans, 'Because of your hard and impenitent heart you are storing up wrath for yourself on the day of wrath when God's righteous judgment will be revealed.' But even in God's wrath on a sinful world, he is still drawing you to him. The prophet Isaiah said, 'Seek the Lord while he may be found; call on him while he is near. Let the wicked forsake their ways and the unrighteous their thoughts. Let them turn to the Lord, and he will have mercy on them, and to our God, for he will freely pardon.'"

He speaks to them as friends. He is sincere and compassionate and full of hope in what feels like a hopeless situation. "A man named Paul was a Jew just like me and he lived over two thousand years ago. He said, 'Now is the time of God's favor, now is the day of salvation.' Don't put off what you can do right here. All who call upon the name of the Lord shall be saved! Now is the time to ask Jesus for salvation."

"Now's the time for this," a man says as he curses and calls Elliott filthy names.

Several in the crowd laugh, but Elliott speaks directly to him. "I was you before all this happened. I never wanted to hear the name of Jesus. We never spoke his name in my home. If I had heard someone say these things I would be as angry as you. You don't have to believe me. Pick up this book and read what God has said. Beginning in the books of the Old Testament, he told us how everything was going to end."

Noise picks up down the street as glass shatters at another business storefront. People in the crowd turn at the commotion, and several run toward the newly available treasures. The man hurls more obscenities at Elliott, disgusted by him and his God, and he follows the pack to ransack the next store.

"God knew this is what we would come to because we're human," Elliott continues to the crowd remaining before him. "He knew we would shut him out of everything. He knew we would want to rule ourselves and that because of that we would destroy ourselves. Look at us. Look at what has happened to our city and country by those who hate us. And look at what we're doing to what's left of our own neighborhood. We're destroying it and ourselves. All around the world we're at war with and killing each other. Several of you have been cursing at me for the last couple of minutes, but for centuries now humans have been cursing at God, telling him to get out of their lives. We've rejected him and his word and we have rebelled against him. From the very beginning, God said that his spirit would not strive with man forever." A group of five men gather along the edge of the crowd to listen.

"God's wrath isn't like man's wrath. If it was, we would have been doomed long ago because of the way we have rebelled against him. God is patient; he doesn't want anyone to die without knowing Jesus, but his cup of wrath is filling up because of our disobedience and sins against him. We read right in the Bible in Hebrews that it is a fearful thing to fall into the hands of the living God. He is good and kind and loving, but he's also called the *lion* of Judah for a reason. Lions are dangerous. He loves you so much that he wants you to repent and turn to him."

"You are an infidel and a liar!" shouts one of the five men who have gathered on the edge of the crowd. His dark face is ridged with lines. "This is the work of the Mahdi." The bodies of the other four men are stiff with rage.

"The Mahdi, your prophesied redeemer…where is he in this mess?" Elliott says as he motions with his arm out toward the street.

"We don't know where he is, but he is working to establish his rule. He will remain hidden until he reappears to bring justice to the world," one of the men says, pushing his way through the crowd.

"How will he do that?"

The men are furious. "We don't know these things," another yells. "They are above us. That is up to the Mahdi and Allah."

Elliott kneels down on the car, facing them as he speaks. "From the beginning, God revealed everything to us about the end. He has held nothing back or kept anything secret. He loves us all so much that he put everything into his holy word that we might know him, that we might know these things, and that we would believe and turn to his son, Jesus."

"You are oppressing these people," another yells as they each scream louder. "Your Jesus is a fascist, Islamophobic, Zionist pig."

Elliott's voice does not rise to meet theirs; he is calm. "The Bible says that we are all made in the image of God and precious in his sight. He doesn't want any of us to perish, but to come to him through Jesus."

The men, revolted by what they've heard, curse and roar out, their voices rising with fury. "Our beloved Mohammed said that a word of truth in front of a tyrant ruler or leader is the best form of jihad," the first man shouts. "Allah will accept this."

The men scream as they leap for Elliott. He falls backward onto the hood of the car, his heart beating against his ribs, but amazingly, the men don't land on him or the car. Instead, they flail to the ground like birds shot from the sky, then scramble to their feet, trying to climb onto the wrecked heap. It's as if they're grasping at air, slippery with oil, and they shout curses. Elliott is breathless as he stands; some in the crowd begin to snicker at the sight of the men thrashing about against each other.

Incensed, one of them pulls out a gun and aims it at Elliott. "Get down from there, Jew, and face us like a man."

Elliott's tone is peaceful, and his eyes are filled with compassion. He is less than a foot away from the man and can see the beads of sweat in his eyebrows and on his upper lip. "I face you like a man. I don't have a gun. All I have is the truth. Jesus said, 'I am the way, the truth, and the life. No one...'"

The man screams and opens fire at Elliott. The crowd shrieks as the bullets are heard hitting the building behind Elliott. He feels the blood drain from his head, looks down at his chest, and then at the building. The bullets missed him and licked at the red brick, leaving five distinct graze marks on the storefront. The man fires again and again, and each time, the bullets pass by Elliott and ricochet off the brick.

The woman who earlier had shoved shoes into the arms of her child cries, "He's a man of God." Others begin to cry at what they've just witnessed.

The man with the gun curses and threatens to kill Elliott, shouting words the crowd can't understand. He and his companions push their way out of the crowd, screaming as they go.

There's no time for Elliott to say anything more to them because people are gathering closer. His head is throbbing; he is in awe. God filled his mouth with his word and protected him from a murderer's gun, just as Jesus said he would do. Elliott looks down the street, which is crackling with chaos, and feels his heart swelling.

These are his streets, and this is his mission.

To discover more about the biblical facts behind the story, read Where in the Word? *on page 223, or continue reading the novel.*

CHAPTER 19

Rome, Italy

With the United Nations gone, the conference of world leaders in Europe has garnered the globe's attention. All world leaders were invited to participate, but Russia, along with Iran, some African countries, parts of Asia, and many countries of the Middle East have declined. In a great move of solidarity, the nations of Europe (many of which have been left weakened and vulnerable since the global disappearances), along with some countries in North Africa, the United States, Canada, and parts of Western Asia, have joined together. After losing much of their populations, many of them have banded together with three, four, or five other countries to form one nation. Many of these "nations" have now come together to form a ten-nation coalition that is being called the European 10, or E10 for short. The formation of the coalition has been miraculous, to say the least, and has given a breath of hope to the world.

In order to become stronger, the United States has joined the coalition, and US president Banes has, in his words, "Felt enormous relief to hear global leaders speak of peace, security, and restoration for the world. Out of chaos, unity is being developed on a scale the world has never known. We will truly have a global, interdependent society."

But it is not President Banes, Chancellor Albrecht of Germany, Prime Minister Clattenberg of the United Kingdom, or any of the seven other E10 leaders who has received the most attention in the last couple of days. Rather, it is the counsel secretary of the E10, a man by the name of Victor Quade, who is generating buzz as the E10's designated spokesperson.

Born to a German father and French mother, and with paternal grandparents in Poland, the thirty-something charismatic blonde had a glorious childhood and education across much of Europe. Quade's work in the private sector, first in marketing and then in finance, made his climb a natural one from the Economic and Financial Affairs Council of the feeble European Union to the current president of the failing European Council. The single, handsome leader found himself on the news on a daily basis as he began to restore life to the bleeding Union. He was charming and magnanimous on screen, and reporters and viewers alike clamored to hear more from him.

Quade soon learned the fine art of manipulation and extending the hand of friendship and comradery across the aisle to those who had once been enemies in the European Union, brokering deals between fighting factions whose countries had long been in turmoil. He fought for open borders across Europe, maintaining that autonomous nations were foes of global peace.

Quade has long been a proponent of socialized medicine and a common currency for not only Europe but the world. "A piece of paper in our wallets should not prevent us from growing stronger and closer together," he was filmed saying at a conference years earlier. "The coins rattling around in our pockets should not keep us from helping a brother or sister in need. All that I have is yours," he said, his voice rising with compassion and humility. "We can only be one in strength, in power, in unity, in kindness, in peace, in security, and in belief if we can share in one another's burdens and joys. There is no greater way to share each other's burdens than through the commonality of our monies."

Quade's views were met with some resistance, but many leaders and nations were already leaning his way before the havoc of the worldwide disappearances. His proposal for a common worldwide currency not only makes the most sense now but may possibly be the only way to ensure survival.

Reporters and TV news crews from around the world cram inside the grand lobby of the Palace of Justice to record the first statements from the E10 leaders. The Italian Supreme Court normally meets and has its offices here, but the vanishings have set the world on a new path for normal.

"A new international order is emerging that is radically different from anything we've ever known," President Banes says from the podium on the landing at the top of the stairs. "It poses enormous challenges, but now is the time to reorder our world." The reporters' clamor echoes throughout the atrium and Banes raises his hands to quiet them.

"How can the E10 do this?" a female reporter from Japan asks, her voice rising above the others.

"That is the challenge, isn't it?" Prime Minister Sophia Clattenberg says. "The challenge is how to build a world order for the first time in history, one that will cover our entire globe and protect all of our citizens."

Before allowing any questions, Quade raises his hand, indicating he has something to add, and steps to the podium. "The E10 has a plan. In these coming days, we will forge for ourselves and for future generations a truly global society. Together we will form a global order that will stop war and famine, hatred and discrimination, an order that will eliminate poverty once and for all and standardize medicine for all. A world order that will be based on one currency for all our citizens. A world order that will work together to feed and clothe and provide a safe home for everyone. We are citizens of the world together, and we must act as one. A peaceful and interdependent world will be built from these ashes of crises. We have been thrust into a great position for global unity, and we will all rise victorious."

"But the world is currently at war," a reporter yells above the noise. "Many countries are attempting to annihilate each other. What…"

"These conflicts," Quade says, refusing to say the word *war*, "will end. Peace and security must be our top priority."

"Without a stable world, life as we know it is doomed, as a next world war would usher the globe into its final conclusion," President Banes says. "We are working with all the nations involved to bring an end to these conflicts. We are working on what is called the Pathway of

Peace, and it is needed now more than ever. We are aware that the Persian Empire, the Russian Empire, and an Arab caliphate could wreak havoc on our global security, and we extend our hands in solidarity to these leaders to join us. We must focus on peace and safety for the citizens of Earth."

"What exactly is the Pathway of Peace?" a reporter with long black hair asks from the front.

"We are no longer enemies," German chancellor George Albrecht says, looking directly into the cameras. "We aren't looking out for our own best interests. We are all friends and neighbors, brothers and sisters. Peace can be achieved through each of us."

Reporters raise their voices, questioning how this can done, when Victor Quade steps to the podium again. "Together we will achieve this. Together we will make the world beautiful. Together we will bring safety and security to the globe. Together we will be strong and unified and like-minded. Together we will usher in a peace that the world has never known. No one could do it before us, but this is our time. This is our time! It is our time to change the world!"

Quade's words rally global support and acceptance as his presence seems to fill each TV screen with confidence and optimism. He sounds as if he's armed with a vision and wisdom for peace that no man before him has ever had. Perhaps the E10 could possibly outline a plan for what no one has ever accomplished…a new world order and peace for mankind.

CHAPTER 20

Israel

The streets of Jerusalem and all of Israel are empty with the exception of the Israel Defense Forces fighting Hamas and members of the Muslim Brotherhood who have been living safely in Palestine since the two-state solution was signed into place. Zerah and his unit have been charged with guarding the Wailing Wall. The men are diligent at their posts; he assumes that most of their thoughts are as consumed as his, wondering about what has taken place in the world, what Israel's enemies are planning at this moment, the likelihood that war is imminent, and how their tiny nation will survive. They are facing the worst existential threat of the Jewish nation since its statehood in 1948. They have held off the faction from Palestine, but they know that at any moment Palestine's allies will see that Israel is still strong and will join the fight for their extermination. Israel pulled down its border walls when President Banes brokered the two-state solution and has lived at peace next to Palestine, but it has been a fragile peace at best, neither country trusting the other; and the Palestinians will not rest until they occupy the entire land of Israel. Zerah's not sure how much the former walls would help anyway should a war begin. Had the United States not struck Tehran following the attacks on New York City and Washington, DC, Iran's Revolutionary Guard would have already been mobilized and fighting against Israel.

The words spoken from members of the E10 have angered Iran's Supreme Leader, the Ayatollah Behnam Mahdavi, and he has in the last hour called for the final extermination of the world's greatest antagonists: the great Satan and the little Satan, the United States and the Zionist dogs of Israel, and the members of the E10. "I have been chosen by Allah to hasten the coming of the Twelfth Iman, our beloved Mahdi, to launch a final holy war against the infidel Christians and Zionist pigs. The day is coming when we will live in a world without America and Israel. We will completely wipe them both from the map!"

Iran's President Fahim Manesh was filmed saying, "It is time to bring an end to the fat, lazy, apathetic Americans, Jews, and the weak leaders of the E10 who know nothing of sacrifice and courage. We will not rest until your blood runs through your streets. We are united against you, and our holy hatred will spread throughout the world and strike like a serpent."

Their words add fuel to the already-raging fires of their allies, long bent on the destruction of Israel and the United States. No peace agreement or group of foreign leaders will hold them back now. An attack could happen at any moment, and Zerah has never been so frightened.

"Zerah."

He jumps at the voice, turning to the soldiers on his left and right, but they're unaware that anyone has spoken.

"Zerah."

He pivots, holding his rifle.

"God is preparing you."

"Blasphemy!" Zerah says aloud, making the soldiers on each side snap to look at him. He looks at them, wild-eyed. "Who has blasphemed the name of Hashem?"

One of the soldiers, a man by the name of Sergeant Jacobs, shakes his head. "No one has said a word."

Zerah's breath comes in short spurts. "I thought I heard something." He shakes it off, breathing out and gripping his rifle tighter. As he turns his attention back to the top of the wall in front of him, he sees that an old man with a long gray beard and a mohair sackcloth robe is staring down at him.

"God is preparing you, Zerah," the old man says, his voice rushing like a river across the expanse.

Zerah lifts his hand to point, but realizes no one else sees the man. No one hears his voice. He turns to look at Jacobs beside him; his eyes are keen on the wall. When Zerah glances again at the top of the wall, the old man is gone. He exhales, shaking it off as a hallucination. Maybe he *is* mad, as Rada suggested. But there is a fire within his heart that believes otherwise.

CHAPTER 21

Queens, NY

The darkness outside Emma's window is frightening beyond description. The lights of the city were always there in the distance, reassuring her that New York was bustling with life. Now it's black for miles, and terror sticks in her throat at what used to be the sight of it.

"Have you been up all night?" Matt asks when he walks out of the bedroom, making her jump.

She's been on the sofa for hours, with several lit candles, and reading from Mrs. Ramos's Bible. She closes the book and looks at him, standing up. "Yes! Matt, there's so much in here," she says, holding the Bible. "It's *all* in here."

He sighs. "All what is in there?"

"About what happened. I discovered that Jesus would come back for his followers, and then a man will become leader of the entire world. Have you heard of the Antichrist?"

Matt looks down at the floor. "Emma. You're exhausted."

"I know, but I can't rest without knowing."

He moves to her, putting his hands on her shoulders and casting long shadows on the wall. "People are on this. Lots of people are trying to figure this out. People with PhDs."

She looks in his eyes. The distance between them is growing with each hour. She is grieving and tired and desperately wants to know what has happened in the world, but Matt finds every reason to belittle her. She presses on. "Are they looking in here?" She says, flipping the pages of the Bible. He shakes his head, about to answer, but she doesn't let him. "The leader, the Antichrist, according to Mrs. Ramos's notes, he's called a bunch of names, but he's in Revelation along with another man, a great religious leader who is a false prophet. They'll lead people astray and away from the truth. At some point they'll force people to take a mark on their hand or their forehead if they want to buy or sell anything. If a person doesn't take the mark, they're killed. But if they do take the mark, they prove that they're against God and won't get into heaven." Matt sighs loudly, but Emma continues. "Mrs. Ramos wrote in her Bible that these two men and Satan make an unholy trinity. Just the opposite of the Holy Trinity. They'll make…"

Matt raises his hand. "Stop it, Emma!" She looks stricken. "Just stop it. This is ridiculous. Antichrist. Taking a mark. Unholy trinity. It's like Grimm's fairy tales or something."

Her voice is quiet. "Why would you say that without looking into…"

"It's not realistic," he says, laughing. "It's not believable, Em! It's really bad science fiction." He works at buttoning his shirt. "I'm going into the city."

She wraps her arms around the Bible and turns to look out the window so he can't see her face. "Why? It's still dark. Don't go, Matt. You shouldn't be out when it's dark. Something could happen."

"You're freaking yourself out because you keep filling your mind with all that creepy stuff in there," he says, indicating the Bible in her hand. "Why don't you give your mind a break?" He looks out the window. "It will be light in a few minutes. I need to see what's left. I need to see if the restaurant is still there, or the university." He fastens the last button and talks to the back of her head. "It might all be gone, and then what? What do I do?"

She's already thought about this and about her own job, and lacks an answer. She turns to look at him; she wants to tell him that he should stay with her, but can tell by his face that he's set on going.

"I'll be back later." He leaves the apartment, and she turns to go lock the door behind him.

She walks back toward the window but stops at the coffee table, lifting the bridal magazines from it, looking at them in the half-light of the candles. Her eyes fill as she stares at the covers of beautiful brides, smiling as if they had swallowed the sun itself. She tosses the magazines into the garbage can in the kitchen and notices a picture of her with her mom and Sarah on the refrigerator. She takes it down and moves near the glow of candlelight, gazing at the image. It was taken last Christmas, and her mom made prints of the picture for each of them to have. "How can you keep up with special pictures on those crazy phones?" her mom had said. "Now you each can have this in front of you every day and remember how much I love you." Tears fall down Emma's face as she looks into her mom's eyes. Emma carries the picture with her and walks to the window, just making out the cratered remains of the city in the first light of dawn.

She slips the picture between the pages of Mrs. Ramos's Bible and reads for nearly two hours, studying Revelation again, and the realization of what is coming in the days ahead makes her stomach feel like it's moving up into her throat. She looks up from the words and her eye catches what looks to be a little boy around nine or ten across the street. He is standing outside an apartment building. She gets up, straining to see if anyone is with the boy, but from what she can make out, it looks like he's alone. There are individuals and a few groups of people on the street, but she can't see what they're doing. She assumes that all looting is done by now. What could possibly be left? And who would leave a child alone out on a city street on a normal day, let alone after everything that's happened? She decides to watch for a few minutes to see if anyone comes for him.

Tired of standing, she sits on the chair and rests her forehead on the window, keeping watch. After several moments she notices a group of people down the road who are getting closer to the boy's apartment building. The boy is still there, and Emma's heart begins to pound harder. *What is he doing?* she wonders. *Who is watching him?* With that she becomes concerned. Who *else* is watching him besides her? She cranes her neck to see the group, and they're now very close to the boy's building and are mostly young men. She can't go outside; she's too terrified to leave the apartment. She pauses a second more, but can't stand the thought any longer and gets up, grabbing her keys from the counter.

Running out the front door of the building, Emma's hair stands up on the back of her neck. The air is filled with the smell of fire and it sends a chill down her spine just thinking about all that lies beneath the ash. The normal street sounds and rumblings of life are missing, replaced instead with a disturbing silence, an eerie quiet that unnerves her. She looks across the street, and two of the young men from the group are talking to the little boy. Her heart races as she runs toward them. "Get back in the apartment," she says, as if she knows the boy. "Go! Go now!"

"What's your problem?" snarls one of the young men, cursing at her.

"He's been out long enough," Emma says, her heart beating wildly, but pulling the little boy up the entry steps of the apartment building and inside. She locks the door and pulls him down the hallway. Up close he seems younger than ten, with skin the color of light cocoa and curly brown hair. "You were standing out there a long time. Do you live in this building?" He nods. "It's not safe for you to be outside." She is unsure of how to ask the next question. "Is your mom home?"

He shakes his head. "She's gone."

Her heart sinks. "I'm so sorry. My mom is gone too."

He looks up at her. "Did she leave when you were four?"

She pauses, letting his words sink in. "No. She was one of the..." She stops. "Do you live with your dad?" He dips his chin. "Is he in your apartment right now?" He nods, and she looks up and down the hallway. "Does he even know that you were outside?" He doesn't answer and she steps closer to him, bending over so she can look him in the eyes. "My name's Emma, and I live in that building across the street. I think your dad needs to know where you are. Can I walk you back to your apartment?"

He won't look at her, but shakes his head no. Emma is uneasy; something isn't right. "Could you tell me your apartment number? I'd like to let your dad know that you're down here."

He gazes at the floor and says, "203."

"Could you come and wait outside your door while I try knocking?"

He follows Emma to the second floor and stops at the end of the hall-way. She turns to look at him, wondering why he won't go any further. "Wait for me?" He nods, and she finds 203 and knocks. She knocks again and again, with no answer. She looks up and down the hallway, so afraid to be here. She realizes there's no possible way she can con-tinue to let the little boy stand outside unsupervised and decides to try the doorknob. It's unlocked, and she opens the door a couple of inches, knocking and calling out into the apartment. "Excuse me, sir! Your lit-tle boy is outside alone!"

She waits for a moment for someone to come to the door, but no one does. She opens it a little more and yells again into the apart-ment. "Is anybody here?" She sticks her head through the doorway and is hit with a powerful odor—a combination of spoiled food, body stench, feces, and marijuana or something else. She yells louder this time, "Hello! Is anybody here?" She opens the door all the way and steps inside, calling out to anyone who may be down the short hallway. "Your little boy is outside!"

The smell is overwhelming, and Emma covers her nose. "Is any-one here?" The hallway spills over into a living room/kitchen area, and Emma gasps. "Oh my God!" There are four…five, six, or maybe more people who are either passed out or sitting in a zombie-like stupor on the floor. Crack pipes lay on the coffee table, and one shirtless man sits with a needle sticking out of his arm, his eyes rolled back into his head. She has no idea whether there are others inside the bedroom but imag-ines there are. She runs back through the short hallway and slams the door to the apartment shut, racing to the little boy.

He has wedged himself into a corner and looks at Emma as she runs toward him, peppering him with questions. "How long have those people been in your apartment?" He shrugs. "How long have you been outside?" He shakes his head. "Are you afraid?" He nods. "Yeah, me too."

Emma kneels down in front of him. "I realize you don't know me, but I really think you should come to my apartment and stay for a while. Just until…" she struggles for words. "Just until we know it's safe for you to go back to your own apartment. Normally, this would be a bad idea. It would never be safe for you to go to a stranger's apartment. On a typical day, it isn't safe for a little boy like you to even talk to a stranger. But this isn't a normal, typical day, is it?" He shakes his head. "When's the last time you've eaten?" He gazes down, thinking, but doesn't answer. "Okay, we don't have much, but I do know we have peanut butter. Could I make you a sandwich?" He nods, and she sticks out her hand. "Like I said, I'm Emma."

"Micah."

"Hi, Micah. How old are you?"

"Nine-and-a-half. How old are you?"

"Twenty-five-and-a-half."

"That's old."

"You know, I've never felt old, but that changed a few days ago."

CHAPTER 22

Queens, NY

Elliott reaches for his phone and runs up to the roof. It's a crazy idea, but maybe there's the possibility of picking up a signal from a far-off cell tower. He dials the number for his dad, hoping that this will work. He's been using a solar charger that his brother gave him for his birthday to charge his cell, and now he prays that he'll get a signal. *Cell phones and computers will help share the word of salvation in Christ with many more people*, he tells himself. His plan doesn't work, so he shifts to the other side of the roof, looking at the signal bars on his phone. Half a bar is lit, and once again he dials his father's number.

"Elliott!" Hearing his father say his name makes him cry. He's so happy to hear his dad's voice, yet knows he is about to grieve his mom and dad's hearts. "We've been so afraid. We didn't know if you were hit in the attack." His dad begins to cry and puts his wife on the phone.

His mother's voice breaks as she asks, "Where are you, Elliott? Are you hurt?"

"No, no! I'm not hurt, Mom."

She's sobbing on the other end. "We made it to your uncle's house and have been trying to call, but…"

"I know! It's so hard to get through right now. Are you and Dad okay?"

"We are. So shaken. So very afraid, but all right. We've been terrified since hearing of the attack on New York. I've been crying out in prayers for you! Are you sure you're okay? Are you almost here?"

Elliott prays again for the right words to say. "I'm not hurt, but I… can't come, Mom."

"What?! You need to get out of the city!"

He stares out at the city's destruction. "I want to be there with you and Dad, and I'm so happy that you're safe with Uncle Harold, but I have to stay here."

His mom's words are full of worry as her voice fills again. "Why? What is happening, Elliott?"

"I know what happened to all the people who disappeared around the world."

"What do you mean? What do you know?"

"Mom, please let Dad hear this too." He can hear her tell his dad that she's putting him on speakerphone. "You both know what I'm like. You know I'm sensible and I'm not gullible or easily persuaded." Looking over the ruins of New York City, Elliott feels a breeze against his skin. "Please listen to me. Just prior to the attack, my apartment was filled with light."

"What do you mean, light?" his dad asks. "What kind of light?"

"I didn't know, but then a man appeared in my apartment and began talking to me. He knew my name. He said that he was Yeshua, our Messiah."

"Blasphemy!" his father says, screaming into the phone. "Our Messiah has not come! You were hit during the attack! You were hallucinating!"

Elliott's heart is beating against his ribs; he talks faster and louder. "No, Dad! I wasn't! My apartment building is standing. Everything about me is fine. Yeshua filled my apartment and told me that all the people who disappeared are with him. Yeshua, our Messiah, came over two thousand years ago. He died and rose again and lives in heaven. He called for his own and he took them there, but he'll return again."

"We can't listen to this!" his mother says, screaming.

"I know you can't listen right now, but please believe me. Please believe that I love you. Jesus has made me one of his 144,000 servants on Earth for this time. I have been sealed for his work."

"Blasphemy!" his father yells, away from the phone. "Go see the rabbi! Go see the rabbi! You've lost your mind!" He is so outraged that his voice is breaking.

"Look up Revelation 7," Elliott begs. "Please Mom! Please read Revelation 7 in the Bible." The line goes dead. Elliott's eyes fill as he looks up into the sky. "Please, Hashem, please. I love them so much."

CHAPTER 23

Queens, NY

Emma opens the door and hurries Micah outside his apartment building, wanting to get back to her apartment. "Without electricity, I can't warm up or cook anything, and I know we don't have any bread. It's probably a long shot, but maybe there's something left at the market."

She glances up into windows and can see some onlookers watching them, while others dart away into the shadows. She wonders again what would have happened to Micah with so many groups of people—or should she call them gangs?—wandering the streets. The trash that was ready for pickup three days ago still sits on the roadside, the smell becoming pungent. Some garbage cans have been overturned, probably in the rush when so many were running to get home, or maybe from dogs that smelled a free meal.

Emma quickens her pace and keeps Micah close to her as they turn the corner for the main road. For the first time, she sees the battered shops and restaurants of her neighborhood and feels sick to her stomach. The exteriors of businesses and restaurants have been scarred and cratered from the attack, like in war zones from pictures she's seen. The insides have been ransacked, making them look more like long-abandoned shops of a ghost town than the brimming city Emma has loved. So many people lived with anger and hate before the disappearances; why would they play nice now? Why would they respect someone else's property if the insides were exposed, free for the taking?

Horrified by the sight, she puts her arm around Micah's shoulder to hurry him along.

Stepping inside a market at the end of the block, Emma notices the cashier holding a gun and she directs Micah through the store. Store owners have had to guard their businesses, sometimes even living inside of them to protect whatever goods are left, which appears to be what this owner has been doing. All the shelves are nearly empty and, as suspected, there isn't any bread. She picks up a can of beans and looks at the price: ten dollars. Anger swells in her chest as she holds up the can for the cashier to see. "You can't charge this kind of money for a can of beans!"

The cashier's anger is equal to hers as he curses her out. "Do you see my shelves? I had to fight to keep what I had." He holds up the gun. "I don't know when the next truck is coming in. I charge what I want!"

Emma feels Micah watching her and realizes there's no point in arguing. Once these few remaining groceries are gone, this store will probably go out of business. Where *are* the trucks with groceries? When would they be coming through again? What if there are no more trucks? What then? She reaches for Micah's hand and hurries to get out of the store and back to the safety of her apartment.

"Okay," she says, opening her cupboards to find something. A nearly empty bag of bread sits in a cupboard next to the peanut butter, and she places it on the kitchen counter. "Feel free to sit on the sofa or here on a stool." She reaches for the peanut butter and sets it down, looking at him. "I'd say you can watch some TV, but there hasn't been electricity since..." She stops.

"Since we were attacked," he says, climbing onto a stool at the counter.

She nods. "Yeah." She pulls out a plate and puts two slices of bread on it, then reaches for jelly out of the refrigerator. They have kept it closed as much as they can to keep the food cold, but there isn't much in it to begin with; she and Matt ate a lot of their meals at restaurants. She spreads some grape jelly onto one of the slices.

"You said you were afraid." It's the loudest Micah has spoken since she has met him, and it takes her by surprise. His eyes are earnest but show fear.

She is honest with him. "Yes, I am. I'm terrified."

"Did a lot of people die when we were attacked?"

She nods, spreading a thick layer of peanut butter on the other slice. "I don't know for certain but…" She pauses, knowing that now is the time for truth. "Yes. Many people died. Much of the city is gone."

He takes the sandwich from her and begins to gobble it down. "Where'd everybody go?"

Emma starts making another sandwich. "After the attack?"

Micah's mouth is full, and he shakes his head no. "Everybody who disappeared. Did bad people take them?"

Emma is unable to wrap her mind around everything that has happened; she can't imagine what it's like for a child. "I'm not sure, but I think they went to heaven."

"How?"

"I'm still trying to figure that out, but I think that Jesus came and he took his followers to heaven. My mom was one of them. So was my friend Mrs. Ramos and her family." She looks for anything else she can put on Micah's plate and finds an apple, some carrot sticks from the fridge, and a half-eaten bag of chips.

Micah reaches for the second sandwich and shoves it into his mouth. "How could Jesus take people?"

Emma fills a glass full of tap water and slides it next to the plate. "Well, that's what I don't know for certain, but from what I've been reading in the Bible, I do know he's powerful."

He sits quietly eating before asking, "Who bombed us?"

"Word is that Iran and Russia attacked the country together." She clears her throat and changes the subject. "How long have those people been in your apartment?" He doesn't answer. "Do you know how long your dad has been…" She doesn't finish the question and Micah doesn't answer, eating the rest of his food in silence.

Two hours and a few pretzels and candy bars later, the sound of a key in the doorknob makes Emma jump. Matt opens the door and looks at her, and then at Micah. His face is not one of joy or even relief in seeing her; rather, he looks irritated. "What's going on?"

"This is my boyfriend, Matt," she says to Micah. "Matt, this is Micah. He lives in the building across the street." She looks at Micah. "I'll be right back."

Matt follows Emma into the bedroom, closing the door. "Why is he here?"

She sits on the bed, looking up at him. "He was standing outside of his building all morning, and I was worried when I saw a gang getting close to him. I went over and discovered that his apartment is filled with drug addicts."

"How do you know that? Is that what he said?"

She stands up, not liking the tone in Matt's voice. "No. I went up to his apartment to tell his dad that his son was out on the street, but I opened the door and found a bunch of crackheads completely stoned out of their minds. I don't even know which one was his dad. The whole apartment smelled like vomit or a toilet. No one was watching him."

Matt walks to the window, looking out. "So now we have to?"

"I'm going to go back later to see if his dad is conscious, but if he's not, I'm not sending that little boy back into that apartment."

Matt turns on her; his face is twisted up and angry. "So what if he's still stoned out of his mind? Are we just going to keep him? He's not our kid, Emma!"

She wants to yell, but controls her voice, keeping it down. "I'm not going to leave a little boy out on the streets. You've been out there. It doesn't even feel like the same street."

Matt paces the bedroom floor, agitated. "I don't want him here for long. The restaurant is gone. The university is gone. I have no work, Emma. We can't pay for another mouth to feed around here." Emma softens and walks to him, reaching for his hand. "It looks like a war zone, Em. We'll never dig out from underneath it. The city is finished."

CHAPTER 24

Israel

Zerah walks with soldiers from his unit as they make their way to their posts at the Wailing Wall.

"Hello, Zerah."

Zerah turns to see who has spoken to him, but the other soldiers are busy talking and heading to their positions. Zerah picks up his pace, muttering under his breath.

"Zerah, you have been chosen by God as one of his servants."

Again, Zerah mutters, "Blasphemy!" Orthodox Jews would never use the name of G-d in speaking to one another. Instead, they would say *Hashem*, which is Hebrew for "the Name." He hurries to pass the other soldiers.

"Zerah." The voice is louder now and Zerah pivots in all directions, seeking out the speaker. He stops when he sees the old man with the long gray beard and sackcloth robe standing ahead on the street and looking at him. "I've been waiting for you, Zerah."

How does the old man know him? How is it that no one else hears him? Zerah's hand has been clutching the assault rifle across his chest and he puts his finger on the trigger. "How do you know my name? What are you doing out here? The whole country is under lockdown."

The old man steps closer. "It is God who knows you, and it is God who has chosen you to be one of his 144,000 servants on this earth." Zerah's grip tightens around the rifle. "You won't need that, my son. God will seal you with his protection."

Zerah's face is red with anger as he says, "Crazy old man! Get off the street! You blaspheme the name of Hashem!" Zerah marches past him, but the old man grabs his arm, stopping him.

"Your coworker, Dr. Haas, is in heaven. You know that, though, don't you?" Heat spreads over Zerah's back and chest. "You know where all the others who have disappeared from Israel and the world are, don't you? But you've been too afraid to speak of it in front of your parents and Rada and Amir."

Zerah stares at the old man, his heart stuck throbbing in his throat. "Who are you?"

The old man releases his grip. "I am a witness."

Zerah turns to see if anyone is watching them. "A witness for what?"

"A witness for the testimony of Yeshua."

"Shut up!" Zerah hisses between his teeth. "You speak blasphemy and lies!"

The old man's mouth turns up into a slight smile. "You know I don't. You know the Truth, Zerah. Hashem has spoken it to your heart. You know that Yeshua has come for his own and that he's coming again, don't you?" Zerah stiffens, keeping his finger on the trigger. "Zerah? He is your Messiah. Do you know that?"

Zerah nods. "I do," he whispers, releasing his grip on the rifle. Flashes of light begin to swirl around Zerah, enclosing him in a tornado of brilliance, gleaming and spinning, and filling his body with heat. A tongue of fire laps across his forehead as a voice speaks from inside the light.

"I am Yeshua. Your Messiah. And you are mine, Zerah. My two witnesses will be here in Jerusalem, but you will go throughout Israel and the Middle East and tell people of my love for them. The Holy Spirit will lead you and teach you. No one can harm you, Zerah. You are mine."

That is the second time he tells Zerah "You are mine."

Zerah smiles, his eyes brimming with hot tears. The burning tempest disappears, and Zerah looks up for the old man. He's gone. The street is empty.

To discover more about the biblical facts behind the story, read Where in the Word? *on page 233, or continue reading the novel.*

CHAPTER 25

Rome, Italy

President Banes steps to the podium with the members of the E10 behind him looking dazed and exhausted. It has been a wearying time for all of them. He raises his hands to quiet the noise inside the Palace of Justice.

"The entire E10 is as distressed and shaken as all of you as a result of recent world events. The crash of global financial markets, the crushing blow to the employment sectors around the world, and rising inflation can be seen as opportunities to prey on one another. However, as we have stressed in days prior, these are the days, more than any other in history, in which we must make a way for peace and unity to bring us together as a new world. We are troubled by the many wars that are being fought, and as one people, we must bring an end to them. We are not enemies. We will no longer be defined by our borders because we are one together in our new world. We will no longer be set apart by the color of our skin, our nationality, or our faith because we are one! As one world we must look inside ourselves for the answer, for the better way, and for peace. We will not know peace until all war ends!"

Reporters shout out, and many have the same question. "What will the E10 do if the wars continue?" But the E10 isn't taking questions today.

Queens, NY

Rick and Brandon are on the sofa. Emma hands each of them a drink and notices they look as exhausted and gaunt as she and Matt do. They have barely slept and have been too frightened and weary to eat much. Since the attack she has only seen Rick and Brandon and wonders how the others in the apartment building are doing, but reasons they are as terrified as she is. She bends over to make sure that Micah is still asleep on the floor. They sit by candlelight each evening, and the images outside their apartment windows and the quiet of life without the noise of all things electric is becoming unnerving. None of them have ever gone this long without use of their phones or computers, and it's driving them crazy.

"Will we ever have electricity again?" Brandon says, his voice low and uncertain.

"Maybe not in the city," Matt says.

"We have to get out of the city," Brandon says. Emma nods, agreeing with him.

"And go where?" Matt asks tersely.

"I don't know," Emma says. "But we'll run out of food and…"

Matt raises his hand. "I don't want to talk about this right now."

Emma looks at Brandon and his eyes are filled with dread. So much uncertainty, so many unanswered questions, and so much fear among all of them.

"When will you be able to take him back?" Rick says, looking at Micah sleeping on the floor. His voice is tinged more with disinterest than concern.

She can feel Matt's eyes on her from the chair. "I'll try again tomorrow, but it doesn't look good. Everybody is stoned."

"That's one way of dealing with it," Rick says.

Emma glares at him. "Getting stoned out of your mind is not a way of dealing with anything, let alone this," she says, pointing outside the window to what's left of the city.

"I was just saying that…"

"It's not going to get any better," Brandon says, interrupting. "It's only going to get worse."

"We don't know that," Matt says.

Brandon looks at him with fear in his eyes. "People have disappeared. The country has been attacked. Most of our city is in piles. There's no food coming in. We have no electricity. People are looting every store and they're fighting in the streets. And we're just one part of the world!" He brushes a tear off his cheek. "If it's happening here, then it's happening everywhere else. Countries are attacking and killing each other. People aren't suddenly going to shape up and everything's going to get better. Can't you feel it?"

Matt shakes his head as he answers. "I just feel like we still don't know anything. I don't know if it's going to get worse."

Brandon looks at Emma. "Do you feel it, Em?"

Matt sighs. "Don't get her going again."

"On what?" Rick asks.

"The boogeyman and his unholy duo or whatever they're called." Matt looks at her, waving his hand in the air as if erasing everything Emma has said to him.

"What does he mean?" Brandon says.

"If darkness can be felt, then yes, I feel it," Emma says. "Something's missing, and something has been let loose on Earth. There's lots of stuff in here about the end," she says, picking up Mrs. Ramos's Bible from the floor by her chair.

"We're at the end?" Rick says, looking at Matt. Matt shakes his head, listening.

"I've found some things in here," Emma says. "Jesus raised up the dead and all the people who were alive who had followed him and took them into heaven."

"How?" Rick says, puzzling over the statement. "Like with a fishing pole?" He and Matt smirk at the thought.

Emma pretends she didn't hear him. "He called to them, and they were all caught up together."

"Really, Emma," Matt says. "Nobody's up for this talk. Not tonight."

"I want to hear," Brandon says, looking at Emma.

"I've been reading so much. I don't understand it all, but Mrs. Ramos wrote in her Bible that God always gives signs before judgment comes, and that he gave us all sorts of signs leading up to the disappearances and everything that comes after."

"What sort of signs?" Rick asks. "Like fire from the skies or something?" Matt sighs, shaking his head and getting aggravated with the conversation.

Emma reads from the Bible, "It says people will be lovers of pleasure more than God and lovers of self and money..."

"That's a sign of judgment?" Rick says, incredulous. "Your God would judge us for loving pleasure and money and ourselves?" He looks at Matt, snickering. "Then we are all doomed."

Emma reads louder, "We would be proud, ungrateful, unholy, always learning but never coming to the truth..."

Matt holds up his hand. "All right. We get the picture. What's wrong with pride? And nobody likes someone who's holier than thou." He stands up. "Learning but not coming to the truth? Whose truth? My truth? Or your truth? And ungrateful?" He paces in front of them. "So God would send judgment because some of us didn't say thanks enough to satisfy him?" He curses and makes Emma feel stupid.

"What else does it say?" Brandon asks, interrupting before Matt can continue his rant.

"A man will come into power and be the leader of the world."

"The entire world?" Brandon says, skeptical. She nods. "That's not possible. One man? The whole world following him? Africa, Europe, Asia, the Americas...every nation following one man?"

"I don't know," Emma says. "Maybe not the entire world—I'm not sure, but much of it will."

Rick laughs. "I don't think so."

"He'll have unbelievable power and control that comes from Satan."

Matt claps his hands. "Oh my God! Stop it, Emma! This sounds crazier every time you talk."

She looks up at him. "I don't know everything, but I'm reading and reading, and I know he's going to be a real man, and people will believe him and follow him."

"An evil man?" Rick says.

"Yes."

He dismisses the idea. "The whole world will follow an evil man? I have no plans to follow evil."

"Nobody ever plans it, Rick," she says. "It happens gradually. He won't tell people he's evil. He'll convince them that he's good and that he has a great plan, and they'll fall for it. Just like Hitler."

Brandon leans forward. "Who is this evil man?"

"I think he's old man Ware from the market," Matt says, walking to the kitchen for another drink.

Emma ignores him. "I don't know who he is. From what I've read, the day will come when we won't be able to buy or sell anything unless we have his mark on our forehead or right hand."

"And if we don't?" Brandon asks.

"Then we're killed."

Matt bangs the counter in the kitchen. "That's it, Emma! No more! I've told you before…these stories are insane."

"We have to know what's ahead," she says, glancing at Micah to see if he's still sleeping. She looks at Brandon and Rick for support.

"All you're doing is scaring them," Matt says, hissing through his teeth.

Brandon hasn't stopped looking at Emma. "So things will get darker." It's not a question.

"It looks like it. But Jesus will come back and set up his kingdom here. The world we know will end, but then God will refurbish this earth and heaven. I don't know exactly what's going to happen. I don't even know if I believe that it's all real, but maybe we can all study the Bible together and figure it…"

"No!" Matt says, slamming a cabinet door and walking into the living room. He shakes his head. "No. We're not going to study the Bible together because not all of us are as…" He stops.

"As what?" she asks.

He looks at her, his voice softening. "We're not as gullible, Em."

She nods. "If gullible means to study and search out, then yes, that's me. I'm not going to wait to see how the end comes. I want to know before it gets here."

Matt shrugs. "Then you're on your own."

CHAPTER 26

Israel

Mossad, Israel's intelligence agency, led by Director Isaac Benesch, is busy tracking movements taking place inside Palestine, Russia, Iran, Syria, and Libya. In Syria, Iran's Revolutionary Guard is moving closer to Israel's border, and Mossad's concerns about movement at the Mezzeh air base in Syria is heightened when the magnification on their cameras goes from cloudy images to clear shots of large containers being driven across the base into a hangar. Mossad's man on the ground in Damascus confirms that nuclear warheads are being lifted from beneath the city. Director Benesch watches the activity with grave concern.

"Inform the defense minister."

Queens, NY

In the streets of New York City, news is spread through bullhorns that churches, rescue missions, and several other types of buildings are being used as places of lodging for anyone whose home was damaged or lost during the attack. Throughout the day, Emma can hear the sound of sirens announcing that news is about to be broadcast, followed by loud voices through the bullhorns with updates about food lines, common necessities, temporary housing, and news from the world. Even though many are encouraged by the meeting in Europe and the United States's inclusion as a member of the E10, Emma continues to have an unsettled feeling beneath her skin. With the ongoing global wars, it's as though the world is still at the brink of collapse…or maybe that's just what she's feeling within the walls of her own apartment. She and Matt are becoming more and more estranged; their nerves are stripped thin and Micah's presence is frustrating Matt.

Brandon is a bright spot. Each time Emma runs to Micah's apartment, she leaves him with Rick and Brandon upstairs. Like Matt, Rick wants little to do with Micah, feeling that he's someone else's responsibility. But Brandon feels as Emma does; the child needs to be protected, even if that means from his own father.

This time when Emma looks inside Micah's apartment, she can tell the people within have changed positions, yet everyone is still in a drug-induced daze and incoherent. "I don't think it's safe for you to be with your dad right now," she tells Micah upon her return. "I think you need to sleep here again. Are you okay with that?" He is. At least he feels safe with her.

Emma sleeps on the sofa, and Micah stretches out on the floor, just within her reach. During Sunday's early-morning hours she awakens with a start; she has slept only one or two hours each day since everyone disappeared. She is weary and still unable to take in much food. She thinks of her sister and tries texting her again. Emma has not been able to talk to her since their last contact, and all she can do is wonder if Sarah is okay. She then reaches for Mrs. Ramos's Bible, using candles and a flashlight to help her see. She flips open the book and looks down at Ephesians 1. She begins to read and finds herself going back over each sentence a couple of times, trying to understand the words. She reads verses 18-20 again.

> I pray that the eyes of your heart may be enlightened in order that you may know the hope to which he has called you, the riches of his glorious inheritance in his holy people, and his incomparably great power for us who believe. That power is the same as the mighty strength he exerted

> when he raised Christ from the dead and seated him at his
> right hand in the heavenly realms…

Each time she reads these verses she stops at the words "when he raised Christ from the dead." All her life, she had known that Jesus was born in a manger, died on a cross, and was resurrected three days later. That seemed like common knowledge among most people she knew. Before, when she was a child and at church with her parents, or even when she would go back and visit and sit next to her mom during a church service, the birth, life, and resurrection of Jesus seemed like a great story to tell, but now it doesn't feel like a mere story; it's beginning to feel real.

Emma looks down at Micah and can hear her heart throbbing in her ears. *God raised Christ from the dead.* He was dead in a tomb with a rock rolled in front of it for three days, but then *God raised him from the dead.* Her mind races back to all the images on TV of open graves around the world.

"God raised them from the dead," she says aloud. She reads the rest of that sentence: *and seated him at his right hand in the heavenly realms.* "God raised them from the dead and now they're in the heavenly realms." Tears begin to fall as she thinks about an empty grave in Indiana. "God raised Dad from the dead and now he's in the heavenly realms, and Mom is there with him." She looks up toward the ceiling. "I miss you both so much."

She looks down again at the chapter and reads verse 17: "I keep asking that the God of our Lord Jesus Christ, the glorious Father, may give you the Spirit of wisdom and revelation, so that you may know him better."

"This is what I want," she says. "Please, God. Give me the Spirit of wisdom and revelation so that I can know you better."

She looks again at the words "when he raised Christ from the dead and seated him at his right hand in the heavenly realms," reading one chapter after another as Micah snores through the night.

✳

Carrying the Bible Kennisha gave him, Elliott walks through the streets, which are worsening by the hour as they become the stomping grounds for thieves, pillagers, and thugs who are banding together in rings to protect themselves, while others are still scrambling for a place to live following the attack. It's Sunday morning, and he walks a few blocks to a church in his neighborhood. He has often passed Solid Ground Chapel, but has never paid attention to the service schedule, the people who come and go there, or even what the building looks like. The structure looks like it possibly started off as a warehouse back in the early 1950s but has changed businesses many times since, and once it became a church has gone from one denomination to another throughout the years.

He's never been inside a church and feels a rush of adrenaline as to what it must be like. He sees 100 or so people standing outside and assumes the service hasn't begun. He's anxious to hear what the pastor or anyone has to say and glances at his watch, realizing the service should have started. When he steps inside, he sees that the vestibule is swollen with people. He makes his way through the middle of them and stands in the back of the sanctuary, pressing in beside others who are lining the walls.

At normal capacity the church looks like it could hold 600 or so, but today the seats are bulging and the stage is overflowing with what he estimates could be 1,500 people, including some who have been living in the basement of the church since the attack. Everyone is waiting for the pastor to come out and explain what has happened to the world. A man holding a guitar and another man behind a keyboard are the only musicians on stage. They look as bewildered and frightened as everyone else.

After several minutes of awkward silence, a man from the seats speaks up. "Where's the pastor?"

"I've come here every day looking for him and he hasn't been here," a woman behind him says.

A moment of nervous quiet passes before the crowd's mood changes from solemnity to fear. "Where is he?" someone yells. "Where is everybody?"

They are becoming anxious and upset as Elliott, emboldened with the same courage he felt on the street, steps to the front. He opens his mouth and realizes again that the words he's about to speak aren't coming from him, but from the Spirit of God himself. "They're no longer here," he says as he looks out at young, weathered, dark, light, and worried faces.

CHAPTER 27

Queens, NY

Emma and Micah listen to the young man at the front of the church as a woman next to her speaks up.

"Where are they?" she asks.

"They're in heaven." The sound of laughter and scoffing are heard throughout the church, but the young man ignores the mockery. "The apostle Paul said that Jesus would descend from heaven with a loud command, with the voice of the archangel and the trumpet call of God, and that the dead in Christ would rise first."

Emma's palms begin to sweat as she remembers the words she read earlier this morning from Ephesians: "when he raised Christ from the dead."

"A loud command?" a man shouts from the back of the church. "A trumpet? Nobody heard anything like that!"

The crowd shouts as one in agreement as the young man raises his hands. "Jesus's followers heard him. He said in the Bible, 'My sheep hear my voice, and I know them, and they follow me. I give them eternal life.' We didn't follow Jesus. We didn't hear his command." People begin to murmur, but he keeps talking. "All around the city—all around this world—graves burst open when the dead in Christ heard the voice of their Savior, and then those who were alive were snatched up and met them in the air with Jesus. I was standing in a cemetery when graves exploded open and security cameras around the globe showed us how quickly people disappeared. Someone may have disappeared right in front of you."

Many in the church are crying, while others are trying to shout Elliott down. "Who are you?" a red-faced man says, standing in the middle of the crowd.

The young man talking to them is not tall or bulky; he has a small frame, a slightly receding hairline, and wears glasses, but there's something unusual about him when he speaks. "My name is Elliott. Until a week ago I was a religious Jew. I'm still a Jew and so is my Messiah, Jesus Christ."

Nobody knows what to think of Elliott. They are feeling incredulous, angry, confused, or scared. The city lies in ruins and the world is so lopsided now that their nerves are stretched tight, their hearts are shattered, their strength is nearly broken, and now this man is making it worse. What he's saying is unscripted and unrestrained.

"Christ came for his people," Elliott says. "He took them to heaven because the time has now come for God to judge the earth for its rebellion and sins against him, but there's still time to know Jesus. There's still time to repent and follow him so you can live with him forever."

The crowd gets noisy. "You need to sit down. You're scaring the hell out of everybody!" a man shouts from the back. "Look at our city! How are we going to live? What you're saying isn't helping."

Elliott nods, talking louder. "I know you're scared. I was too. Many of you no longer have your loved ones with you. Some entire families are gone, and that's too much to bear."

Emma begins to cry, and she notices that many people can't hold their tears at bay either. Losing so many loved ones has been crippling.

"Much of the city is gone," Elliott says. "But we're still here, and we have to help each other like never before. We have to spread the truth about Christ before he comes back again."

"It's not true," someone yells from the back, and others raise their voices, shouting that Elliott is lying.

"He's telling the truth," a man calls out who is around forty and standing along the wall with a boy about eight or so at his side. "My dad kept telling me. Someone you know probably tried to tell you," he says, his arm making a sweeping motion to point to everyone in the room. "I thought my dad was a crazy old man. I thought he was ignorant." His words catch in his throat and he doesn't say anything more.

"What are you talking about?" asks a woman who is about fifty. "If it's true, then why didn't the pastor ever tell us any of that?" The man shrugs, unable to answer.

"Maybe he didn't think you would believe it. Maybe he thought that calling you a sinner was too hard for you to hear," Elliott says. "There are kinder messages to hear. Maybe he knew you wanted to hear pleasant things and not hard truths. But the truth is, our sins separate us from God. Jesus became sin for us and hung on a cross for us." He holds up the Bible. "It's all right here. I've been reading this Bible ever since it was given to me after the attack. Jesus said he would prepare a place in his Father's house for his own, and that he would come back and take them there. Read it in John 14. That's what he's done. He has come, and he has snatched his followers out of this world and taken them there. But he'll be back! And then those who believe and follow him will live with him forever."

"Why would anybody want to live with him?" the same angry man in the middle yells. "You're saying he took some and not others?!" He curses at Elliott and his face darkens. "Nobody wants that kind of God!" He's physically agitated and rallies others in the crowd, who stand and shout over one another. "That kind of God is vindictive and cruel!" The vitriol builds as the uproar grows louder, their rage directed at Elliott, but he continues to speak.

"It would be cruel if God never brought an end to murder, rape, genocide, sex trafficking, abuse, drug addiction, destruction, pain, suffering, evil of all kinds. All of that was brought into the world through our sin!" Elliott is louder now, trying to be heard above the crowd. "How is God good if there's never an end to those things? To sin? *That* would be cruel! There has to be an end to evil. He'll judge the earth of these sins against him, and Jesus will come back with all those who are in heaven with him, and this world will be made clean and new and put under his authority. No more suffering. No more pain. No more rebellion. It's because of God's goodness that he's judging evil. It's the goodness of God that leads people to repentance. While there's still time, he calls us to repent."

"Repent of what?" a confused young woman from the second row yells. "What have we done that all those who disappeared didn't?"

"We were separated from God by our sins. We followed our own desires," Elliott says.

"Shut up and sit down!" a woman screams while holding her little girl on her lap.

Elliott responds to her in kindness. "I can speak for myself and say that I didn't believe or obey what God says is true. I didn't believe Jesus was the Messiah, but now I do. He said he was coming back to take his followers to his Father's house, yet very few taught about that, thinking it sounded either like a fairy tale or a horror story. But he did exactly what he said he would!" He lifts the Bible over his head. "In here he said to stay close to him, stay in his word, obey his word, but we all wanted to do things our way, not his. Now this is our time to believe and obey and follow before he comes back *again* at the end of the age, but the next time He won't come back in the blink of an eye. At that time, *every eye will see him!*"

A woman with two teenagers speaks up. "But we still don't have a clear answer. How do we know that you're telling the truth?"

"He's not telling the truth!" a man roars from the stage behind Elliott. The heated voices blur together, hurling insults and curses and trying to thunder over Elliott, but he doesn't waver.

Elliott's eyes are full of compassion. "How does this message benefit me? Why did any of you come here today? To hear myths? To hear something that would magically take away the terror of the last four days? Either I'm telling the truth or I'm insane. Either Jesus told the truth in this book or he was insane. Either that man's father," he says, pointing to the man along the wall, "was an ignorant old fool, or he was telling his son the truth. Jesus said, 'I am the way, and the truth, and the life. No one comes to the Father except through me.'

"We didn't want to believe that because we didn't think it was fair," he says, directing his comment to the man who brought up the issue of fairness in the first place. "There *had* to be more ways to heaven than just through Jesus. As for me, I reasoned that I wasn't a murderer or a rapist and that I was a good person, but that was by my own measurement, my own rules, not God's." He stops to take in their faces, but many in the crowd are becoming furious and screaming over him.

"The time ahead of us is dark and dangerous, but the light of Christ still shines today as it has for over two thousand years. Peter said Christ is patient with us, not wanting anyone to perish, but for everyone to come to repentance. Jesus is coming again, and on that day there will be no more chances to repent. No more chances to follow him. This is your time!" Many men and women and children begin to weep, falling to their knees.

"Or what?" a man standing along the wall shouts.

Elliott looks at him. "Jesus said, 'Do not be afraid of those who kill the body but cannot kill the soul. Rather, be afraid of the One who can destroy both soul and body in hell.'"

"Fearmongering won't work," the man says. "Look at these people," he says, pointing to the ones on their knees. "They're sniveling."

Elliott takes a step toward the man. "These people aren't under my conviction, but the conviction of the Holy Spirit. They feel the presence of God."

"Nobody wants your God," the man sneers. Others join him in screaming and jeering at Elliott. Outraged by what he's heard, and empowered by the mutinous clamor inside the church, the man runs for Elliott, cursing as he lunges for him. His body bounces off the air and lands on the floor with a thud. Stunned, the man curses louder, lunging again, only to be held at a distance by an unseen force.

Elliott continues to speak, calling people to repentance. Emma and Micah watch in astonishment as the man flails alone before others join in to help, a mob hell-bent on inflicting physical harm to Elliott, but their blows miss him and strike each other. It is a brutal fight bordering on the absurd as time and again fists fly through the air past Elliott, cracking the jaw or eye socket of someone else. One man picks up a folding chair and strikes at Elliott, but the chair hurls back at the man, knocking him down.

For those who believe, there is a palpable presence in the room, and Emma's eyes fill as she reaches over and takes hold of Micah's hand.

"Do you believe that Jesus is the Son of God?" Elliott says, making his voice heard above the clamor. "Do you believe that God raised him from the dead and that he's coming again? Tell him! Follow him! Repent while there's still time."

Many of the people who have been screaming choose to leave, while others, like the man who had flung the folding chair and the red-faced man in the middle of the pews, decide to stay. Emma and Micah hold hands, and Emma begins to talk aloud. "Forgive me, God," she says. "I do believe that Jesus is your Son, and I do believe that you raised him from the dead, just as you raised my dad. I believe, God. Forgive me. Please. I believe and want you, Jesus, to be my Lord."

Micah looks up at Emma and prays the same words, and she hugs him. She then pulls him toward the front, through the crowd of people to Elliott. She yells at him over the noise. "Could you come and talk to the people in my apartment building?"

To discover more about the biblical facts behind the story, read Where in the Word? *on page 243, or continue reading the novel.*

CHAPTER 28

Queens, NY

Emma runs, shouting through her apartment building as she pounds on doors. "Piya," she says, breathless with Micah at her side. "Bring your family to my apartment in twenty minutes. It's urgent," she says, running to the next door. Micah helps, banging on doors up ahead and people reluctantly look out into the hallway.

"Everybody come to my apartment in twenty minutes," Emma yells.

"What's this about?" old man Gruebber says.

"Just come! A man will be explaining everything that's happened!"

Emma and Micah run to the second floor, delivering the same news, and then up to the third floor, where she knocks on Rick and Brandon's door. Brandon sees her through the peephole and opens the door. She hugs him. "Brandon! You have to come to my apartment in twenty minutes!"

Brandon looks at Micah, noticing his face. It's as bright as Emma's. "What's going on?"

"We just heard a man. A Jewish man who has explained everything about what has happened." She grabs him by the shoulders, looking at her dear friend. "He's not crazy, Brandon, and neither am I."

"Neither am I," Micah says.

"Tell Rick and come," she says, running to the next apartment.

When Emma opens the door to her apartment, there are just a few minutes left before Elliott is due to arrive. Matt is wearing a

T-shirt with jeans and is looking out over the devastated city. When he turns to look at her, Emma can see that his mood is dark. "Something amazing has happened!" she says. He doesn't ask what, but stands looking at her, unable to feign interest. "We heard a Jewish man speak today, and he told us about Jesus and about how he called his followers to…"

Matt cuts her off. "Not this again, Emma. I'm not up for it today."

She steps toward him. "Please Matt! This man knows what happened. I invited him to come here so that he can tell everyone in the building…"

"You what?!" He raises his hands in the air as he tries to stay calm. "Why would you invite someone here to talk to the entire building?"

Her voice gets softer. "Because he's right."

His words come out heated and stressed: "You don't know that! You only believe that!"

"You know me, Matt! I don't fall for things. This guy is not making things up just to help people feel better. When he talks, he's actually speaking the very word of God about Jesus."

Matt snickers. "A Jewish guy is speaking about Jesus and telling people exactly what happened in this world?" She nods. "That's great, Emma! You're wasting my time and everybody else's."

"It's not a waste of time," says Micah. Emma turns to look at him. He steps next to her and holds her hand. "It's not a waste of time," he says again.

Matt glares at him, shaking his head. They are interrupted as Rick and Brandon step inside the apartment. Brandon can sense that they have intruded on a strained moment and he looks at Emma.

She smiles and waves them to the couch. "Come on, sit!"

As the other residents gather, Matt avoids eye contact with Emma. He is so disgusted that he can't even look at her. His anger simmers just beneath the surface as the apartment fills up. The last to arrive is Elliott, and Emma runs to him, grabbing his hand and leading him into the middle of everyone. "This is Elliott." She pauses, looking at him. "I'm sorry. I don't know your last name."

"Hirsch," he says, smiling.

"Micah and I heard Elliott this morning, and I just had to bring him back here so that all of you could hear the same words that we did." She turns to him. "Please."

As he speaks, Emma feels her heart swelling again. Looking at these familiar faces from within her apartment building, she realizes that she loves each and every one of these people. She can't imagine what the next few years hold in store for planet Earth, but she does know that she wants all of these individuals to be rescued by Christ.

The Kleins are angry that a Jewish man would dare speak of Jesus, but Elliott implores them to stay. "I'm Jewish! I stood at a Jewish funeral wearing my yarmulke when graves burst open. Jesus came to me in my apartment and told me that he was my Messiah. Either I'm nuts or I'm telling the truth." Mrs. Klein sets her hand on her husband's arm, pleading with her eyes for him to stay and listen.

Piya is visibly moved as Elliott speaks and tears begin to roll down her face. Even old man Gruebber's eyes fill as he grips his cane. Brandon listens intently, but Rick is annoyed and stays quiet to be polite to his longtime friends. The Kramers and their son Brody look upset and cross but listen without saying a word. Matt stares at the floor, embarrassed that Emma has done this.

"When is Christ coming again?" Piya asks.

Elliott shrugs. "There are many things that have to happen first. We know that a man whom the apostle John identified as the Antichrist will rise to world power. He'll confirm a peace covenant that's put in place with Israel."

"What do you mean, he'll confirm a peace covenant?" Mr. Kramer asks. "It's already in place."

"Israel's enemies have been striving since 1948 to annihilate her. The bombs that are flying toward Israel today tell you that the current peace agreement that President Banes crafted between Israel and the Palestinians means nothing. The Antichrist will somehow strengthen the covenant."

"So this…this world leader confirms the agreement," Piya's husband says. "So what?"

Elliott nods. "The confirmation of that peace treaty will begin the earth's final seven years, but even then, no one knows the day or the hour of Christ's return, yet we're told to be ready."

"How do you know this?" Mr. Gruebber asks, clutching his wife's hand.

"It's all right here," Elliott says, lifting the Bible. "Wars will rage. Nations will all come against Israel. According to the book of Daniel, the world leader will confirm the peace agreement with Israel and all will seem well at first. But that will begin seven years of tribulation. Halfway through that time he will break the agreement, and even greater troubles will come."

"Who is the world leader?" Brandon asks, his eyes dark and tired.

Elliott shakes his head. "We don't know yet, but we'll know who he is as soon as that peace agreement is confirmed."

"When?" Mr. Klein asks.

"I don't know," Elliott says. "We just have to keep our eyes and ears open." He looks at the small group and smiles. "We haven't been left alone. If you accept Jesus as Lord of your life, you will never be alone. His is an everlasting love."

Emma smiles for the first time since the disappearances as Piya and her family, the Kleins, the Kramers and Mr. and Mrs. Gruebber eagerly claim Christ as their Lord. The single mom and her two children pray aloud as Matt moves away from the group, catching Rick's eye before he slips away from Brandon and into the bedroom.

Less than an hour later, everyone is leaving to go back to their own apartment. Emma hugs the people one by one as they leave, and Elliott urges them to read the Bible and meet together so they can learn what's happening. Mr. and Mrs. Klein hold Elliott like a long-lost brother and smile at him through tears.

"Pray for my parents and brother," Elliott says to them. "That they might also know what you do."

The Kramers thank Emma and Elliott as they leave, and Emma's face clouds over with thoughts of Rick and Matt. She had wanted everyone to come to know Christ. Before the single mom leaves, Emma gives her a hug. She pulls back and says, "I'm so sorry! I never learned your name."

"Lydia."

Emma smiles. "That was my mom's name. I wish I'd known that was yours a long time ago." She looks at her children. "And what are your names?"

"I'm Benton," says her son, who looks about nine. Pointing to his little sister, he adds, "That's Cam."

Emma pulls both toward her and hugs them. "I'm so glad to know you." She reaches for Lydia and pulls Micah into the hug as well.

After they leave, Emma shuts the door. She looks up and sees Matt in the middle of the living room looking at her. There's nothing left between them. "It's time for me to go," she says.

"I agree." He walks past her without making eye contact. "Get what you need, and come back later for what's left," he says before walking out the door.

Tears swim in her eyes as she looks at Elliott. "I just wanted him to know what we know. I wanted him to know Jesus."

Elliott nods, and she goes into the bedroom, gathering a few things in a bag, her hands shaking as she collects them. Where can she go? It feels like her heart is being squeezed inside her chest, but she makes sure that she packs every picture of her mom and dad and Sarah and reaches for each special gift her family ever gave her. Elliott and Micah each carry a duffel bag filled with her belongings when they leave the apartment. Emma's head is reeling as she closes the door and walks down the stairs. What has she done? She needs Matt. She needs the apartment. Approaching the front door, she hears someone running down the stairs and calling out to her. Emma looks up to see Brandon with a backpack over his shoulder.

"Matt came upstairs and said you were leaving," he says breathlessly. "I need to leave too."

She hugs him and turns to look at Micah. "I didn't think this through," she says, her voice catching. "I have no idea where to go."

"I know a place," Elliott says.

CHAPTER 29

Israel

Zerah enters his parents' home and goes below to the bomb shelter. They gasp as he opens the door. Rada and her children are still there, and they all look tired and much older, their faces creased with worry. Fear and uncertainty are taking their toll. "Zerah," his father says, "where have you been? Two soldiers have been here looking for you. They said you did not report for duty yesterday."

Zerah has such love for his family that it's hard to imagine the gulf that will come between them now, but he has no choice; he's no longer his own. "I was headed to my post," he says, taking in their faces. "I was headed there when an old man stopped me."

"What old man?" his mother Ada asks.

"An old man of Hashem."

His father waves his trembling hand in the air. "What are you saying? Why did an old man stop you? And why didn't you report for duty?"

He reaches for his mother's hand and takes a breath. "There were soldiers on the street. We were walking to our posts when I heard my name. It wasn't the soldiers who were calling me. It was the old man. As I was about to pass him, he grabbed my arm, calling me by name again."

His mother looks confused. "I don't understand. Was he someone from work?"

Zerah shakes his head. "No, Mom. He was a man of Hashem. He

told me things that I had been thinking. He even brought up all of you. He told me that I am one of Hashem's 144,000 servants for this time."

"For what time?" his father says, looking quizzically at him.

"This time of the end." His family is speechless. "We are in the end. Time is running out."

"He was a crazy old fool, and you were a fool for listening to him!" his father bellows, angry at his son.

"He also brought up Dr. Haas."

"Why?" Rada asks, hanging on to his words.

"He told me that she and the others who have disappeared from here in Israel and around the world are with Yeshua."

"Blasphemy!" his father screams, covering his ears and moving away from them.

"Papa, listen!"

"Get out! Get out of my house!" he roars. Zerah's mother begs Chaim to hear him out, but his father's shouts intensify.

"Yeshua surrounded me with a great light," Zerah yells, hoping his family can hear him. "He sealed me for his work."

His father screams, tearing his shirt. "You are dead to me. Get out! Leave and never come back to this home!" Zerah's mother and sister and niece and nephew plead with him to stop.

Zerah's eyes fill as he opens the door. He walks upstairs to leave, and his mother and Rada and her two children follow, begging him to stay. He turns to them and, glancing to his mother, says, "I'm no fool. You and Dad didn't raise fools. I am educated. I'm a doctor and researcher. I've never trusted the shifting of the winds. Everything had to be calculated and reasonable and have an intellectual conclusion. This has none of those things, Mom." She's crying, and he holds her hand. "Yeshua came to me on the road and he sealed me for His service." Rada covers her mouth, weeping. "Don't cry, Rada. Everyone who is in Yeshua will live with him forever."

A pounding on the door makes them jump, and Zerah's mother grabs his arm when he moves to open it. "Don't," she whispers.

He lays his hand on top of hers and leans in to give her a kiss. "It's okay. I have to do what Yeshua has asked of me."

Two armed soldiers are at the door. "Sergeant Zerah Adler?" One of them says.

"Yes."

"We're here to escort you back to your post." They couldn't officially designate him a deserter; for all they knew, he had been in an accident or was in the hospital.

"I'm sorry. I can't go with you."

The soldiers don't flinch. "We are under fire and on the brink of war, Sergeant, and you're to come with us."

"I love my country. I gave service to my country and would do it again, but I can't do it now. Hashem has called me to his service."

Zerah's mother steps in behind him, putting her hand on his back. "Please, Zerah. Please go with these men."

He turns and kisses her head and reaches for his sister, kissing her forehead, before stepping outside. The soldiers turn to the left, indicating the direction of their vehicle, but Zerah turns to the right, walking away from them. "Sergeant Adler!" one of them yells after him.

He doesn't stop, and the two soldiers run after him. Zerah's mother and Rada step out onto the stoop, closing the door to keep the children inside. "Zerah!" his mother shouts.

One of the soldiers reaches for Zerah's arm but misses. "Stop!" he yells, trying to grab him again.

"Zerah, stop!" Rada screams. She and her mother shout out his name and the other soldier grabs his arm, only to lose his grip. They run after him again and jump for him, their bodies landing hard on the ground. They scramble to their feet and try to secure him, their arms swinging in the air but never making contact with him.

"Sergeant Adler! Stop where you are!" Zerah turns to look at the soldiers as Rada and his mother plead with him to stop while the soldier barks, "Get in the vehicle!"

"I can't do that," Zerah says. "I haven't lost my mind. I'm not turning my back on my country, but guarding the Wailing Wall isn't my post anymore. That's not what Yeshua sealed me for. I'm sealed for his work."

The soldiers rush to him and one of them says, "You're a deserter, Sergeant Adler!"

Zerah shakes his head, smiling. "I am not. I'm not deserting my country. I'm here to give life and truth to my country."

The soldiers try to grab Zerah's arms from behind in order to escort him to the vehicle, but they end up stumbling into and wrestling with each other. Zerah turns to walk down the road as one of the soldiers puts his hand on the Jericho 941 in its holster, but the second soldier stops him, shaking his head.

Rada and her mother stand astonished, their bodies shaking. "What just happened?" Ada asks, breathless.

"Hashem protected him, Mother," Rada whispers. "Just as he said. Hashem protected him."

They stand crying and holding one another.

CHAPTER 30

Queens, NY

As Emma and Micah settle into Kennisha's apartment and Brandon unloads a few things inside Elliott's, Elliott climbs to the roof of the building and holds his phone just so, trying to pick up any news. A story partially loads: *Israel Destroys Damascus.*

Israel launched two short-range ballistic missiles fitted with nuclear warheads, an action that has never been taken in the history of the nation. Due to the warheads that were being brought up from under Damascus, the resulting nuclear explosion levelled the city, completely destroying it. The article says Syria was "blindsided" and calls Israel's actions "sinister and deadly in an already-volatile climate." Images from Syria show smoke and ash smoldering over what once was the world's oldest city. Israel is named the aggressor and its people called murderers, while Syria's, Iran's, and Palestine's culpability are denied.

The rest of the story doesn't load, and despite walking to each corner of the roof, Elliott can't pick up any more signal. He saves the story as a photo before it disappears off his phone. He takes time to pray, then runs back down the stairs. "It's Isaiah 17," he says, bursting through the door at Kennisha's and reading the news story to her, Brandon, and Emma. They look at him, waiting for an explanation. "Damascus will no longer be a city but will become a heap of ruins. That's Isaiah 17," he says, opening his Bible and finding the chapter. "In the evening, sudden terror! Before the morning, they are gone!" He glances up at them. "Damascus has been attacked before. It's been damaged, but it's always been rebuilt; it's always been on the map. Isaiah 17 said that one day it will no longer be a city but a heap of ruins. This is fulfilled today. Damascus has been destroyed."

"What's going to happen now?" Brandon asks, his voice laced with dread.

"The entire Middle East will be at war," Kennisha says, whispering.

Emma feels as if she has been reunited with a long-lost friend with Kennisha. They are a ragamuffin group, barely hanging on, but Emma senses that they could be strong together…even now, as war erupts around Israel and throughout the world.

To discover more about the biblical facts behind the story, read Where in the Word? *on page 253, or continue reading the novel.*

CHAPTER 31

Rome, Italy

Following the destruction of Damascus, war is raging against Israel and loss of life is mounting on all sides. Lebanon has joined in the fight with what's left of Syria, and President Khoury of Lebanon and Syria's President Kalif speak venomously at a news conference, saying, "The Zionist pigs will be destroyed once and for all," and the media surrounding them cheer. "We will finally take back the land that belongs to every Arab!" Kalif shouts above the applause. There is no room for misinterpretation: They are speaking for all nations who hate Israel; they seek the total extermination of the Jewish state and her people.

Iran's President Manesh hails Presidents Khoury and Kalif and other fellow leaders as heroes because they "will not rest until the annihilation of Israel is complete and the Mediterranean Sea runs red with the blood of the Jews." Many of Iran's Revolutionary Guard died in Damascus, cutting short their immediate plan of destroying Israel with nuclear force, but Iran is moving weapons and thousands more of the Revolutionary Guard into northern Syria to bring an end to Israel once and for all. Iran's leaders and military advisors, along with those of Russia, Turkey, Sudan, and other countries, are meeting to determine the swiftest possible action for bringing total extermination.

In Rome, Prime Minister Sophia Clattenberg takes the podium inside the Palace of Justice on behalf of the E10 leaders. "These are tumultuous and frightening days, which call for rational thinking and global cooperation," she says. "There can only be peace across the globe as we are willing to offer peace to our brothers and sisters around the world. We must tear down the walls of animosity and hatred in Africa, in North and South Korea, in Iran, Pakistan, China, India, the United States, South America, and in the Middle East as we come together as a unified globe, extending the hand of help and belief to one another. Our thoughts go out to the people of Syria for their great loss, but this is not the day of vengeance. There can and there must be peace and safety, or our days will be marked only by destruction. We cannot care for the citizens of the earth without global stability."

Reporters yell above one another for clarification, and the E10's counsel secretary, Victor Quade, steps beside Clattenberg, bending closer to the microphone on the podium. "As we lock arms together in our new world, we will be stronger together. We must tear down the borders of hatred and bitterness, anger and vengeance, and replace them with help and hope, kindness and generosity. The great citizens of our world will survive, but only as we unify ourselves together. We are one world with one goal: peace. It is within our reach, and we must strive for it as never before. The E10 has begun a dialogue with North and South Korea and with many leaders in Africa, China, India, Pakistan, and other counties to stop all wars. The members have reached out to Israeli prime minister Ari and to the presidents of Syria, Lebanon, and leaders with the Hamas government and the Fatah government of Palestine, and we are dialoguing with the president of Egypt and with the king of Jordan to help us bring all fighting in the Middle East to an end. Without a strong, unified, and stable Middle East, we cannot be a strong, stable, and unified world. Peace is on our horizon. We will have peace. And we will have it together."

Quade steps away from the podium, and for a moment, hearts seem to swell with belief around the world.

CHAPTER 32

Queens, NY

Since the disappearances, millions of people have crossed the southern border of the United States into Texas, Arizona, New Mexico, and California looking for housing and food. Trucking and rail companies have been figuratively derailed, and many farms and ranches have been shorthanded, making food scarce and with fewer ways to transport it. Farms struggled prior to the vanishings to stay in business, many farmers exhausting their savings to keep their farms afloat and many more taking their own lives at two times the rate of veterans. How could the farming industry in America endure this? Factories have shut down; train engineers, barge crews, and truckers are missing. The demand for food has gotten greater but the supplies and the ways to get it to people are limited like never before.

Between looting, price gouging, and a run on the banks, Emma and Kennisha have reason for concern. The vanishings, unemployment, and rising inflation have thrown the country into a depression. The food on Kennisha's shelves won't last long, and the loss of electricity has ruined the perishables in her refrigerator and freezer. Water is now coming out of the pipes in spurts, and they know it's just a matter of time before it stops running altogether. Food lines have been created throughout the city, but the food is in short supply right now and the prices are too high for them to afford the most basic of items. They had not thought about getting their money out of the bank when the upheaval occurred, and now, due to the run on banks throughout the city, they're all closed (not that a big wad of money would help anyway, with store shelves looted and bare). They have to come up with a plan for what to do next, and come up with it soon. Kennisha has worked at the front desk of a hotel in Manhattan for the last four years but hasn't gone back since her sister and niece disappeared, too afraid to leave her apartment. She doesn't even know if the hotel is standing anymore.

"I'm going to see Micah's dad, and then I need to go to Thrive to see if it's still standing," Emma says. "Maybe there's the possibility of some work. We need money and food."

"I've been thinking that too," Kennisha says, sitting on the sofa next to her. "We can't stay in the city much longer."

"I agree," Emma says. "But where could we all go?"

Kennisha shakes her head, her face clouding over. "If Kaala was here I'd ask her," she says, looking down at her hands.

"What would she say?" Emma asks.

"She would say ask God for wisdom. She would tell me that it was about time that I grow up and start making hard decisions like an adult." She smiles, glancing up. "Kaala never minced words."

Emma sighs. "We've all been pulled into this, and we'll all make the hard decisions together. And we'll all learn to pray."

"Now I really wish Kaala was here because that woman could pray!" Kennisha says, laughing as she cries.

"Kennisha," Emma says, pondering how to best ask the question weighing on her mind. "What if Micah's dad can't take care of him? What if he still…"

"Then he'll stay here," Kennisha says, bobbing her head. "That was an easy decision." Emma nods, gets up, and grabs the keys. "Be careful, Emma." The door closes and Kennisha jumps up to lock it, praying as she does.

As Emma approaches Micah's apartment building, she feels a knot in the pit of her stomach at the sight of her own apartment window across the street. She wonders if Matt is standing at the window, but pushes that thought out of her mind as she runs into Micah's apartment building and up the stairs. She knocks on the door and discovers that this time, the door is locked. She keeps pounding until she hears someone on the other side. The door opens, and a drawn-looking woman of about thirty glares out at her. She reeks of smoke and her eyes are glassy, trying to focus on Emma.

"I'm here to see Micah's dad." The woman doesn't respond. "I need to talk to his dad. Is he here?" The woman acts as if she's trying to wake up from a thick dream. "Hey!" Emma shouts in her face. "Go get Micah's dad!"

Instead of closing the door and fetching Micah's dad, the woman opens it, letting Emma inside. Emma covers her nose at the smell. She walks down the small hallway that leads to the living room and looks at the same wasted faces who have been here during her prior visits. "Which one is Micah's dad?" she asks the woman behind her.

The woman points at a man splayed out at the end of the sofa. His shirtless body reveals ribs sticking out from his lanky frame. His frizzy black hair hasn't been washed in days. Emma walks to the curtains and throws them open before stepping over two people who move more like zombies than human beings as she gets closer to Micah's dad.

"Wake up!" she says in his face. "Hey! Wake up!" She jostles his shoulder, yelling louder. "Wake up!" She feels anger begin to fan across her chest and she pats the man's face. "I need to talk to you. Wake up!" She slaps harder and realizes she doesn't care how hard she's hitting him. "Hey! Hey! Wake up!" The man moans and his eyes begin to flutter open. "Look at me! Can you hear me?"

He covers his eyes, shielding them from the light in the room.

"Are you Micah's dad?" Emma shouts. He nods. "Do you know where he is?" He strains to see her through the fog, pointing toward another room. Emma shakes her head. "No! He's not in there. He's not been here for days. Do you even know that?" She's so infuriated she can feel herself shaking. He tries to sit up but is unable. "Do you know where he is?"

"No," he whispers.

She looks at his face and around the room at the others who have kept themselves stoned since the mass disappearances, and her tone changes. "He's been with me. I've been taking care of your son. I can't bring him back here. No one should live like this, especially a little boy. Do you want me to continue to take care of him?" The man nods. Emma looks in his eyes, small and black and unfocused. "Did you understand what I said?"

"You asked if I wanted you to take care of Micah." He nods again. "Yeah. I can't."

For the first time since she arrived, Emma doesn't feel rage; instead, she feels like crying. "I can bring him back in a few weeks to see if you're straightened out."

The man shakes his head. "I can't do it." He points to the other room. "His things are in there." He rests his head on the back of the sofa and closes his eyes.

Emma watches him for a few moments before stepping back. Her stomach churns with nausea and she steps over the same two people again as she heads toward the bedroom. There she finds two people on a mattress on the floor half awake or half dead, she's not sure which; she steps over them and begins to open drawers. She finds a plastic bin that is partly filled with miscellaneous toys and throws underwear, socks, shirts, and pants into it. A tote bag that was probably given out at a school event sits empty on the closet floor; she fills it with the rest of Micah's clothes and his shoes.

A picture of Micah and his dad sits on top of the plastic chest of drawers, and she picks it up. Micah looks only a year or two younger and is wearing his backpack in front of a school. His dad looks healthy and strong, and is wearing a suit and nice shoes, with a leather brief-case over his shoulder. He's kneeling beside Micah with his arm around his shoulder and both are beaming in the picture. Emma can't take her eyes off the man in the photo. He wasn't always like this, what she sees in this apartment. He was a good dad who walked Micah to school and took the time to take a picture on the first day. Somehow, something went wrong, life spiraled downward faster than he thought, and now he's turning his son over to a stranger.

Emma looks around the room for anything else that might be Micah's and spots a backpack crumpled in the corner. In it are a notebook and a couple of schoolbooks. She reaches for the last few Legos that are scattered on the floor, throwing them inside. She pulls the backpack straps over her shoulders and sets the tote bag on top of the plastic bin as she leaves the room. Stepping into the living room, she notices that Micah's dad is watching her. She pauses, waiting for him to speak, but he doesn't say anything. Her mouth edges up a bit in a sad smile before she heads toward the door.

"Take this." Emma stops and turns to see the woman who had answered the door. She's holding two grocery sacks. "These were some things that Micah liked to eat."

Emma thinks about refusing the sacks because she is already so loaded down, but there is no way she can refuse food. "What about you and the others?"

"We don't eat much." Her face is sharp and angular, and her eyes look like nothing more than small beads in large sockets.

"You have to eat or you're going to die," Emma says with urgency in her voice. The woman doesn't say anything, and hands the grocery sacks to Emma, who is still talking. "This isn't the time to give up. You need to…"

"Thanks for taking care of Micah."

Emma pleads with the woman. "Don't do this. Don't give up."

The woman shuts the door and Emma stands there, breathless, listening to her heart pound in her ears. She hurries to the end of the hallway and stops, staring at the stairs and wondering how she'll manage to get down them and walk the few blocks to Kennisha's apartment.

"Are you taking care of the little boy?"

Emma jumps at the voice and turns to see a man about thirty or so with dark skin, hair, and eyes. "Why are you asking?"

"I've seen him by himself. Long before all of this. He's by himself a lot. It's good what you're doing…if you're going to take care of him."

On a normal day, Emma would think this man was handsome in a boyish way, but this isn't a normal day. He reminds her of Mrs. Ramos's son, Luis. "Are you from Puerto Rico?"

"Guatemala," he says, extending his hand. "Lerenzo. My parents and I came here ten years ago."

She shakes his hand. "Emma."

He looks at her load. "Can I help you get to wherever you're going?" He notices her hesitation. "I don't think you're going to be able to walk through the streets carrying all of that." She isn't taking him up on it. "I'm an honest person." He pauses. "Honest!" She hands him the bin. "We all have to watch out for each other, you know," he says, following her on the stairs.

"Did you know anyone who was snatched away?" she says, looking over her shoulder.

He stops outside the door. "Why did you say snatched away?"

He looks eager for her response, and she knows he understands. "Because Christ snatched His followers…"

Lerenzo reacts with excitement and surprise. "You have family who were followers?"

"My mom."

"My grandmother in Guatemala is gone, but my parents are here along with my brothers and sisters."

They begin to walk on the street toward Kennisha's apartment. "Did your grandmother try to tell you?" Emma says.

"Yes. It was just crazy talk to me. Some old lady insanity. But as soon as the shock wore off that day, I knew."

She stops. "Right away?"

He nods. "I'm a truck driver. The highway was a mess. Empty cars and trucks. Or a passenger left without a driver, or a driver without passengers. It felt like everything was taking place in slow motion as I walked along the road, but deep down, I knew what had happened."

The pain in his voice is as real as her heartbreak and she gets a lump in her throat as she listens to him. "What did you do?"

"My knees gave out. I fell on the road and sobbed." He shakes his head. "I'd never cried like that in my life. I became a follower right then. All my family too. We finally found each other, and every single one of us became followers."

As with the people in her apartment building, Emma wishes she had met and gotten to know Lerenzo earlier. She needs him as a friend, and she believes he needs her friendship too.

"Can we keep in touch?" he asks.

CHAPTER 33

Ashdod, Israel

After Zerah leaves his parents' house he makes his way to Dr. Haas's home in Ashdod. The doors are locked; it appears as if no one has been inside the home since the disappearances. Zerah manages to get in through an unlocked window; it doesn't take him long to find what he had come for. He opens the Bible that is sitting on a bedroom nightstand and discovers it had belonged to Dr. Haas.

"You would never believe what I'm standing here looking at, Miriam," he says aloud. He glances around the rest of the small home and regards for a final time the face of his longtime colleague looking out at him from pictures. "Thank you for this," he says, looking at her bright face surrounded by her husband and two children on vacation at the sea.

Through his life, Zerah has read the Torah, or the first five books of the Bible, many times. He begins his reading today beyond Deuteronomy in the Old Testament and devours the New Testament as well, nearly finishing both in two days. He reads again from Daniel and flips to Revelation. The very Spirit of God leads him, teaching and guiding him from one book to another. As he listens to thunderous explosions taking place all across the country and as missiles shriek toward his beloved nation, he prays again that he will be prepared.

✳

The E10's talk of peace has further fueled outrage from the nations engaged in war with Israel; they have fired on her relentlessly, but Israel holds off each attack, fighting for her life. Israel's laser-guided missiles, which have a strike accuracy of twenty-three feet or less, hit armament locations in Lebanon; giant explosions are felt for miles as enormous fireballs blaze into the sky, devastating the armament supplies, much of it provided by Iran.

Fighter, bomber, and remotely piloted aircraft conduct strike after strike, destroying terrorist headquarters in Lebanon and Syria and taking out mortar systems, tanks, artillery systems, command and control nodes, bomb-making facilities, and terminating or suppressing several tactical units. Israeli fighters drop air-to-surface missiles on military fortifications, air bases, and airports in Syria where Iran has stored munitions, while Israeli soldiers and snipers target and kill militants in Palestine and terrorists who have infiltrated Israel.

As the war is broadcast around the world and casualties reach into the thousands, the media applauds the Arab coalition's ceaseless pounding of Israel. Yet Israel's defense has been so swift, so strong and unyielding, that it has caused her enemies to stagger and left the media speechless. As missiles are launched at Israel, destroying life and land, Israel's antiaircraft and antimissile defense systems intervene, saving her and her people, but she has no ally to offer help, and the brutality of the war is taking a toll on the tiny nation.

The cry from her enemies to "Drown the Zionist pigs in the sea" and the data newly retrieved by satellites has left Israel with no other choice. The Jewish nation will launch two long-range ballistic missiles fitted with nuclear warheads and fire them toward Iran, knowing that a monstrous giant is coming together against them.

To discover more about the biblical facts behind the story, read Where in the Word? *on page 269, or continue reading the novel.*

CHAPTER 34

Queens, NY

Upon returning to Kennisha's apartment, Emma finds Micah eating cereal from a box. He eyes his belongings and moves to claim them, looking up at her. "Was my dad there?"

Emma nods and leads him to the sofa. Micah sits with the box of cereal on his lap, looking uncertain and afraid. "I talked to him," she says. His eyes are wide, waiting. "He said he can't take care of you." Micah's brown eyes look intent as he ponders what this means. "He asked if I would, and I said yes." She puts her hand on his knee. "I realize we don't know each other very well and if you are uncomfortable, I understand. Do you have any other place you want to go?"

He shakes his head. "I'm not uncomfortable."

"I'm not sure if I need to contact child services or if they even exist now, or…"

"No!" Micah says, cutting her off. "I want to stay with you." Kennisha enters from the bedroom and sits down next to Micah as his lip begins to quiver. "Can we ever go back and see my dad?"

"Absolutely," Emma says, putting an arm around him and looking at Kennisha. "And we want you to know that we'll do whatever it takes to fight for you. We're all part of a team now." She pulls him closer, then adds, "We're part of a family. You and me and Brandon and Kennisha and Elliott."

A tear leaks from the corner of his eye and she kisses him on the head, letting him grieve.

Emma eats a few bites of cereal before heading into Brooklyn to check on Thrive. She has to see if there's any possibility of work. She wonders if there's any food at 316 Deli and grabs Mrs. Ramos's bag, putting her own pepper spray into it, then concealing the bag under her jacket. The subway system is still shut down and the line for bus service would require hours of waiting, so she borrows Kennisha's bicycle, pushing it out of the apartment, down the stairs, and onto the street. She figured it would probably take less than an hour to ride the few miles to Brooklyn. She's never ridden a bike through the streets of New York and prays she'll be able to maneuver through traffic, which has become so much worse since everyone was snatched away. Many are leaving the city, which has created total gridlock. Violent mobs have been prowling like dogs, and she prays they won't notice her.

Emma's legs burn and her lungs feel as if they could burst, but she keeps pedaling until she reaches 316 Deli. Her heart sinks when she sees that the windows are broken and the restaurant has been vandalized. Deep down she knew there probably wouldn't be anything left, hoping against hope that looting hadn't happened, but in the absence of respect it doesn't take long for human nature to reveal itself. It seems that the millions of people who disappeared also took laughter and chatter and general kindness along with them.

She pushes the bike inside the restaurant and discovers that all the food has been taken from the shelves, walk-in refrigerator, and freezer. Sorrow grips at her lungs as she remembers the Ramos family members babbling away with their customers and serving up the food they loved here. The wonderful smells, the sight of the beautiful breads and pastries and desserts, and the sound of customers enjoying good conversation and delicious food won't be heard here again. She steps between the broken tables and chairs and is unsettled by the sound of shattered glass crunching beneath her feet. She's so glad that Mrs. Ramos is not here to see this.

The door to Thrive is locked, a good sign that no one has broken in; Emma uses her key to get inside. The building is mostly dark, with the exception of light pouring in through the front doors. She doesn't dare leave the bicycle on the street and carries it up the stairs, using the key to open the door to the office. She locks it behind her and steps through the waiting room, calling out to anyone who might be there.

"Emma! What are you doing here?" Linda says from behind the reception desk, holding one hand to her chest. "You scared me to death!" She moves out from behind the desk, looking spent, her eyes hollowed and dark. "I'm so jumpy. Everything scares me now. How are you?"

"Hanging on." Emma looks out over the floor of the rehabilitation room and sees that someone has been here, taking whatever they wanted. "I came to see if there's any work."

Linda shakes her head. "Look at it. The computers are gone. A lot of the equipment is gone. Who would do that? How is any of our equipment useful to some guy off the street?"

"They didn't take it because it was useful. They took it because they could." Emma looks at the files on the reception desk. "What are you doing?"

"Arlen wanted me to see if there's any way we can stay open. He was here with me up until a few minutes ago. He doesn't like to leave his family for too long."

Emma looks at the stacks of files. "Any luck?"

Linda shakes her head. "I can't make calls. I might know more if I could, but right now it's impossible."

Emma sighs. "It's doubtful there will ever be work here again, isn't it?"

Linda shrugs, her eyes looking frightened. "Maybe on some sort of cash level, but even then, I don't know how Arlen could get equipment again. He'll have to file an insurance claim, and I don't know if our insurance company exists anymore. Everybody could be gone, for all I know. Even if some of them are still around, do they even have records anymore?" Looking over at the spot where Mrs. Ramos had disappeared, Emma feels a tug at her heart, wishing she could be with her mom and dad and Mrs. Ramos today. Linda notices the look on her face and says, "I'm sorry about your mom, Emma."

She looks at Linda and tries to smile. "I'm not. I'm sorry that I'm here. My mom's in heaven along with Carrie and Reggie, Mrs. Ramos, and all the others who disappeared."

Linda's face reveals discomfort over what Emma said. "I've heard people say that, but why would you think it's true?"

"Because in the Bible, God said it's true. Jesus called for his followers, just like he said he would."

Linda isn't buying any of this and Emma steps toward her, thinking out loud. "If there's a big building in your neighborhood, like a church or school, I could bring someone who can explain it all."

Linda looks uncertain, but her eyes brighten enough to give Emma hope.

CHAPTER 35

Queens, NY

Hatred for the Jews is no longer isolated to the Middle East; venom for Israel is hurled throughout each news broadcast. Ever since the war began in the Middle East, anti-Semitism has escalated across the world. Jews have been called thieves, murderers, pillagers, barbarians, butchers, invaders, antagonists, dogs, and swine who are stinking up Arab land, creating a growing intolerance for their existence around the globe. Iran, Russia, Turkey, Sudan, and parts of central Asia have mobilized, threatening Israel at every turn and promising complete annihilation.

As a Jew, Elliott's life is in danger, but he goes out each day to preach, protected by Christ. He rides his bicycle for miles, shouting as he goes, telling people about the love of Christ, how he received his own followers, and how he will return again. He preaches inside apartment buildings, churches, rescue missions that are housing the homeless, hotel lobbies, bars, on street corners, at food lines, or anywhere there's a group of people.

It's not his own life as a Jew that Elliott is concerned about when he takes his phone and runs up to the roof, praying that the call will go through. It doesn't. He tries texting and prays that will work, sending a simple message: *Are you there?*

His heart races when the screen on his phone fills with words: *Yes! It's Mom. Don't have long. Can't let your father know I'm texting u*

Elliott's heart beats faster. *Are u safe at Uncle Harold's?*

Yes. Are u safe? Getting more dangerous every day. I keep praying the war against Israel will end soon

Elliott knows he has to tell her as much as possible. *This is just the beginning. Russia, Iran, Turkey, and other countries will come to fight against Israel, but Hashem will save Israel*

I pray u r right

Elliott continues. *A man will rise to power who will confirm the peace treaty that Pres Banes made with Israel*

I hope soon

No. Many in the world will b deceived by this man. He'll say the right things, but he's evil. He's against Hashem. Will kill more people than any man in history. Elliott wants to tell his mother that the Bible calls this man the Antichrist because he's anti-Christ, against Christ, but she's not able to hear those words yet. *He'll confirm treaty with Israel. Will seem he's on Israel's side but he'll break the treaty 3 1/2 years later and will set out to kill every Jew on Earth*

Don't scare me Elliott! U r wrong

I'm not wrong. Did you read Revelation 7?

No

Brandon opens the door to the roof and Elliott glances up at him, texting: *Plz read it. It's who I am. You'll understand if u read it. Plz read Daniel, all of Revelation, 2 Thessalonians 2. All are in the Bible*

I don't have those books! I need to go before ur father knows

U do have them! On phone or computer. Promise me. Plz promise u'll read them. I'm your son. Plz

There is no response, and after several moments, he can only assume that his final text didn't go through.

Brandon hasn't yet seen the devastated city from this view, how it rests grave-like and silent, and it feels like he's been punched in the gut. He bends over, resting his hands on his knees.

"You okay?" Elliott asks, placing his hand on Brandon's back.

Brandon shakes his head. "I was afraid to see what the city really looked like." He puts his hands on his head, exhaling. "Keep it together, Brandon. Keep it together," he tells himself. "What do you do up here?"

Elliott holds up his phone. "Sometimes I can catch a signal up here. Can you text?"

"No. My phone died hours after everybody disappeared. I should have bought an extra battery or solar charger years ago. I hope we get power again soon. I haven't heard anything from my mom since that day." His face grows solemn. "That day." He glances over the guts of the city. "Those are our stories now, right? *Where were you that day? What happened to the people you love on that day? This is what happened to me on that day.*" He shakes his head. "Man, I wish I had been out of here on that day."

Elliott touches his shoulder. "You will be out of here. We all will. Very soon."

Brandon's face clouds over. "I want to tell my mom about Jesus. She doesn't have an Elliott."

"There are 144,000 of us out there. There could be an Elliott in Louisville!"

"I'm praying that there is. I never prayed before, but I'm praying now." Brandon closes his eyes, letting the wind lap at his face. "For the longest time I felt it, you know?" He looks at Elliott. "I felt like the world was just spinning out of control. Every day the news just screamed it at us, but I couldn't listen. Didn't want to listen. I didn't want to think about it."

"Me neither."

Brandon lifts the Bible he's holding in his hand. "I've been trying to read the Bible. I've never done that before."

Elliott smiles. "*You* haven't done that before! At least you probably had one in your house growing up."

"I don't know much about it, but last night I was reading in Matthew, about Jesus, you know, the night that he was in the garden. He asked his disciples to pray for him, and three times he found them sleeping. I could see him there, you know? I could see him counting on his friends to pray, but they were so tired that they couldn't stay awake and they didn't get it. They didn't understand what was at stake, what was happening. He had no one to count on. He was all alone there in the garden." Brandon looks at Elliott, hoping he's making sense. "All he had was his Father in heaven, and he's begging God to take the cup away because that cup was his death." He pauses. "And then Jesus said, 'Not my will, but yours.'" He looks up to the sky, thinking. "All my life I've done what I've wanted. You know, my will. I never considered God's will."

"Me neither."

"Jesus was in such torment that he sweat drops of blood. His body was saying, 'No, no, no! Not this!' But he didn't do what his flesh wanted, and he said, 'Not my will, but yours.' He was alone. He was constantly rejected by people. He was facing crucifixion and still said, 'Not my will. Yours.'" Brandon rubs his hand over his arm as he continues to think out loud. "For the first time in my life I want to do God's will, Elliott. I can't live with myself if I don't. It might mean that I'm all alone, but I want to do it. I have to do it if I follow him."

Elliott smiles. "You won't be alone."

"But I'm afraid."

"I think Jesus must have been afraid too. You said yourself he sweat drops of blood."

"Then I read this in Matthew," Brandon says, finishing his thoughts. "Jesus said that whoever wants to be his disciple must deny himself and take up his cross daily and follow him." He smirks at the thought. "Deny myself and take up my cross daily to follow Jesus. I never denied myself anything. Take up my cross? You mean that thing that I'm denying? Those *things* that I'm denying? That cross? It never happened! Not once." Brandon pauses for a moment, realizing something for the first time. "If somebody would have told me that I had to deny myself and take up my cross to follow Jesus, I would have said that's not love. How is that love if I'm denying myself? God doesn't love me if he wants me to deny myself. If God is love, then he would *want* me to have what I want!" He looks at Elliott. "Right?"

"That's how I saw it."

"Before that day, I wouldn't have understood denying myself or 'not my will but yours,'" Brandon says, looking out at the rubble that was New York City. "I never understood anything about surrender." He turns to Elliott. "But I get it now. I don't know if I said that right. I haven't been to church in a long time."

"You're in church right now," Elliott says. His phone buzzes in his hand and he glances down at it.

Ok I will

He smiles at the text. His Jewish mother is going to read the Bible.

CHAPTER 36

Brooklyn, NY

Emma carries the bike back down the stairs from Thrive, adjusting Mrs. Ramos's bag over her shoulder and stands for a moment, thinking. She digs through the bag, pulling out the wallet and opens it, looking at Mrs. Ramos's driver's license. She quickly turns her head to check the street signs and jumps on the bicycle, peddling away.

When she gets to Mrs. Ramos's address, she looks down at the license again and compares it to the street number above the door. It's a small brick walk-up with neighboring homes close on each side. Her heart races when she sees that none of the windows have been broken. She doesn't want to draw attention to herself trying to get inside the front door, so she rides her bike up the driveway to the back of the house, pulling out a set of keys. Emma's hands shake as she begins to try each key that looks like it would fit this particular doorknob. The third key opens the door, and she can hear her heart in her ears as she pushes the bike inside, then locks the door.

Along the back hall are pictures of Mrs. Ramos's children and grandchildren, and Emma picks up a picture of the entire family and stares at Mrs. Ramos. "Please forgive me for coming into your home like this. You were so kind to me that I thought maybe…" She doesn't finish and considers leaving, but she can't. Emma and her friends need food and anything else that will help them get through the days ahead.

She makes her way into the kitchen and opens the cabinets and the pantry door, smiling. There are soup mixes, noodles, canned vegetables, rice, flour, crackers, sugar, peanut butter, jellies, oatmeal, cereals, nuts, a flashlight, and more that Emma can't see. "Thank you," she whispers, standing in the middle of the kitchen and looking at all the open cupboards. Her mind spins as she wonders how she can get all this back to Kennisha's apartment, and she realizes she'll have to make several trips. She looks for a rolling cart, the kind people often use on the subway to carry groceries or lots of packages, but how could she get it home? There's no way to attach it to the bicycle. She would be an obvious target for thieves if she pulled a loaded cart on the streets.

She opens a door that leads out of the kitchen and holds her breath when she hears the voice of a man coming from inside the windowless garage. She listens in the dark as she creeps down the stairs, then realizes she's hearing some sort of foreign news broadcast. She runs back into the kitchen for the flashlight she found and is relieved to see that it works. Emma hurries back into the garage and sitting on a shelf amidst car oil, garbage bags, gardening spades, and plant fertilizer is a shortwave radio. She lifts it and guesses she's probably listening to a man broadcasting from Puerto Rico. She can envision Mr. Ramos tinkering in his garage while listening to news from his beloved country and her eyes get misty, knowing that now she and her friends can hear the news from around the world.

She turns a knob on the radio and stops when she hears what sounds like the voice of President Banes. "The E10 assures you that we are dialoguing with leaders to bring an end to this war in the Middle East and we are actively involved in ending the wars throughout the world. Over the last few days we have seen unprecedented turmoil around the globe, which has caused us to be interconnected as never before in history. We cannot fight against one another because we *are* one, and as one, we must reason together to end all conflicts. We must have peace and security, and the only way to achieve this is to see our neighbors as ourselves. The life of our planet depends on each one of us."

Reporters begin to shout out questions, but Emma turns off the radio; there's no time to listen, and what she heard makes her feel sick to her stomach. The death toll in New York City alone proves that the world is not one, and "peace and security" is nothing more than a hollow soundbite.

She shines the light in front of her and her eyes widen at the sight of a car. It's obviously old with much wear and tear and lots of miles, but she yanks open the driver's door, sliding behind the wheel. She fingers the keys on Mrs. Ramos's keychain again and grabs the one that's marked *Ford*. She puts it in the ignition and turns it; the sound of the engine almost makes her cry. She shines the flashlight onto the gas gauge and the tank is almost full. Through the front windshield she notices garage shelves that are packed with huge bags of flour, sugar, salt, lard, rice, dried beans, cornmeal, and noodles. The Ramos family must have stored some of the food for the deli here. Emma turns off the car, stunned by all she's discovered. Then she starts laughing. She has an audacious idea and runs back into the house and up the stairs.

There are three bedrooms. She checks the water in the two bathrooms, then in the kitchen. Water pours from all the faucets! Emma looks at the open cupboards and her mind is firing too many ideas at once. She's so hungry; she can't remember the last time she's eaten. Cans of tuna fish sit in an open cupboard in front of her and she opens one, finding a jar of mayonnaise to mix into it. "Thank you, God," she says.

Emma doesn't want to take more time looking for more to eat, searching instead for any money that may have been kept in the home. She apologizes again to Mrs. Ramos and her husband. "This isn't me," she says. She finds a hundred dollars or so in a small wooden box in their bedroom closet, and fifty-some dollars in a jar in the kitchen. She shoves the money into her pocket and returns to the garage, locking the house door behind her. She holds her breath as she lifts open the garage door, backs the car out, races out to pull down the garage door, and prays that no one will break into this house.

Her eyes track all movement on the sidewalks and the alleys and she's fearful as she drives, not wanting anyone to take this car from her. As she passes one alley she does a double take, looking behind her as she passes. She thought she saw a little girl near the dumpster in the alley. Emma tries to shake it off, but the feeling nags at her that the little girl is alone, and she finds a place to turn around. She parks in the alley and exits the car, locking the doors. She looks down the alleyway and sees the little girl, who appears to be around eight or so and has long black hair and light brown skin. She's sitting against a building and there are mounds of garbage around the dumpster.

"Are you out here with anyone?" The little girl jumps at hearing Emma's voice and gapes at her. "You need to be inside. Do you live in this building?" The girl shakes her head. "Well, where do you live? Is it close?"

Her little shoulders lift in a shrug. "I don't know."

Emma turns to make sure the car is okay and they're alone in the alley. "Where is your mom or dad?"

"I don't have a dad, and my mom said she'll be back."

Emma steps closer to the girl, looking back over her shoulder as she does. "Where did she go?" The girl doesn't answer. "Did she just drop you off here?" The girl nods. "When?"

She lifts her shoulders again. "The moon was out."

Emma's eyes widen. "How many nights have you been here?" The girl doesn't answer, and Emma looks around. "Where did you sleep?"

The girl points to the dumpster. "Behind that."

Emma imagines the rats that must be feeding on the trash and her stomach turns at the thought of a little girl sleeping among them. "Is there any place you can go? Do you have a grandma and grandpa?"

"I have a grandma, and she left with everybody. Mommy tried to take me there, but she was gone."

Emma glances again at the car before kneeling down. She needs to get out of this alley and back into the car before someone sees it. "My name's Emma. What's yours?"

"Lia."

"Lia. Are you afraid out here?" Lia nods. "Yeah, I would be too. Do you think your mom is coming back?" Lia looks at the ground, unable to respond, but Emma knows the answer. "I'm sure your grandma told you never to talk to strangers or ever get in their car with them, and I would tell you the same thing, but I'm afraid to leave you here on the street. There's a little boy in our apartment named Micah and I bet he would love to meet you. Would you like to come meet him? I can give you something to eat, and then I promise that we'll come back to see if your mom is here."

Lia nods, and Emma hurries her to the car. She looks so tiny sitting in the passenger seat. Emma doesn't know what she's done, but as she imagines leaving Lia with the rats and the dumpster and in the darkness of the alleyway, she shudders at what could never be undone and drives for home.

To discover more about the biblical facts behind the story, read Where in the Word? *on page 277, or continue reading the novel.*

CHAPTER 37

Queens, NY

Brandon walks with Elliott out on the streets, and as they pass the many people shuffling by to stand in a food line or wait outside the doors of a church or mission for a place to sleep, he notices that Elliott is looking each man and woman in the face. He can't simply walk from here to there anymore because it's not about his destination, but theirs. These people whose faces are etched with concern, worry, fear, loss, and pain take Elliott to the streets all day every day.

Brandon is jostled from behind as people pass them, and Elliott looks at him. "There are a lot of people here. I can't let them slip by." He puts his hand on Brandon's shoulder. "You need to know that nothing can harm me. You don't need to help me." Brandon opens his mouth, but Elliott steps up on a light pole, watching the people coming toward him, racing for the food line that won't have enough food for most of them to buy. He wraps his arm around the pole and adjusts his glasses with the other hand, while holding his Bible.

"Please know that God loves you very much," he says to the passing crowd. Most people ignore him. "He loves you very much and wants you to know what's ahead. Many of you no longer have loved ones here." That stops many people. "Jesus called for his own, and that's why they were snatched away." He holds up the Bible. "God told us in the beginning what would happen in the end." Several more stop and look up at him. "None of this is a surprise. God knows how all this is going to end. He's known it since the beginning and has tried to tell us.

He wants you to know today that he loves you very much and that his Son Jesus is coming again."

Brandon notices that a couple of young men bolt away from the group and wonders why they took off so fast, but a few moments later he understands when a mob of people with knives and guns show up. It's obvious that the two young men had gone to find these assailants, who are brandishing weapons and cursing and screaming at Elliott and anyone listening to him. These hostiles perfectly reflect the gangland violence that is erupting in the streets of New York City and around the country every day.

"You're a Jew!" a young man with fierce features and pronounced eyebrows shouts.

Elliott steps down from the pole, facing him. "I am a Jew. My Savior and Messiah Jesus Christ is a Jew, and he died so that all of us could live, and he's coming back for…" The armed mob is outraged at his words, and many in the crowd shrink back in fear. "Don't let them frighten you," Elliott shouts. "This message is for you, it's for them, it's for anyone with ears to hear. Today is the day of salvation in Jesus."

The mob screeches at his words, yelling on top of one another. "You Jew pigs are killing people!" one screams.

Brandon shouts from the back of the crowd to warn Elliott, but the attackers are already lunging at him with knives. Many in the crowd run and scream as sharp blades, long and glistening, slice through the air at Elliott, only to stab bystanders and other assailants, their roars becoming more vicious with each failed and bloody attempt to knife Elliott. Brandon shouts for them to stop; his heart feels like it will burst through his ribs as he prays, climbing up onto a window ledge to get a view of Elliott. He can't believe what he's seeing; Elliott is unharmed.

"Please put away your weapons," Elliott says in the midst of the clash. "I'm not here to harm you or anyone else. I'm here to tell you that Jesus is coming back again for all who believe."

The fierce man who was the first to shout at Elliott screams curses and fires his gun, but Elliott is unfazed, the bullet striking a gang member right behind him. The man falls to the ground, shrieking, and the man with the gun pulls the trigger again and again as he aims at Elliott's chest, only to shoot another armed assailant behind him. The man crumples to the sidewalk. "Please put away your weapons before you kill each other," Elliott says, addressing the attackers more like a diplomat than someone whose life is in danger.

Brandon looks on in wonder and amazement while one man on the periphery of the violence records it on his cell phone. In the end, the attackers are bloodied, stunned, and raging against one another while the crowd grows and gathers closer around Elliott, astonished by what they've witnessed. The sidewalk looks like a crime scene covered with so much gore, the blood-soaked reality of the city's new normal. While some in the defeated pack limp away, holding hands over their injuries or dragging away their wounded as they curse and scream at Elliott, others of the bloodstained horde turn their backs on their comrades and listen to Elliott. He speaks to the growing mass of onlookers, numbering at least a hundred or more by now.

Elliott speaks for less than ten minutes, saying things like *believe, love, repent, turn from sin, seek, look up, follow Jesus,* and *He's coming again.* The words don't fall on the listeners like lies, exaggerations, or madness, but rather like truth from a friend, and although some walk away dismayed or disgusted, most of them believe. Elliott tells the crowd to get together in groups and pray and read Scripture so they can help one another in the coming days and tell others about Jesus.

A man rushes from the back of the crowd toward Elliott and Brandon opens his mouth to shout a warning, but realizes his words are feeble here amidst the crowd and the noise. The man stands in front of Elliott for a moment before embracing him, lifting him off his feet. Elliott laughs and pats the back of the man's head as they hold on to each other.

"It's Simon!" Elliott shouts to Brandon.

CHAPTER 38

Queens, NY

Brandon and Simon walk through the streets with Elliott, stopping to watch and listen as he preaches along the way. The time is coming when he will no longer have a place to call his home, and who knows…some of these people may offer him food, help, or a bed for the night.

Simon is mesmerized as he listens to his longtime friend. For as long as he has known Elliott, he has been quiet and shy, happiest just mulling about in the shadows. But now he's bold and unafraid of anybody or what they could possibly do to him. Every word out of his mouth is spoken with courage and power and great compassion. When people curse at him, it doesn't faze him. When they scoff and laugh, he talks louder. They aren't in control of him; God is, and this leaves Simon speechless. To ponder the greatness of God and the power of Christ has left Simon undone, and his eyes pool over while watching his friend. "How did those knives and bullets miss you?" he asks when Elliott finishes with a group.

Elliott shakes his head, still amazed by it all. "I'm sealed with Hashem's protection." He uses the Jewish words for God and Jesus when speaking to Simon.

"You're not afraid?" Brandon asks, trying to keep pace with them on the crowded sidewalk.

Elliott stops, thinking. "I was afraid the first time I went out to the streets, but not anymore. I see the weapons and hear the anger and hatred of many people, but Yeshua sealed me for this work, and I'm no longer afraid."

"How do you know what to say?" Simon asks. "You've answered so many questions. How do you know how to do that?"

"I've already read through the Bible and Hashem brings the verses back to me. The Spirit of Hashem speaks through me. He even teaches me in my dreams."

Simon snaps his head to look directly at him. Dreams have always been a vital part of their culture, but he's never experienced any like Elliott is talking about. "Every day?"

Elliott nods. "Hashem says he's going to pour out dreams and visions all over the world."

A middle-aged man and a young girl catch Brandon's eye as they walk past. She appears to be his daughter, but there's something in the way that the man handles her with his arm wrapped firmly around her waist, seeming to drag her along, that makes Brandon take notice. He watches as the man and the girl walk further down the street and meet another man who is around forty or so. Brandon can't see exactly what's happening, but it looks like something is exchanged between the two men before the first man walks on without the girl. The second man grips her arm and leads her across the street to avoid the crowd that's gathering around Elliott, who's preaching again. Brandon moves around the group to see where the man and girl are going, breaking into a run when he sees the door of a passenger van open with what appears to be other young girls inside. "Elliott!" he screams, darting across the street.

Elliott leaves the group, bolting after Brandon. As the young girl is being forced inside the van, Brandon leaps for the man, pulling him away from the girl before he can get her inside. Elliott yanks open the driver's-side door and tries to pull a man the size of King Kong out of his seat. Unaccustomed to fighting, Brandon takes solid, heavy blows to the face as the abductor curses at him.

Simon runs to help and smashes his fist against the side of the abductor's head. Elliott scrambles over the driver to grab the keys, and the driver attempts to beat him off; his punches land hard into the van door, steering wheel, and windshield. A couple of men from the crowd Elliott was speaking to realize what is happening and rush in to help Brandon and Simon, hitting the abductor in the head and the stomach to keep him away from the girl. He runs down the street and the driver flees from the van as well, running through an alleyway.

Elliott turns to see two young girls, no older than eleven or twelve, staring at him from the back of the van. "It's all right now," he says. He gets out of the van to check on Brandon and the girl. Brandon is gasping for air and his face is swollen and red; his left eye, nose, and lips are bleeding. "Are you okay?" Brandon nods, leaning over with his hands on his knees to catch his breath. Elliott looks at the young girl and can see that she's no older than the two inside the van. He puts his hand on her shoulder. "Have you been hurt?" She shakes her head. "Do you have parents?"

She nods and begins to cry. "My mom."

"We'll get you back to her." He leans his head inside the van, looking at the two girls. "Do you live here with your mom and dad or a family member?" They shake their heads, and Elliott turns back to Brandon and Simon.

"What do we do?" Brandon asks.

They use the van and drive the young girl, Lorena, back to her mother, who falls to the ground when she hears about what happened. Elliott speaks with both of them before leaving, and they place their fears and lives in the hands of Christ. Lorena's mother hugs all of them again, even the other two young girls, kissing one cheek and then the other before she lets them go. Elliott drives to the closest police station, but there's no use in getting out. The line to get in winds down the street, and he and Brandon and Simon know it won't do them any good once they are inside anyway. The lack of police officers is clearly evident in the streets, which means there is a lack of them inside the precinct as well.

"If we were Emma, she would bring them home," Brandon says, his eye swelling shut.

They drop Simon off near his home, and Elliott gets out to say good-bye, hugging his friend.

"Thank you, Elliott." Simon's voice is full of emotion.

"The Holy Spirit helps lead you through the Bible," Elliott says, gripping Simon's shoulders. "Read it. Share the gospel of Yeshua with your family and friends." He hugs Simon, pounding him on the back. "Hashem will give you dreams, Simon. He will pour out His Spirit on you."

CHAPTER 39

Ashdod, Israel

The sounds of explosions fill the air outside Dr. Haas's house. Zerah keeps his eyes on the Bible, reading every word again in Ezekiel 38:

> After many days you will be summoned; in the latter years you will come into the land that is restored from the sword, whose inhabitants have been gathered from many nations to the mountains of Israel...Its people were brought out from the nations, and they are living securely, all of them. You will go up, you will come like a storm; you will be like a cloud covering the land, you and all your troops, and many peoples with you...you will say, "I will go up against the land of unwalled villages. I will go against those who are at rest, that live securely, all of them living without walls and having no bars or gates"...Thus says the Lord GoD, "On that day when my people Israel are living securely, will you not know it?...and you will come up against My people Israel like a cloud to cover the land. It shall come about in the last days that I will bring you against My land, so that the nations may know Me when I am sanctified through you before their eyes..."

Zerah looks up from the Bible, glancing outside to the empty street. These words were here within this book his entire life, but he never knew about them until now. Israel was brought out from the nations. There is no other country on the planet whose people were dispersed around the world, only to come back into their land nearly two thousand years later. Up until the two-state solution was implemented with the Palestinians under the guidance of President Banes, Israel was protected by barrier walls along the Gaza Strip and West Bank, but those walls came down in a good-faith effort to show that the people of Israel believed in both the treaty and the Palestinians. They were now a people without walls protecting them from terrorist groups like Hamas, Palestine Islamic Jihad, and the Palestinian Liberation Front, among others, but because of the peace covenant, had been living securely, just as Ezekiel foretold. Zerah glances down at the Bible, reading again: "You will come up against My people Israel like a cloud to cover the land. It shall come about in the last days that I will bring you against My land." According to Scripture, Israel would be attacked by many nations gathered against them.

As Zerah contemplates this, he raises his arms and drops to his knees.

Queens, NY

When Kennisha opens the door, she gasps at the sight of Brandon's face, reaching for him before she notices the two young girls. She spots them and glances at Elliott before ushering the girls inside. "What are your names?" she asks, leading them into the apartment.

"Signe," one of them says with a soft accent. She has fair skin, small features, and blondish-brown hair. Emma is in the living room with Micah and Lia and she jumps up at hearing their voices.

"Are your parents here, Signe?" Kennisha asks.

She shakes her head. "I came here with my uncle after my mom died, and he..."

Emma kneels down in front of Signe as Micah and Lia stand behind Emma, looking at Signe. With so many eyes on her, Signe's lips begin to tremble. Lia steps from behind Emma and puts her arm around Signe's small shoulders. Emma and Kennisha don't need Signe to say that her uncle sold her to make money. The pain is fixed on her face. "What's your name?" Emma asks, looking at the other girl, who has charcoal-black skin and long, plated braids.

"Ines," she says with a Haitian tone.

"This is Micah," Kennisha says. "And this is our new friend, Lia. We were just going to make something to eat."

"Are you hungry?" Micah asks. He leads all the girls into the kitchen.

Emma directs Brandon and Elliott into the bathroom, signaling for Kennisha to join them once the children are settled. She hands a flashlight to Elliott so he can help her see better in the mostly dark bathroom and instructs Brandon to sit down on the toilet lid, then reaches for a washcloth to begin cleaning his face. "What happened?"

"I saw a girl get sold on the street." He winces when Emma touches his face.

"She would've been gone…They all would have been gone if not for Brandon," Elliott says, moving the flashlight around as he talks with his hands.

Emma lifts a bottle of alcohol, the only disinfectant she can find, out of the cabinet and looks for cotton balls. "All of them? How many were there?"

"Three," Brandon says. "We were able to take the first girl home."

"How did you get them?" Emma dabs at Brandon's swollen left eye and each time she does, he flinches.

"The first girl was about to be shoved into a van when Brandon, like Superman, jumped on the guy," Elliott says, fist-bumping Brandon and making the flashlight shine onto the ceiling.

"He must have been a pretty big guy to do this to you," Emma says, patting the bloody cheek, lips, and eye with a cotton ball.

"You should have seen what I did to him," Brandon says, smiling.

"Really?!"

Brandon shakes his head. "No. He would have killed me if not for Elliott and Simon and two guys from the street. But he didn't get the girls!"

"Simon?" Emma asks.

"A friend," Elliott says.

"He saw the crowd on the street in his neighborhood," Brandon says. "One guy was taking a video—obviously, the only one who had an extra cell battery or solar charger. Hopefully he'll upload it when we have Internet again and you can see what happened."

"Why did he video it? What happened?" Emma asks, looking at Elliott.

Before Elliott has a chance to answer, Kennisha peers into the doorway, trying to see Brandon's face. "Brandon and Elliott saved the girls' lives," Emma says. She reaches for the flashlight and Elliott hands it to her; she finds an antibiotic ointment in the cabinet and dabs it around Brandon's wounds.

Kennisha leans against the door, shaking her head. "How many more kids are out there like that? There are probably rings all over the city that have been operating for years. They'll only get bigger now with so many people and police officers gone. And we can't save them all."

"But we can save a lot," Emma says. The weight of what she has said invades the small space between them with a combination of fear and hope, and they can hear each other breathe. "I can't leave any child out on the streets."

"We can't take in all of them," Kennisha says.

"I've been thinking," Emma says, then pauses, gathering her thoughts. "I took money and a car from Mrs. Ramos's house," she says, almost as a confession, looking at Elliott.

He nods as a look of shame crosses Emma's face. "It's all right, Emma."

"I'm no better than thugs on the street."

"Everything you've said about Mrs. Ramos tells me that she would want you to have the money and the car to help you and all those children."

She nods. "I know. I just feel so bad for what I've been thinking." They all look at her, wondering what she means. "We have to get out of the city, but right now it would take days to get through the traffic, and besides, where would we go? We don't have anything to help us get started somewhere else." All eyes are on her, waiting. "This apartment is too small for all of us. What if we move into the Ramos's house?" Kennisha opens her mouth, but Emma cuts her off before she has a chance to say anything. "The house has three bedrooms, two bath-rooms, a basement, and running water. We could find more mattresses and bring them in."

"But they probably have a mortgage," Kennisha says.

Emma's already thought about this. "What if the mortgage company no longer exists?"

"Even if it does exist," Brandon says, his eyes widening, "it would take them months to sort through all their files. They would have to figure out who's gone and who's left here with a mortgage to pay."

Emma is talking faster now. "Before everything's stolen, what if we found the homes or apartments of those who disappeared and…" She can't bring herself to say it.

"And take what we could find and move it to the Ramos's house?" Brandon asks.

She shakes her head. "Hearing you say it makes it sound worse than I thought."

"No it doesn't," Kennisha says. "She was your friend."

"You're going to need medicine too," Elliott says. Emma looks at him as he finishes his thought. "How easy will it be to see a doctor now and how much will they charge? How much will medicine cost?"

Emma leans against the door. "I'm sure Mrs. Ramos has her kid's addresses in her phone," she says to Brandon. "If we can get hold of a solar charger, I could charge her phone enough to get their addresses. We can go to their homes."

Brandon nods. "Maybe there are other people listed in her phone that she went to church with."

Emma's eyes light up. "Maybe even a doctor or two. We need to go before it gets dark. Can we all pack what we need?"

Elliott raises his hand. "What you can't pack you can store in my apartment."

Emma looks stricken. "You're not coming with us?"

"I won't be in New York forever."

Emma is saddened by the thought, but nods at Elliott's decision. "We need to get back to Brooklyn right away, before somebody else breaks into the house."

CHAPTER 40

Brooklyn, NY

As suspected, Lia's mom is nowhere to be found in the area where she had left Lia. Emma drops her, Kennisha, and the other children off at Mrs. Ramos's house, and they all unload the car together. Emma and Brandon waste no time in hunting down addresses inside Mrs. Ramos's home and are soon on their way to her son Carlos's apartment; they gasp when a key on her keychain fits the door.

As their "family" is expanding, Emma knows they don't have enough of the most basic items, and she and Brandon fan out, collecting medicines, food, towels, sheets, blankets, kids' clothes, money, soap, toothpaste, shampoo, plates, cups, and more silverware, putting it all in garbage bags, boxes, pillowcases, or whatever they can find. Again, they take the time to find other family members' and friends' addresses and are thrilled during their search to find a cell phone solar charger. Thankfully, others in the same apartment building are moving out, so they blend in among the movement. There's a sense of urgency in the air and people are running up and down the stairs and through the hallways, rushing their things into waiting vehicles on the street.

Emma wants to get back to Mrs. Ramos's house to unload before finding where Viviana, Angel, or Luis lived. She and Brandon are cramming the last few items into the trunk when a voice from behind curses at them. "Give me the keys!"

Emma turns to see a man around nineteen or twenty pointing a gun at them. People on the street scramble away, but Emma feels fury raging in her gut. He is not going to take these things. "The keys are in my purse in the apartment. If you want the car, go get them yourself!" He steps toward them, heading for the car to look inside when Emma grabs his arm. "Go get the keys if you want them!" He shouts curses, hovering over her and pointing the gun in her face, screaming. He doesn't like being told what to do. "God help us!" Emma yells, slamming the base of her hand up into his nose, drawing blood.

The man stumbles backward, blood squirting out his nose and over his hand. Brandon rushes behind him, locking his arm around the man's neck. Emma rushes forward, kicking the man hard in the groin. She moves for the gun when he drops it, using it to smash the man in his face. In pain and desperate for air, he falls to the street, and Emma and Brandon race to the car, jumping inside. Emma is still shaking as she hands the gun to Brandon. They are too frightened to speak, but know they will do this again and again in search of what they need to survive.

They unload the car at Mrs. Ramos's house, then Emma sinks into the sofa. She is shaking, hungry, and exhausted. There has been no time to grieve so much loss in her life, and she feels tears begin to well up. Brandon drops next to her, his face swollen and red. "Maybe we can eat something, then see if that solar charger will charge Mrs. Ramos's phone," he says, looking at her. "In the meantime, we can look in the desk and files we saw upstairs and check for more addresses for one of her kids or a friend who might have lived near here. I don't want to be on the streets when it gets dark. It's getting too…" He looks at her face, then stops. Brandon doesn't need to tell Emma it's getting too dangerous. He doesn't need to explain to her the risk of being out on the street. He simply holds out his hand, and she clasps it.

Kennisha and the children enter the living room, and Kennisha holds out her hands to Lia and Signe. They each grab hold and extend their hands to Micah and Ines. Together they form a small circle, each holding on to the others' hands. It is so quiet they can hear each other breathe.

Elliott arrives the next morning as Emma and the others are sharing a makeshift breakfast of stale sweet rolls found in Mrs. Ramos's pantry, along with a few apples. "Mr. and Mrs. Ramos would be blessed to see all of you safe inside these walls," he says, watching them eat. Emma hands him a sweet roll. "I've eaten," he says. Her face indicates that she doesn't believe him. "Keep it for the kids."

Elliott doesn't stay long, and Emma wonders if she'll ever see him again. Has it only been since Sunday that they met? Their bond makes it seem it's been much longer. He says good-bye, first to the children, then to Brandon and Kennisha, but Brandon won't let him leave until they pray for him. Praying is still so strange to them, but Brandon talks with God as if he's standing right here next to them as he prays for Elliott and the people of New York City. "Come, Lord Jesus," he says, finishing, and hugs Elliott good-bye.

Elliott steps outside with Emma, and she closes the door so no one can hear. "Last night I was reading, Elliott. Reading the Bible again and…" She looks in his eyes and realizes that he already knows what she's thinking. "The years ahead…many of us will be killed."

"And will be instantly before the throne."

Her voice catches. "All these kids."

Elliott puts his hands on her shoulders. "They will be loved and cared for, some of them for the first time in their lives."

She realizes how tired she is and a tear streams from her eye; she shakes her head as he takes his hands off her shoulders. "But how can they…?" She fumbles for the words. "How can we…?" She looks over her shoulder into the living room. "Where will we house them all? This place will get crowded and we need to get out of the city, but I don't know how we could…How will we feed and clothe them? How many more will we find? I can't do it, Elliott."

"Yes, you can. God said I will pour out my Spirit in those days. The very Spirit of God is on you, Emma. He's inside of you and Kennisha and Brandon. Do you think he wants those kids on the street? He needs people to go out and bring them in and take care of them." He smiles. "You and Kennisha and Brandon are just the founding members of this great organization."

She tries to smile. "One of our founders looks like he got the stuffing beat out of him."

They laugh together for the first time in days, and Emma cries again, looking at him. "I sure could talk to my mom right now."

"All of her prayers for you throughout your life are still alive," Elliott says. "They didn't disappear just because she's in heaven. They're perpetual. They'll go on and on. And I have a feeling that your mom prayed some powerful prayers for you. Prayers for belief and strength and great courage. The same kind of prayers that you'll be praying over these kids now."

Emma hugs him good-bye and watches as he gets on his bike and rides away. Knowing that he'll be out on the streets of Brooklyn today gives her a sense of peace. As long as Elliott is on the streets, the truth is being shared, and others like her and Brandon and Kennisha are being saved. She thinks of the children just inside this front door, her kids, and wonders how many more there will be.

To discover more about the biblical facts behind the story, read Where in the Word? *on page 283, or continue reading the novel.*

CHAPTER 41

Ashdod, Israel

The noise from a squadron of jets rattles the windows at Dr. Haas's house, and Zerah jumps up, peering into the sky. He walks to the door and opens it, straining to see the aircraft overhead. He can't see them yet, but the noise is deafening as they draw near.

When he does finally see them come into view, he is taken aback. The Mediterranean Sea darkens as the great swarm of aircraft from Russia, Turkey, Iran, Libya, Sudan, and other nations cluster together like a sinister cloud over the sea. On the northern end of Israel, fighter planes, helicopters, and a great horde of armored vehicles, all too numerous to count, advance from the border of Syria. This invasion of armies is unprecedented in history, and Zerah cranes his neck upward for a better look.

"It's happening," he whispers.

To discover more about the biblical facts behind the story, read Where in the Word? *on page 287.*

WHERE IN
THE WORD?

WHERE IN THE WORD?

I love stories; I always have. I love to hear them, read, and write them. My list of favorite books is long, but at the top is the greatest story given to man, the truest story that has ever been written, of how an awesome God pursues, loves, forgives, disciplines, redeems, renews, and cares for humanity all the way from Genesis through Revelation.

When I was a little girl growing up in Ohio, our pastor and visiting pastors spoke often about the return of Christ. I knew what the "catching up" of believers in Christ and the second coming was as early as when I was five or six years old, but somewhere along the way, those kinds of messages have largely disappeared from the Western church. It has been decades since I've heard anyone in a pulpit say something like, "Jesus is returning!" or "Jesus is coming soon!" If it's been decades, that means there is an entire generation that has heard little or nothing about Christ's return in their church, Christian high school or university, or even in their seminary. For the most part, this message and that of Bible prophecy have not been proclaimed as they should be.

SOMETHING IS MISSING

About twenty-seven percent of the Bible is prophecy. Why are these Scripture passages rarely taught anymore? For some, perhaps it's

187

because there was a string of bestsellers that some people used to make Bible prophecy into a part of pop culture, and when Jesus didn't return immediately, others scoffed at and derided the whole idea of Jesus snatching away those who are in Christ, thinking it too campy to be taken seriously.

And there have always been pastors who have backed away from teaching Bible prophecy and the return of Jesus for a variety of reasons (pastor Tom Hughes has addressed five of those reasons in an informative article).[1] Perhaps they believe it is perceived as cheesy or farce-like, maybe they see Bible prophecy as something to be interpreted symbolically and not literally, or they feel it is too scary for many in their congregation to hear, too complicated to understand, or too judgmental to proclaim.

Whatever the reason, that means more than one-fourth of the Bible is being overlooked. Who would pick up the latest bestseller and not read twenty-seven percent of the book? If you were reading a book, would you read a few pages and then skip to somewhere in the middle, and then skip some more pages, not even bothering to read the end? I doubt you would, but that's the way many people read Scripture. How can they tie all of God's Word together without reading that twenty-seven percent?

In the Western church, we hear many wonderful sermons about love, forgiveness, unity, compassion, service, hope, mercy, and grace, but seldom hear messages from the neglected twenty-seven percent of the Bible.

This hasn't gone unnoticed. It seems people know that something's not quite right; something is missing. They know that there are vital plot points and important people left out of this great story of God, and they're hungry to know more. There is an urgency in the air, and believers and unbelievers alike feel it. What is happening? Where are we headed? I'm writing this series for people like me, people who for many years have sat in church Sunday after Sunday and have heard the same topics or life lessons given by a variety of speakers, but we know there's more. We want to read and hear and learn about the twenty-seven percent of the story that's been absent in our midst for far too long.

I'm writing these three books for people like me who love stories but who also love the truth and, when they're side by side, it's a perfect day of reading! I'm writing this series for anyone who wants to dig deeper into Scripture, who wants a closer walk with Jesus, and feels the urgency to tell others about Him.

I'm also writing these books for those inside and outside the church who doubt that God can be trusted or that the Bible is true. I'm writing for those who are unchurched or who have been gone from church for longer than they can remember. Perhaps that applies to you. Within yourself you feel as though you have misplaced or overlooked something of importance, or you sense a deep longing for what you've lost. May this series of books with their fictional storyline and Scripture-based study notes be just the beginning of finding what you are searching for.

BE LIKE THE BEREANS

The Time of Jacob's Trouble is a fictional account of what will take place during Earth's final years, but make no mistake: The prophecies, as revealed in the pages of the Bible, are true. When I realized that I wasn't learning about some twenty-seven percent of the Bible in church, I became a student of that twenty-seven percent. As you read through each Where in the Word? section in this part of the book, I encourage you to become a student, too, and ask the Spirit of God for help and understanding as you open your own Bible to learn what the Scriptures say. For myself, I didn't want to take someone else's word or theory about the end of the age; I wanted God's Word as the final authority and studied it, comparing each theory against the Bible.

Regarding the return of Jesus, I determined that I believed as Paul and the early church leaders believed, who were expecting their Lord's return at any moment. Paul said, "Our citizenship is in heaven. And *we eagerly await a Savior from there*, the Lord Jesus Christ" (Philippians 3:20). Peter said they "were waiting for and hastening the coming of the day of God…waiting…to be found by him without spot or blemish, and at peace" (2 Peter 3:12, 14 ESV). They were "looking for the blessed hope and the appearing of the glory of our great God and Savior, Christ Jesus" (Titus 2:13 NASB).

Don't take my word for anything you read in this book! Be like the Bereans in Thessalonica, who "received the message with great eagerness and *examined the Scriptures every day* to see if what Paul said was true" (Acts 17:11). I understand that there are varying opinions about the snatching away of those in Christ and return of Jesus, but I don't understand the anger and vitriol that often accompany those opinions. This isn't a salvation issue. The study of biblical prophecy is not meant to ignite fury, anger, or hatred.

Instead, Bible prophecy has been given to us to…

- *stimulate holiness in our lives* and to *teach us to say no to worldly passions and live self-controlled, upright, blameless, and godly lives* (see Colossians 3:4-5; 1 Thessalonians 3:13; 4:3-5; Titus 2:11-14; 1 Peter 1:13-16; 2 Peter 3:11-14), because "without holiness no one will see the Lord" (Hebrews 12:14).

- *embolden us to be salt and light* and to share the gospel message with others (see Matthew 5:13-16).

- *remind us to wake up* because the day is almost here. We must strap on the armor of light and *live to glorify Jesus, not gratify the flesh* (see Romans 13:11-14; 1 Thessalonians 5:6-8).

- clarify that we must not only wake up from our slumber but *be alert, watch out that we are not deceived, and be on our guard* (Mark 13:5, 9, 23, 33, 35-37).

- urge us to *use our bodies in righteous ways because we are united with Christ* (1 Corinthians 6:9-10, 13-20; 2 Corinthians 5:10; Ephesians 5:3-5).

- *spur us on to love and good deeds, to assemble together, and encouraging one another*—"all the more as you see the Day approaching" (Hebrews 10:24-25).

- *encourage us to purify ourselves that we may be more like Jesus* (1 John 3:2-3).

There are so many other verses I could include, but it's clear from the pages of the Bible that the return of Jesus should affect the way we live today because He asks, "When the Son of Man comes, will he find faith on earth?" (Luke 18:8).

There isn't enough space to cover all the basics about Bible prophecy and the last days here (we'll cover more in the two books following this one), but these notes are meant to reveal the truth behind the novel portion of this book. Whether you are a believer in Christ or you're on a journey to discover who He is, I hope these pages encourage your heart, strengthen your faith, bring your doubts into the pages of God's Word, deepen your walk, fill you with hope, and calm your fears. Perfect love casts out fear, and we should not be afraid at the prospect of Christ's return, but anticipating it.

SOMETHING ISN'T RIGHT

A couple of years ago I listened to a radio broadcast in which the host was reading from an article about a poll conducted among university professors from around the world. Although the professors couldn't put their finger on why they felt this way, the majority of them believed that the world was escalating toward some sort of conclusion. Any casual chat among people in general will reveal the same. When we read headlines from around the globe of wars, genocide, terrorism, sex trafficking, murders, the refugee crises, natural disasters, hunger, abortion, drug use, the loss of innocence, and the rise of racism, anti-Semitism, persecution, hatred, rebellion, and anarchy, we feel something in the air; we think, *Something isn't right*.

In Matthew 24, Jesus's disciples ask about the sign of His coming *and* of the end of the age. Jesus first named deception, wars and rumors of wars, nation rising against nation, famines, and earthquakes, saying that those were "the beginning of birth pains" (Matthew 24:8), which means other birth pains will come. And if there are birth pains, that means something is about to birthed, after which the pains will end.

What many don't know is that God has laid out for us, in His Word, the plan of that ending.

> I make known the end from the beginning,
>   from ancient times, what is still to come.
> I say, "My purpose will stand,
>   and I will do all that I please."…
> What I have said, that I will bring about;
>   what I have planned, that I will do (Isaiah 46:10-11).

The end that is spoken of in the Bible is really a beautiful beginning. God will make all things new: a new refurbished earth with Jesus to rule over it, and it's all laid out within the pages of Scripture. The Greek word *heuriskó* means "to discover, to find, to celebrate." Proverbs 25:2 says, "It is the glory of God to conceal a matter; to search out a matter is the glory of kings." And in 2 Timothy 2:15 we read, "Be diligent to present yourself approved to God, a worker who does not need to be ashamed, rightly dividing the word of truth" (NKJV).

God designed each of us to *heuriskó*. We are meant to study, discover, search out, find, and celebrate the Word of God. As we do, we come to know who He is, uncover great treasures of wisdom and knowledge, receive answers to our questions, and learn of His plans for His creation. We don't need a college education or PhD to study God's Word; there's no greater teacher than the Holy Spirit, and I encourage you to ask Him to teach and lead you.

As you *heuriskó* with me, you'll discover that what happens in the end has been known from the beginning.

AN ANCIENT JEWISH WEDDING

"Do not let your hearts be troubled. You believe in God; believe also in me. My Father's house has many rooms; if that were not so, would I have told you that I am going there to prepare a place for you? And if I go and prepare a place for you, I will come back and take you to be with me that you also may be where I am" (John 14:1-3).

In John 14, Jesus promises to

- prepare a place in His Father's house for you
- come back
- take you to be where He is

When Jesus talked of His Father's house and said that He would "come back and take you to be with me," He was using an analogy that the Jewish people would easily understand, which is based on an ancient Jewish wedding ceremony and consists of several steps. Follow along, and you'll see where this is heading.

Step 1: A Marriage Covenant Is Established

In ancient Israel, the groom's father chose the bride through an agent of the father. On behalf of his son Isaac, Abraham sent his servant, Eliezer, to seek out a bride (Genesis 24:2-4). Rebekah agreed to marry Isaac before meeting him (verse 58).

Today, in the church age, God works through the Holy Spirit to draw people to Christ. Jesus said,

> You did not choose me, but I chose you (John 15:16).

And when we ask Jesus to be our Lord and Savior, we become part of the bride of Christ, even though we have not yet seen Him.

"Though you have not seen him, you love him; and even though you do not see him now, you believe in him and are filled with an inexpressible and glorious joy" (1 Peter 1:8).

In the same way that Abraham had Eliezer search for a bride for Isaac, God uses the Holy Spirit to call us to become the bride of Christ.

Step 2: A Bride Price Is Set and the Bride and Groom Are Betrothed

Once a bride was selected, the groom would leave his father's house and travel to the home of his prospective bride so he could negotiate a purchase price with her father. When the price, or dowry, was paid, he would return to his father's home.

Just as the Jewish groom had to pay a price to obtain his bride, Jesus had to pay a price to acquire us. That price was His blood on the cross.

> You are not your own; you were bought at a price (1 Corinthians 6:19-20).

> It was not with perishable things such as silver or gold that you were redeemed from the empty way of life handed

down to you from your ancestors, but with the precious
blood of Christ (1 Peter 1:18-19).

In ancient Galilee, the groom would offer the bride a cup of wine,
and she would drink from the cup. The groom would then drink from
the cup, solidifying their covenant, and would say to her, "You are now
consecrated to me by the laws of Moses, and I will not drink from this
cup again until I drink it anew with you in my Father's house." In the
same way, during the Last Supper, Jesus offered His apostles a cup of
wine to signify a new covenant with them. After the apostles drank
from the cup, Jesus said what the Galileans (with the exception of Judas
Iscariot, the 12 apostles were Galilean) would have heard in that day:
"But I say to you, I will not drink of this fruit of the vine from now on
until that day when I drink it new with you in My Father's kingdom"
(NKJV). This was a new covenant that would be made in Jesus's blood
and was marked by drinking the wine. Pastor J.D. Farag, who is from
Lebanon, says, "In my Arab culture, you eat from the same bread. You
drink from the same cup. The thought is, 'That which is in you, is
in me.' It is a *common union*. Communion. No longer two, but one.
When Jesus says at that last supper, 'This is my body given for you—
broken for you'—He's talking as a bridegroom to His bride. When He
says, 'This is the cup of My blood in the new covenant,' that's how they
would seal the betrothed in the ancient wedding."[2]

The bride and groom are now legally bound in a marriage contract,
but they don't yet live together. Next comes a time of preparation. The
groom builds and adds living accommodations to his father's house,
to which he can bring his bride. He will remain there for about a year.
The bride undergoes a ritual cleansing bath called a *mikvah* to demon-
strate her purity. During all this, the day when the groom will come for
his bride is not yet known.

Although we who are the bride of Christ are not yet with Him physically in heaven, we are bound to live a pure life for Him while living
on Earth. The hope of His future calling to take us home with Him
should motivate us to throw off the chains of sin that bind us and keep
us separated from Him.

I am jealous for you with a godly jealousy. I promised you to one husband, to Christ, so that I might present you as a pure virgin to him (2 Corinthians 11:2).

We know that when Christ appears, we shall be like him, for we shall see him as he is. All who have this hope in him purify themselves, just as he is pure (1 John 3:2-3).

It teaches us to say no to ungodliness and worldly passions, and to live self-controlled, upright and godly lives in this present age, while we await for the blessed hope—the glorious appearing of our great God and Savior, Jesus Christ (Titus 2:12-13).

The realization that Christ will call His followers to Him at an unknown hour should encourage us to live prayerful and watchful lives. Be on your guard! Be ready! Be alert! Don't be asleep! Stay awake! Keep watch! (see Matthew 24:42-44; 15:1-13; Mark 13:5, 9, 23, 32-37).

Step 3: Gathering the Bride

Before the groom could go claim his bride, he had to wait until his father declared satisfaction with the bridal chamber. The groom didn't know when his father would give consent to send for his bride, which meant that the bride didn't know when her groom would come! She always had to be ready and prepared, like the wise virgins waiting for the bridegroom in Matthew 25, ready with oil and a lamp at hand.

The taking of the bride would often occur in the middle of the night, when she would be whisked away by her groom. This might sound rude, but it was considered very romantic. According to Renald Showers,

The bride never knew exactly what night it would be. The groom would call his best man and escorts to his father's house and they would begin a torchlight procession through the city to come and take the bride. As they were

coming, bystanders would recognize what was going on
and shout, "Behold the bridegroom comes!" The purpose
of that shout was to forewarn the bride to get ready.[3]

The groom would go up to the bride's door, and he and his escorts
would wait outside. Someone would blow a shofar (a trumpet-type
instrument made from a ram's horn), announcing the groom's arrival.
When the bride was ready, she and her bridesmaids would come out
and meet the groom. Showers notes that when Jesus comes for His
bride, "He doesn't come the whole way down to planet Earth where
the church has been dwelling, but waits outside the earth, in the air,
and will catch up His bride to meet Him in the air."[4] (Showers refers to
1 Thessalonians 4:16-18 here, and we'll dig deeper into these verses later.)

Step 4: The Groom Takes His Bride Back to His Father's House

Upon returning to the groom's father's house, the groom took his
bride into what is called a *chuppah* (the bridal chamber), and it was in
the privacy of that room that they entered into a physical union with
each other for the first time, consummating their marriage.

> If I go and prepare a place for you, I will come back and
> take you to be with me that you also may be where I am
> (John 14:3).

One day God will tell Jesus to go get His bride, and Jesus will gather
her up and take her to His Father's house. Christ's bride will be with
Him in the bridal chamber during "the hour of trial that is going to
come on the whole world" (Revelation 3:10). This is the tribulation
period, and we'll learn more about it later in this book.

God is going to remove His Son's bride from Earth before the tribulation begins—He is not going to bloody, beat up, and execute His
Son's bride, who has kept herself pure as she waited for Him. Ephesians 5:29 tells us, "No one ever hated his own flesh, but nourishes
and cherishes it, just as Christ does the church" (ESV). God won't pour
out His wrath on the bride of Christ. He nourishes us and cherishes

us. Before pouring out His judgment on a rebellious and wicked world, the Father will say to His Son, "Go get Your bride and bring her home."

At the end of the ancient Jewish wedding, the bride and groom were presented to the world as man and wife and a feast began, a feast that could last seven days filled with food, dancing, music, and celebration. At the end of the seven-year tribulation (there isn't space in this book to discover how it boils down to seven years, but we'll dig deeper into that in one of the future books), after a huge celebration in heaven, Jesus will return to Earth at His second coming and will bring His bride with Him (Revelation 19:7-8, 11, 14).

When Jesus spoke the words in John 14:1-3, every Jewish listener would have understood the analogy, and of course only the Jewish believers at that time would have taken His words to heart following His death and resurrection, looking up and anticipating His return. Just days following Jesus's ascension back to heaven, Peter said this in Acts 3:19-21: "...and that he may send the Messiah, who has been appointed for you—even Jesus. Heaven must receive him *until the time comes for God to restore everything*, as he promised long ago through his holy prophets."

More than 2,000 years ago, Peter was already looking for Jesus's return! He said heaven must receive Him "until..." Until what? "*Until the time comes for God to restore everything.*" Heaven can only keep Jesus for so long. Peter and the early church were already looking up for the return of Jesus to restore everything. Are we so heavenly minded? Or are we like the scoffers Peter warned us about in 2 Peter 3:3-4, questioning and doubting Christ's return?

> Above all, you must understand that in the last days scoffers will come, scoffing and following their own evil desires. They will say, "Where is this 'coming' he promised? Ever since our ancestors died, everything goes on as it has since the beginning of creation."

In *Mere Christianity*, C.S. Lewis wrote,

If you read history you will find that the Christians who

did most for the present world were just those who thought most of the next. It is since Christians have largely ceased to think of the other world that they have become so ineffective in this one. Aim at heaven and you will get earth "thrown in"; aim at earth and you will get neither.[5]

Amazing Facts

This Where in the Word? section is a bit longer than the others, but it's important to lay a foundation before continuing, so let's look at some amazing facts together.

The Bible contains:

- 1,239 prophecies in the Old Testament
- 578 prophecies in the New Testament

More than 27 percent of the entire Bible is prophetic in nature. The facts proclaim:

- 500 of these prophecies have already been fulfilled
- all 500 were fulfilled with 100 percent accuracy
- there are 333 prophecies concerning Jesus
- 109 of the 333 were fulfilled by Jesus's birth, life, and resurrection
- all of them have been fulfilled with 100 percent accuracy

These statistics are staggering and amazing! According to mathematicians who have taken the time to figure this out, it is a mathematical impossibility for one person to fulfill 109 prophecies with 100 percent accuracy. With 109 prophecies fulfilled, this leaves 224 prophecies for

Christ to fulfill in His second coming, which is not to be confused with the snatching away of all those who are in Christ (the New Testament Greek word *harpazo*, which means "to catch up, seize, carry off by force, claim for one's self eagerly, to snatch out or away"). This is often referred to as the rapture and is a separate phase from the second coming. There are two phases of Christ's return, which we'll explore more, but let's not get ahead of ourselves.

If 500 of the entire Bible's prophecies have already been fulfilled with 100 percent accuracy, then that should ease any doubt about the remaining prophecies being fulfilled with 100 percent accuracy. God has already carried out His promises 500 times, and He will continue to do so until every single Bible prophecy is fulfilled.

There have been plenty of people throughout history who have made predictions about the future, but none of them have seen every single one of their predictions fulfilled with 100 percent accuracy. A prediction isn't prophecy; many confuse the two. And when a crying-wolf prediction doesn't come to pass (such as those associated with Y2K, when many predicted that the beginning of the new millennium would mean devastation and destruction for the world), people become skeptical and don't want to hear about prophecy. There are even many Christians who confuse predictions with prophecy because they haven't been taught the difference.

As David Reagan has pointed out, there is no other book—no other ancient or modern religious text in the world, including the Qur'an (Islam), the Vedas (Hindu), The Book of Mormon (The Church of Jesus Christ of Latter-day Saints)—that contains fulfilled prophecies, *thus confirming the supremacy of the God of the Bible.*[1] Only the one true God can prophesy the future with 100 percent accuracy.

PROPHECY UNFOLDS

Another misunderstanding is that many people assume a prophecy will be fulfilled relatively quickly. But the prophecies found in the Bible frequently aren't fulfilled for a long period of time, and some of them have fulfillments that unfold over time. For example, Isaiah prophesied about the birth and rulership of Jesus 700 years before He was born in Bethlehem. The prophecy wasn't fulfilled overnight. It was fulfilled in part when Jesus was born, and part of it remains to be fulfilled in the future.

Recently I read an article written by a respected radio host/author, and he wrote about a bestselling book from the 1970s about the second coming of Christ, saying, "But that was a long time ago, almost 50 years now. And still, Jesus hasn't returned." He then mentioned a series of bestselling books from the nineties and early 2000s about Christ's return, and stated, "But still, with all the talk of Jesus coming any day now, with all the excitement about the prophecies being fulfilled, the Lord has not yet returned."[2]

Just because we as Christians are expectant of Christ's return doesn't mean it will happen right away. Prophecy unfolds over time. We are still waiting for hundreds of prophecies to be fulfilled! If 700 years divided Isaiah's prophecy about the birth of Christ and His actual birth, we can be assured that God will fulfill His promise about Christ's return at the right time, even if some 2,000 years have gone by. "The Lord is not slow in keeping his promise, as some understand slowness. Instead he is patient with you, not wanting anyone to perish, but everyone to come to repentance" (2 Peter 3:9).

God—and Only God—Can Do It

Time and again the Israelites rejected God, turning instead to idols. In Isaiah 41 we find God mocking their idols. Could they prophesy what would happen in the future?

> Tell us, you idols,
>> what is going to happen…
> Or declare to us the things to come,
>> tell us what the future holds,
>> so we may know that you are gods.
> I look but there is no one—
>> no one among the gods to give counsel,
>> no one to give answer when I ask them.
> See, they are all false!
>> Their deeds amount to nothing;

their images are but wind and confusion
(Isaiah 41:22, 23, 28-29).

In contrast, God says that *He will tell us about things before they happen.*

I am the LORD. That is my name...
The things I said would happen have happened,
    and now I tell you about new things.
Before those things happen,
    I tell you about them (Isaiah 42:8-9 NCV).

God placed prophecies all throughout the Bible! That His fulfillment rate is 100 percent proves that He alone is God. It's impossible for so many prophecies to be accurately fulfilled by chance. They serve as the evidence that our doubting hearts need to confirm that *God has done and will do exactly what He has said He will do.* God went to great lengths to reveal His plans to us—to reveal, from the very beginning, what will happen in the end.

I make known the end from the beginning,
    from ancient times, what is still to come.
I say, "My purpose will stand,
    and I will do all that I please" (Isaiah 46:10).

And in verse 11:

What I have said, that I will bring about;
    what I have planned, that I will do.

WHAT IF EVIL CONTINUED?

From the beginning, God has known the heart of man. When left to ourselves, we are capable of the most heinous acts. In Genesis 6:3 God said, "My Spirit shall not strive with man forever" (NASB). Just as it was in the days of Noah, there will be a boiling point for God in the end of days, at which time He will judge the earth for evil and wickedness. How could we ever call God good, or call Him a loving Father, if there was no judgment for evil—if wickedness, suffering, pain, rape, murder, torture, genocide, bombings, terrorism, rebellion, etc., were allowed to continue forever? That's not what a good parent would do. That's cruel. There must be an end to this earth, which has been corrupted by sin, and there must come a new, refurbished earth, where sin is abolished. Again, in His goodness, God lays out that plan for us through His Word, and we know that His Word can be trusted to be 100 percent accurate because of the prophecies that have already been fulfilled.

EXAMPLES OF OLD TESTAMENT PROPHECIES THAT HAVE BEEN FULFILLED:

- Abram's descendants would be strangers in a land not their own and slaves for 400 years (Genesis 15:13-16). Fulfilled.

- Babylon would fall to the Medes (Isaiah 13:17-19). Fulfilled.

- Judah would be taken captive by Babylon for 70 years (Jeremiah 25:1-14). Fulfilled.

- The Jews would not only survive captivity but return to their homeland (Jeremiah 32:36-37). Fulfilled.

- Four great empires would rule the world successively (Daniel 2 and 7: they were Babylon, Persia, Greece and Rome). Fulfilled.

- The coming of The Messiah (some verses include: Daniel 9:25, Psalm 2:1-12, Numbers 24:17, 2 Samuel 7:12-16). Fulfilled.

- Jerusalem would be a heap of ruins and the Temple Mount overgrown (Micah 3:12). Fulfilled.

EXAMPLES OF OLD TESTAMENT PROPHECIES THAT CHRIST FULFILLED

- A Deliverer who will crush our great enemy, Satan (Genesis 3:15). The arrival of this Deliverer, Jesus, is confirmed in Luke 2:4-11 and Galatians 4:4. From the time of Adam, the first man, to Christ, 4,000 years went by, so you can see that this prophecy didn't come to fruition overnight!

- He was a descendant of Abraham (Genesis 12:3, 7; 22:18) and of the tribe of Judah (Genesis 49:10). Matthew 1:1 confirms that Jesus fulfilled these prophecies.

- He was of the house of David and would have a throne, a kingdom, and a dynasty that would start with King David and last forever (2 Samuel 7:12-13, 16; Jeremiah 23:5). The New Testament fulfillment is found in Matthew 1:1, 6, Luke 1:32-33; and Revelation 22:16.

- He would be born of a virgin and called Immanuel (Isaiah 7:14). We read about the fulfillment of the virgin birth in Matthew 1:22-23.

- He would be born and called "Wonderful Counselor, Mighty God, Everlasting Father, Prince of Peace," and "the government will be on his shoulders" (Isaiah 9:6-7). This prophecy was given 700 years before the birth of Jesus, and we are still waiting for the fulfillment of the prophecy in its entirety. The first part of the prophecy has been fulfilled: a child has been born; a Son has been given. But the government is not yet on the shoulders of Jesus. He isn't on the throne of David, upholding justice and righteousness over a kingdom of peace. We are still waiting for that part of the prophecy to be fulfilled. It is in this sense that we see prophecy continuing to unfold.

- He would be born in the specific location of Bethlehem Ephrathah (Micah 5:2) in Judea, so as not to be confused with Bethlehem near the Sea of Galilee. Fulfilled in Luke 2:4.

- Infants would be slaughtered in His birthplace (Jeremiah 31:15). This was fulfilled in Matthew 2:16-18.

- He was forsaken by His disciples (Zechariah 13:7). Fulfilled in Matthew 26:56 and Mark 14:50.

- A friend would betray Him (Psalm 41:9). Judas fulfilled this in Matthew 26:47-50, Luke 22:47-48, and John 18:1-6.

- He was treated like a criminal (Isaiah 53:12), and lots were thrown for His clothes (Psalm 22:18). Fulfilled in Matthew 26:47-48, Mark 14:53-65, Luke 23, and John 18–19.

- His sacrificial death would pay the price for the sins of mankind (Isaiah 53). Fulfilled in passages like Matthew 20:28, Romans 5:8, Galatians 2:20, and Hebrews 9:22.

- He would have a forerunner (Isaiah 40:3-5 and Malachi 3:1). John the Baptist fulfilled this in John 1:23, Matthew 3:1-3 and 11:14.

- He was in Egypt for a time (Hosea 11:1). Fulfilled in Matthew 2:14-15.

These are just a small sampling of prophecies that have been fulfilled. We can be assured that the Bible prophecies that *are* remaining to be fulfilled *will* come true in time!

WHAT IS BIBLE PROPHECY?

Simply put, prophecy reveals God's plans for the future. Mark Hitchcock says,

> Bible prophecy is important because it tells us the end of the story. It is our guidance system and tells us where we are going. It reveals that just as our world had a definite beginning in Genesis 1:1, it will also have an ending. This world will not continue on forever through infinite cycles of history. Bible prophecy reveals to us that there is an end.[3]

He further states, "Predicting events before they come to pass is the proof that the Bible is the inerrant, inspired Word of God. More than that, it's the bottom-line basis for believing in Jesus."[4]

Ron Rhodes says that "when we study Bible prophecy our faith in God greatly increases, our confidence in Him grows, spiritual lethargy is cured and we become powerfully motivated to live our lives for the Lord."[5] The *Holman New Testament Commentary* on Matthew says the purpose of prophecy isn't to satisfy our curiosity about the future, but to stimulate holiness in our present lives. When we study and learn about prophecy, we get excited because we realize that God says what He means and does what He says, and we want to share those truths with others.

REVELATION

The Time of Jacob's Trouble will use passages from all throughout the Bible to lay out God's plan for the end of days, and much will be taken from the last book in the Bible, the book of Revelation, also known as "the Revelation of Jesus Christ." To understand Revelation, we need to draw understanding from verses in both the Old and New Testaments. Warren Wiersbe said that of the 404 verses of Revelation, 278 contain references to the Old Testament. So you can see there is a great need for us to have an understanding of the Bible as a whole when we open the pages of Revelation.

Revelation is translated from the Greek word *apokalypsis*, which translated to English is the word *apocalypse*. When we hear the word *apocalypse*, we typically associate it with Hollywood disaster movies dealing with the end of the world. In the original Greek text of the New Testament, the word means "an uncovering, an unveiling, a manifestation of." In simple terms, the book of the Revelation of Jesus Christ is the uncovering or unveiling or manifestation of Jesus. David Jeremiah says, "The primary purpose of the book of Revelation is not to paint a picture of the end times, although it does do that. It was written primarily to unveil, or uncover, the majesty and power of Jesus Christ."[6]

When you read through Revelation, it's interesting to note that the word *and* is used 1,200 times, and according to Ed Hindson,

> This is the little Greek word *kai* that connects the book together to say this is not a cyclical prophecy going around in circles. It's moving from one event to another to another to another. This happens and then this and then this. It

creates anticipation as you read the book. Something exciting is coming in the future, and it's Jesus![7]

TRIFOLD BLESSING

In the opening of Revelation we read, "Blessed is the one who reads aloud the words of this prophecy, and blessed are those who hear it and take to heart what is written in it, because the time is near" (Revelation 1:3).

This is the *only* book in the Bible that promises not just a blessing, but a trifold blessing for

> those who read it aloud
>
> those who hear the words of the prophecy
>
> and for those who take to heart what is written in this book

Notice that the words in verse three don't say, "Be afraid—be very afraid for what you're about to read!" There's no other book in the Bible that says we're blessed for reading it aloud. *Aloud!* My husband and I and our three children read it aloud one evening, and not one of us was afraid. I encourage you to read it aloud as well.

Revelation is meant to be a blessing as it unveils Christ to us. For far too long, people have feared the book. Pulpits have been mostly silent concerning the last pages of the Bible and have missed the blessing. We weren't meant to be kept in the dark, but it has been decades since I've heard a pastor teach from Revelation, with the exception of sermons about the letters written to the seven churches found in Revelation chapters 2 and 3, the only chapters that many pastors are willing to teach from.

The promise of Revelation's blessing is so important that John, the writer of the book, repeats it again in chapter 22:

> "These words can be trusted and are true." The Lord, the God of the spirits of the prophets, sent his angel to show his servants the things that must happen soon.

"Listen! I am coming soon! *Blessed is the one who obeys the words of prophecy in this book*" (verses 6-7 NCV).

Jesus tells us three times in Revelation 22 that He is "coming soon" (verses 7, 12, 20). That's a blessing in itself! We are reminded to keep our hearts looking up for and anticipating His coming.

CONFUSION SURROUNDING REVELATION

An Allegory

There are some who suggest that the book of Revelation is allegory, nothing more than metaphors, but if that were true, then John would have told us that beforehand, just as Paul did in Galatians 4:24 when he specifically said, "Now this may be interpreted allegorically: these women are two covenants" (ESV). Or as Ezekiel did in Ezekiel 17:2: "Son of man, set forth an allegory and tell it to the Israelites as a parable."

A Parable

If Revelation was meant to be a collection of parables, John would have told us that, just as Matthew said in Matthew 13:34-35: "Jesus spoke all these things to the crowd in parables; he did not say anything to them without using a parable. So was fulfilled what was spoken through the prophet: 'I will open my mouth in parables, I will utter things hidden since the creation of the world.'"

A Song

If Revelation was meant to be a song, then John would have said that, as Solomon said in Song of Solomon 1:1: "The Song of Songs, which is Solomon's" (ESV), or John would have labeled it as something like the Song of Moses, which is what we read in the opening verse of Exodus 15. The book of Psalms served as a hymnal for the Hebrew people, containing songs of praise, thanksgiving, and lament.

A Prophecy

If John was writing in any of the above-listed styles of literature he would have told us, but he never alerts us that what he has written is allegory, parable, song, or anything other than prophecy as stated in Revelation 1:3: "Blessed is the one who reads aloud the words of this *prophecy*" (emphasis added), so we must interpret Revelation literally.

John stresses five additional times that Revelation is a book of prophecy:

- "It is the Spirit of *prophecy* who bears testimony to Jesus" (Revelation 19:10).

- "Look, I am coming soon! Blessed is the one who keeps the words of the *prophecy* written in this scroll" (Revelation 22:7).

- "Then he told me, 'Do not seal up the words of the *prophecy* of this scroll, because the time is near'" (Revelation 22:10).

- "I warn everyone who hears the words of the *prophecy* of this scroll: If anyone adds anything to them, God will add to that person the plagues described in this scroll" (Revelation 22:18).

- "If anyone takes words away from this scroll of *prophecy*, God will take away from that person any share in the tree of life and in the Holy City, which are described in this scroll" (Revelation 22:19).

John didn't intend for Revelation to be taken figuratively. People tend to resort to allegorical assumptions when the literal meaning of Revelation's prophecies are difficult to accept, or hard to explain, and they feel they must interpret the book in a less literal, offensive, or frightening way. But we're told in Revelation 22:6 that "these words can be trusted and are true" (NCV). John goes on further and issues a word of warning to us.

ALL OF GOD'S WORD CAN BE TRUSTED

We are informed that the words of Revelation are trustworthy and true, and we are warned not to add or take away anything "from the words of this book of prophecy" (Revelation 22:19 NCV). If anyone does so, God will take away that person's "share of the tree of life and of the holy city" (verse 19 NCV). He doesn't want or need us to water down the prophecies to make them more bearable. Proverbs 30:5 says, "Every word of God proves true" (ESV), and verse 6 states, "Do not add to his words, lest he rebuke you and you be found a liar."

Jesus said that what John recorded in Revelation *is* true, and that He's coming soon. The end-time events laid out in Revelation, or any other book of the Bible, are not allegory. They aren't make-believe or metaphors. If they were, God would have given us some indication of that. Through the prophetic portions of Scripture, God has declared the end from the beginning (Isaiah 46:10), and His Word can be trusted as truth. If we can't trust or believe one part of the Bible, then how can we trust any other part of it? But because the Word comes from God Himself, because it is God-breathed, as 2 Timothy 3:16-17 says, we can trust it: "All Scripture is God-breathed and is useful for teaching, rebuking, correcting and training in righteousness, so that the servant of God may be thoroughly equipped for every good work."

LED BY THE HOLY SPIRIT

It's important to understand that the prophecies in the Bible weren't given to us through the prophets' own understandings, opinions, ideas, or interpretations, but through the Spirit of God. There were times when even a prophet didn't understand what was being proclaimed. For example, Daniel asked about a prophecy he was given concerning the end times:

> I heard the answer, but I did not really understand, so I asked, "Master, what will happen after all these things come true?" He answered, *"Go your way, Daniel. The message is closed up and sealed until the time of the end"* (Daniel 12:8-9 NCV).

Daniel didn't understand, and he wasn't given the answer, but was faithful to write down the prophecy.

Second Peter 1:20-21 assures us, "Most of all, you must understand this: No prophecy in the Scriptures ever comes from the prophet's own interpretation. No prophecy ever came from what a person wanted to say, but people led by the Holy Spirit spoke words from God."

Jesus said that prophecy is true and serves as proof of who He is.

> I tell you this beforehand, so that when it happens you will believe that I AM the Messiah (John 13:19 NLT).

> I have told you these things before they happen so that when they do happen, you will believe (John 14:29 NLT).

In the pages ahead, we'll use the entirety of Scripture to help us grasp what it says about the end of the age. Remember, 109 prophecies concerning Jesus have already been fulfilled with 100 percent accuracy, leaving 224 prophecies to be fulfilled. Without any doubt, we can be assured that they will come to pass according to God's Word.

Everything that's written in *The Time of Jacob's Trouble* and the two books that follow is meant to encourage us to share Jesus with those who don't know Him, to follow Christ faithfully, and to keep looking up in anticipation for His coming so that "when Christ appears, we shall be like him, for we shall see him as he is. All who have this hope in him purify themselves, just as he is pure" (1 John 3:2).

AMERICA IN THE END TIMES

People often wonder if America will play a big part in the end times. Given the fact that the United States is not mentioned in Scripture as a key player in the end times, it is only conjecture what happens to the country from an international perspective. *The Time of Jacob's Trouble* has been written as if America has been weakened due to the mass disappearances of millions, which, in turn, will leave the nation vulnerable to attack. It is estimated that there are over 27,000 nuclear weapons in the world.[1] With that in mind, I created a story in which America is struck by foreign enemies that are determined to destroy the world's superpower and cripple the great nation. Mark Hitchcock has said the United States will probably lose more people per capita than any other nation in the world.[2] I think we can suggest that if foreign enemies can bring her down, then those enemies can rise to greater world power without America's interference. A weakened America will also leave Israel vulnerable to attack, prompting her enemies to strike there as well.

There are some who believe that references to an eagle in Daniel 7:4 and Revelation 12:14 are nods to America, but if we look closely at just the verse in Revelation, we will notice it says, "The woman was given the two wings of a great eagle, so that she might fly to the place prepared for her in the wilderness, where she would be taken care of for a time, times and half a time, out of the serpent's reach." The "woman" referred to here is Israel, not a singular woman. As the Antichrist pursues and persecutes the Jews they will flee for their lives, just as Jesus told them to do in Matthew 24:16-18. We can be certain that the eagle isn't America because God tells us in Zecheriah 14:2, "I will gather all the nations against Jerusalem to battle…" (ESV). Joel 3:2 also mentions "all nations." *All nations* will turn against Jerusalem in the latter half of the tribulation. America won't save the Jews; God will.

America isn't mentioned by name in Bible prophecy, and most other modern nations aren't mentioned either. For instance, we don't see Canada, Japan, or Australia. If America was still a mighty force on the world scene, it seems that the country would be mentioned. Prophecy scholar John Walvoord says, "Scriptural evidence is sufficient to conclude that America in that day will not be a major power and apparently does not figure largely in either the political, economic, or religious aspects of the world."[3]

It's difficult for some to fathom that America will no longer hold a major spot on the world's stage. However, the end times aren't about America, but Israel. We'll examine this a bit more in this book, and in greater detail in the next two books.

PEACE IN THE TRIBULATION?

The world is living in turbulent times; riots and rebellion are in the daily news all over the globe, and that's with law enforcement and peacekeeping agencies in full operation! Imagine what will happen when millions or billions of people are removed from the earth; it will throw the world into chaos. No one will then suddenly decide to *play nice and get along.* Rather, evil will rise; and chaos, rebellion, and lawlessness will only increase.

I've heard some pastors and teachers say that the first few years of the tribulation will be rather peaceful, which is contrary to what we already see in the world. At the time of this writing, according to CNN and PBS Newshour, Haiti is experiencing the tenth day of "violent protests and unrest" as demonstrators call for the president to resign. The entire country is on lockdown as demonstrators block roads, stone emergency vehicles, and destroy businesses by vandalizing and looting them. "People can't get out to find water and are running out of basic supplies."⁴ Many people have been killed, tourists have been evacuated, hospitals are running out of medicine, and "aid workers remain cut off as Haiti braces for another bout of chaos and bloodletting."⁵

Also happening at the time of this writing: India and Pakistan are threatening war against each other after a Pakistan-based terrorist group fired on Indian paramilitary soldiers, killing 40. India retaliated with airstrikes, causing tensions to escalate between the two countries. Farmer-herder conflicts in Kaduna, a state in Nigeria, are raging again, with 120 dead and 140 homes destroyed.⁶ In Christchurch, New Zealand, a 28-year-old white supremacist opened fire on Muslims worshipping in two mosques, killing 51 people and injuring 49 others in what is described as the deadliest mass killing in New Zealand since 1943.⁷

All of this is happening at a time when the world, for the most part, is at peace and gatekeepers are in place. Imagine how people will respond when millions or billions who possess the restraining power of the Holy Spirit inside of them vanish, many of whom are presently gatekeepers on the world scene. Due to the resulting tumult in the world, conditions will be such that it will be virtually impossible to keep warring nations or people groups in check. Chaos will cover the globe. The many tensions in our current world do not point to peace in the future.

Consider the 18 sects in Lebanon who have been embroiled in conflicts for hundreds of years, or the warring people groups in Africa, the Middle East, or other parts of the world. Are they suddenly going to get along? Chaos breeds confusion and anarchy, not peace. With all the gatekeepers gone, the world will become a thieves' paradise. Enemy combatants will seize the moment to attack one another. Countries with nuclear weapons will use them at will because there won't be global gatekeepers holding them accountable.

This notion of peace during the first few years of the tribulation also opposes what the first few seals in Revelation reveal. When Jesus takes the scroll from God and begins opening the seal judgments in

Revelation 6, the wrath of God begins to fall upon the earth. Some believe the first few years of chaos during the tribulation will be due to man's wrath being poured out upon other people, but the Bible makes it clear that it is Jesus, the Lamb of God, who is opening the seals— see Revelation 5:5-7; 6:1, 3, 5, 7, 9, 12. With the opening of the first two seals alone we see the arrival of the Antichrist (verse 2) and peace disrupted as people kill each other (verse 4). There's nothing calm or peaceful about that.

In response, a coalition of ten nations will arise (a revived Roman Empire under the Antichrist, symbolized as ten toes in Daniel 7:7 and ten horns in 7:24; Revelation 13:1; 17:3, 12-13) in the hopes of bringing calm and order to the world. (It's possible that what is left of America will be part of that confederacy, given its history with European allies, as I've suggested in the fiction portion of this book.)

THE 144,000

If God is a God of mercy, compassion, and grace, how could He possibly leave a world to itself without someone to point the way to salvation? God's love never ceases, and as J. Vernon McGee once said in a radio broadcast, "He never leaves Himself without a witness." After Jesus snatches away all those who are in Him, the world will be left with Bibles, Christ-based podcasts, Internet material, Christian books, and videos that will lead people to the cross. People will also hear the gospel message from the two witnesses in Jerusalem and the 144,000 Jewish evangelists who are specially sealed and appointed by God to serve a crucial role in end-time events.

The Time of Jacob's Trouble features Elliott, a Jewish man in New York City, and Zerah, a Jew in Israel, who are sealed for the purpose of proclaiming the gospel. They and the others of the 144,000 will be "purchased from among mankind and offered as firstfruits to God and the Lamb" (Revelation 14:4). Like all who put their faith in Christ, these men will be bought with the blood of the Lamb, and they will be offered as firstfruits, which in Scripture refers to the first part of a harvest. The 144,000 are the firstfruits of the harvest of souls that will come out of the tribulation.

We find the 144,000 mentioned in Revelation 7:1-8 and again in Revelation 14:1-5. Chapter 7 is one of the chapters which breaks the chronological sequence of the events taking place during the end times. Instead of advancing the narrative, it introduces some key players.

Here is what chapter 7 says about the 144,000:

> "Do not harm the land or the sea or the trees until we put a seal on the foreheads of the servants of our God." Then I heard the number of those who were sealed: 144,000 from all the tribes of Israel.
>
> From the tribe of Judah 12,000 were sealed,
> from the tribe of Reuben 12,000,
> from the tribe of Gad 12,000,
> from the tribe of Asher 12,000,
> from the tribe of Naphtali 12,000,
> from the tribe of Manasseh 12,000,
> from the tribe of Simeon 12,000,
> from the tribe of Levi 12,000,
> from the tribe of Issachar 12,000,
> from the tribe of Zebulun 12,000,
> from the tribe of Joseph 12,000,
> from the tribe of Benjamin 12,000 (Revelation 7:3-8).

WHY JEWISH MEN FROM THE 12 TRIBES OF ISRAEL?

Some people believe these 144,000 men represent the church, but as we read through Scripture, the words *Israel* and *tribe* are never used to mean "church," and in Revelation 7 we see that John used "tribe" repeatedly. There are 323 uses of the words *tribe* or *tribes* in the Bible, and none of them refer to the church. The men listed in Revelation 7 are descendants of the 12 tribes of Israel.

Bible scholar J.A. Seiss says, "I know of no instance in which the descendants of the 12 tribes of Israel include the Gentiles."[8] There are 65 uses of the word *Israel* in the New Testament, and each time, they refer to Jews. John Walvoord adds, "The word *Israel* is never used of Gentiles and refers only to those who are racially descendants of Israel, or Jacob. The remnant of Israel, as portrayed in Revelation, should not therefore be taken as meaning the church."[9]

THE CHURCH AND ISRAEL

Throughout the entirety of Scripture, the church and Israel are two distinct groups (when a Jewish person becomes one with Christ, he or she is still Jewish but also part of the church). This distinction is made clear by John in Revelation, for he describes the 144,000 as being from "all the tribes of Israel," not the church. The number 12 is consistently associated with Israel throughout Scripture, and never with the church.

John is very specific in not only mentioning that the 144,000 will come from the 12 tribes of Israel, but goes on to list that 12,000 will come from each tribe. When the Bible speaks of the *12 tribes of Israel*, it always literally means the 12 tribes of Israel, leaving no room for confusion with the church.

We must keep in mind that the church is absent beginning in Revelation 4. Prior to that, in chapters 2 and 3, we read seven times, "Whoever has ears, let them hear what the Spirit says *to the churches*." However, beginning in Revelation 13:9, the word *church* is missing from the phrase "Whoever has ears, let them hear." Scripture doesn't say, "What the Spirit says *to the churches*," which tells us the church is no longer on Earth to be addressed. Because the church is gone and no longer proclaims the gospel, there is a vacuum that needs to be filled. The 144,000 Jewish evangelists and the two witnesses in Revelation 11 will fill that void.

A LIGHT FOR THE GENTILES

God had originally chosen the Jews to show Gentiles the way to Him.

> I, the LORD, have called you in righteousness;
>   I will take hold of your hand.
> I will keep you and will make you
>   to be a covenant for the people
>   and a light for the Gentiles (Isaiah 42:6).

"You are my witnesses," declares the LORD,
"and my servant whom I have chosen…
You are my witnesses," declares the LORD,
"that I am God" (Isaiah 43:10, 12).

Ron Rhodes says that during the future tribulation, these 144,000 Jews will fulfill this mandate from God and serve as His witnesses around the world.

WHEN ARE THE 144,000 SEALED?

In Revelation 7:3, an angel says, "Do not harm the land or the sea or the trees until we put a seal on the foreheads of the servants of our God." In Scripture, we see that winds are used by God to fulfill His purposes. The four destructive winds spoken of earlier in verse 1 are not allowed to blow until His servants are sealed. Nothing, and no one, can harm these 144,000; God will supernaturally protect them.

Once these witnesses are sealed, the four destructive winds will be unleashed as God's judgment falls, but we see His love manifested in the 144,000 as they cover the earth, proclaiming the love of God and salvation through His Son. Robert Jeffress asks, "If God were simply interested in annihilating unbelievers, why would He dispatch 144,000 missionaries to proclaim His message of salvation?"[10]

THE CHARACTERISTICS OF THE 144,000

1. They Are Virgins

In Revelation 14:4, John is again specific regarding the identity of the 144,000, saying, "These are those who did not defile themselves with women, for they remained virgins."

A lot of people struggle with this fact about the 144,000. How could *all* of them be celibate? Given the intensity and violence of the tribulation, it makes perfect sense that God would choose men who are free of the worries of caring for a wife and children and protecting them from horrific bloodshed, wars, plagues, famines, persecution, etc. A married man's heart and concern would be at home, not out in the streets and the world.

In 1 Corinthians 7, Paul says this about singleness:

> I would like you to be free from concern. An unmarried man is concerned about the Lord's affairs—how he can please the Lord. But a married man is concerned about the affairs of this world—how he can please his wife—and his interests are divided…I am saying this for your own good, not to restrict you, but that you may live in a right way in undivided devotion to the Lord (verses 32-33, 35).

These 144,000 Jewish evangelists will be able to live in complete devotion to the Lord during the most turbulent time on Earth because they won't be torn between family and service to God.

2. They Are Devoted to Christ

The extent of their devotion is further clarified in Revelation 14:4-5: "They follow the Lamb wherever he goes…No lie was found in their mouths; they are blameless."

These are men of outstanding character and integrity. They will be blameless in the midst of the most corrupt, deceptive, murderous, and evil time on Earth. David Jeremiah says, "Think of the spiritual power that would be harnessed by 144,000 evangelists who are unspotted by the world and pure in their thoughts and words."[11]

We aren't told how each of these 144,000 will come to Christ, but we can imagine for some it will be much like Paul's Damascus Road experience (Acts 9:1-19), after which God removed the scales of unbelief from Paul's eyes.

3. They Are Sealed

In Revelation 7:2-3, we read that a group of four angels are instructed not to harm the land, sea, or trees "until we put a seal on the foreheads of the servants of our God." The 144,000 are identified as "servants of our God," and they will be sealed before any judgment falls on Earth.

In Revelation 14:1, we see the 144,000 at the end of the tribulation. Jesus has come from heaven at His second coming and is standing on Mount Zion. "Then I looked, and there before me was the Lamb, standing on Mount Zion, and with him 144,000 who had his name and his Father's name written on their foreheads."

In this verse, we learn more about the seal as the 144,000 stand together with the Lamb (Jesus), with "his name and his Father's name written on their foreheads." Both the names of Jesus and the Father are on their foreheads. Now, take note of the number that is standing there with Jesus: all 144,000 are present and accounted for!

The angels will have gathered them, and all those who put their faith in Christ during the tribulation, from every corner of the earth, and brought them before Jesus at Mt. Zion: "He will send his angels with a loud trumpet call, and they will gather his elect from the four winds, from one end of the heavens to the other" (Matthew 24:31). As they stand there, it will be clear that nothing, and no one, has harmed or destroyed them. The seal supernaturally protected all 144,000 through the entirety of the tribulation!

4. They Have a Mission

During the tribulation the 144,000 will be spread throughout the world, preaching the salvation message of Christ, and Revelation 7:9-10 tells us the results of their evangelizing:

> After this I looked, and there before me was *a great multitude that no one could count, from every nation, tribe, people and language,* standing before the throne and before the Lamb. They were wearing white robes and were holding palm branches in their hands. And they cried out in a loud voice:
>
> > "Salvation belongs to our God,
> > who sits on the throne,
> > and to the Lamb."

What a remarkable harvest of souls! There is such an enormous multitude before the throne that no one could possibly count them. To further confirm the effective reach of the 144,000, we read that this multitude is "from every nation, tribe, people and language"! The

144,000 took the gospel message of salvation throughout the entire world, and as a result, that great multitude is praising God in heaven.

5. They Have Their Own Song

As the 144,000 stand on Mount Zion with Jesus, John hears a sound and writes, "The sound I heard was like that of harpists playing their harps. And *they sang a new song* before the throne and before the four living creatures and the elders. *No one could learn the song except the 144,000* who had been redeemed from the earth" (Revelation 14:2-3).

The 144,000 have their very own song that no one else can learn! Given the fact that they have just lived through hell on Earth and witnessed things that no one should ever see, I think we can suggest that some of the words to the song might be, "Hallelujah!" "Praise You, Lord!" "Thank You, Father!" "You are awesome and powerful and mighty to save!" "You have delivered us!" The unimaginably beautiful voices of this choir will rise with unspeakable joy and eternal gratitude as they sing their very own song of praise.

THE END
OF THE AGE

The Time of Jacob's Trouble deals with the mass disappearance of millions or billions of people from around the world. That event will close out the last days of the church age and usher in the end times, which Jesus spoke of, and writers of the New Testament anticipated and even asked about.

- "*The end of the world* is coming soon" (1 Peter 4:7 NLT).

- "Tell us," they said, "when will this happen, and what will be the sign of your coming and of the *end of the age*?" (Matthew 24:3).

- Jesus said, "Surely I am with you always, to the very *end of the age*" (Matthew 28:20).

- "This gospel of the kingdom will be preached in all the world as a witness to all the nations, and then *the end will come*" (Matthew 24:14).

Jesus said that "the end will come." There will be a conclusion to what we sometimes think is the never-ending story of planet Earth. It will end and, thankfully, that end will actually herald a new beginning. God will refurbish this earth, creating a new heaven and a new Earth that has been purified of sin (Revelation 21). But what will happen before that takes place?

THOSE "IN CHRIST" ARE CAUGHT UP

As mentioned earlier, the last days for the church will end with the event in the Bible that many refer to as the rapture. The word *rapture* isn't found in Scripture, and that is a point of argument for some who deny the rapture, but the words *Trinity, missions, incarnation, omnipotent, Christmas, Easter, Sunday, communion*, or even the word *Bible* aren't found in Scripture either. The words *Christian* and *born again* are used only three times each.

Where, then, does the word *rapture* come from, and can its use be supported scripturally?

Let's look at 1 Thessalonians 4:17, a key passage for understanding the rapture: "After that, we who are still alive and are left will be caught up together with them in the clouds to meet the Lord in the air." The phrase "caught up" is the Greek word *harpazo*, which means "to catch up, seize, carry off by force, claim for one's self eagerly, to snatch out or away" (in the pages ahead, I will return to this definition frequently). When the Latin translation of the Bible was written, known as the Latin Vulgate, the Greek word *harpazo* was translated *rapturo*. *Rapturo* is translated into English as *rapture*, and by the very definition of this term we can certainly call this event the "catching up" or "seizing of" believers, the "snatching away," or "taking by force" of those who are in Christ.

I personally love the definition of "claim for one's self eagerly." Before the tribulation begins, Jesus will eagerly claim for Himself all those who are in Him. *Harpazo* is used thirteen times in the New Testament, sometimes referring to the actual snatching away of people or the seizing/taking of them by force: Matthew 11:12; 13:19; John 6:15; 10:12, 28, 29; Acts 8:39; 23:10; 2 Corinthians 12:2, 4; 1 Thessalonians 4:17; Jude 1:23; and Revelation 12:5.

The idea of a mass disappearance of millions or billions of people around the world is hard for many people to accept, including even followers of Christ. Some try to refute the idea by arguing that nothing like this has happened before, so it wouldn't make sense for such a thing to occur in the future. However, the Bible mentions several raptures that have already taken place:

Enoch

We first read about Enoch's being snatched away in Genesis 5:24: "Enoch walked with God: and he was not; for God took him" (ESV).

And it's mentioned again in Hebrews 11:5: "By faith Enoch was taken from this life, so that he did not experience death: 'He could not be found, because God had taken him away.'"

Elijah

This Old Testament prophet didn't die but was snatched up to heaven. He was taken up in a chariot led by horses (for all animal lovers, yes, there are animals in heaven)!

> When the LORD was about to take Elijah up to heaven in a
> whirlwind, Elijah and Elisha were on their way from Gilgal...
> As they were walking along and talking together, suddenly a
> chariot of fire and horses of fire appeared and separated the
> two of them, and Elijah went up to heaven in a whirlwind...
> And Elisha saw him no more (2 Kings 2:1, 11-12).

Philip

The Greek word *harpazo* ("to catch up, seize, carry off by force, claim for one's self eagerly, to snatch out or away"), describes Philip vanishing in thin air. His body was changed from one geographical location to another that was 20 miles away. How awesome is that?

> The Spirit of the Lord suddenly took Philip away, and
> the eunuch did not see him again, but went on his way
> rejoicing. Philip, however, appeared at Azotus and trav-
> eled about, preaching the gospel in all the towns until he
> reached Caesarea (Acts 8:39-40).

Paul

The word *harpazo* describes Paul being "caught up" to paradise in

2 Corinthians 12:2: "I know a man in Christ who fourteen years ago was *caught up* to the third heaven."

Who better to describe being "caught up" to the believers in 1 Thessalonians 4:17 than Paul? A bit later, we'll take a closer look at 1 Thessalonians 4.

Jesus

The word *harpazo* is also used to describe the ascension of Jesus back to heaven: "She gave birth to a son, a male child, who 'will rule all the nations with an iron scepter.' And her child was snatched up to God and to his throne" (Revelation 12:5).

Some people respond to these verses by saying these are examples of *individual* people being caught up to heaven, not millions or even billions. But we limit God's power and might when we make the assumption He isn't capable of seizing or snatching away billions. The restriction of ability and strength doesn't lie with God, but in our own minds; we are the ones who put boundaries around what He can do.

Those Who Are Left

First Thessalonians 4:17 uses *harpazo* to describe a future seizing/catching up/snatching away of all those who are still alive and left on Earth following the rising of "the dead in Christ" (1 Thessalonians 4:16). Verse 17 reads, "After that, we who are still alive and are left will be caught up together with them in the clouds to meet the Lord in the air. And so we will be with the Lord forever." One day, Jesus will step out from heaven and into the air, giving a command that will *harpazo* all those who are "in Christ" so that they can be with Him. First "the dead in Christ" will rise, and then those who are still alive. It's not just any dead who will come out of their graves, but those who are "in Christ" (more on this later). Will you be among those who hear that command?

The Two Witnesses

According to Revelation 11, there will come a point when the two witnesses who proclaim the gospel from Jerusalem will be killed by the

Antichrist. Verses 11-12 tell us what will happen after their bodies lie in the street for three-and-a-half days:

> The breath of life from God entered them, and they stood on their feet, and terror struck those who saw them. Then they heard a loud voice from heaven saying to them, "Come up here." And they went up to heaven in a cloud, while their enemies looked on (verses 11-12).

Although the word *harpazo* is not used here, these two witnesses will ascend into heaven in a cloud; this very event will surely remind all those who have been left on Earth of the great seizing up/snatching away that took place only a few short years earlier.

THE LAST DAYS VS. THE END TIMES

For many years I was confused about the terms "the last days" and "the end times." I never knew if these meant the same thing or if there was a distinction, and I've found that this confusion exists for many people. For clarity, there are last days for the church and last days for Israel.

In the Old Testament, when we read about the last days in reference to Israel, that has to do with events that begin after Jesus seizes all of those who are "in Christ"—that is, the tribulation. For example, Ezekiel 38:8 and 16 refer to the "latter years" and "latter days" (ESV), and Isaiah 2:2 and Micah 4:1 refer to "the last days" for Israel. In Jeremiah 30:7 the tribulation is called "the time of Jacob's trouble" (NKJV), referring to God dealing with Israel at that time. So, for Israel, the last days will begin after the church is caught up.

In e-mail correspondence I received from Ron Rhodes, he quoted a passage from his *Bible Prophecy Answer Book* regarding God's dealing with Israel during the tribulation:

> The Old Testament usage of such terms as "latter days," "last days," "latter years," "end of time," and "end of the age" all refer to a time when Israel is in her time of tribulation. Deuteronomy 4:30—"When you are in tribulation and

all these things come upon you in the latter days, you will return to the LORD your God and obey his voice" (ESV)—will find its ultimate fulfillment in the final restoration of Israel, which will take place at the second coming of Jesus Christ.

Again, the last days for Israel will begin after the church is caught up and will continue through the second coming of Christ. But what about the last days for the church? In the Old Testament, God spoke through the prophets to the people of Israel. In the New Testament, He spoke through His Son. In that same e-mail from Ron Rhodes, he said,

> A number of New Testament passages use "last days," "last times," and "last time" to refer to the present church age in which we now live. For example, the writer of Hebrews said, "Long ago, at many times and in many ways, God spoke to our fathers by the prophets, but in these last days he has spoken to us by his Son" (Hebrews 1:1-2). We also see this in 1 Peter 1:20, where we are told that Christ, in the incarnation, "was made manifest in the last times for the sake of you who through him are believers in God." This means that people in New Testament times up to the present day—all who have lived and are now living in the church age—are, in one sense, in the "last days."

What is called "the end times" will arrive following the *end* of the church age, *after* the church is caught up with Christ. Those will be the earth's final years. (Again, there isn't space in this book to take a closer look at the timeline of the earth's final years as presented in Daniel, but we'll cover that in the subsequent books.)

CHARACTERISTICS OF THE LAST DAYS

Paul and Peter wrote of the characteristics that would mark people during the last days:

> The Spirit clearly says that in later times some will abandon the faith and follow deceiving spirits and things taught by

demons. Such teachings come through hypocritical liars, whose consciences have been seared as with a hot iron (1 Timothy 4:1-2).

People will be lovers of themselves, lovers of money, boastful, proud, abusive, disobedient to their parents, ungrateful, unholy, without love, unforgiving, slanderous, without self-control, brutal, not lovers of the good, treacherous, rash, conceited, lovers of pleasure rather than lovers of God—having a form of godliness but denying its power (2 Timothy 3:1-5).

They will say, "Where is this 'coming' he promised? Ever since our ancestors died, everything goes on as it has since the beginning of creation" (2 Peter 3:4).

All of these were already happening at the time of their writing. When we read through the characteristics listed above, we can see that they are intensifying in this current age and are carried out by our culture without reservation and with great pride. Our culture is like the people described in Jeremiah 6:15, which says, "Were they ashamed when they committed abomination? No, they were not at all ashamed; they did not know how to blush" (ESV). The apostle Paul describes them as those whose "god is their stomach, and their glory is in their shame" (Philippians 3:19). Paul and the other founders of the early church probably never could have imagined that one day a device would be created that could be slipped into our back pocket that would allow our love of pleasure to be fulfilled at our fingertips at any time of the day or night. Would they have believed that such a device would make sexual immorality of every kind available with the click of a button or a voice command with little regard for self-control? In regard to being lovers of self, would they have imagined that people would one day have entire pages dedicated to themselves on social media, where they can post perfect pictures of themselves and spout off whatever is on their mind 24 hours a day?

WITHOUT LOVE

Let's look at just one of these last-days characteristics. Second

Timothy 3 reads, "But mark this: There will be terrible times in the last days. People will be…without love" (verses 1-3). The Greek word translated "love" isn't *agape* love, or a godly or Christian kind of love. Rather, it's *astorgos*, which means "without natural love and affection for family/flesh and blood, inhuman." There's no greater example of this lack of natural love and affection toward flesh and blood than abortion, which has killed more than 60 million babies here in the US and was the number one killer of people worldwide in 2018, taking the lives of 41 million babies.[1]

The New York state senate passed a law that made it legal to abort a baby right up to the day of birth. (New York joined seven additional states and the District of Columbia, which previously legalized abortion up to the day of birth.[2] Similar legislation was followed by Illinois.[3]) Generations before us would never have thought such a mass slaughter of babies would occur, let alone be celebrated with cheers, a parade, and lighting the spire of One World Trade Center with pink lights.[4] As Paul said, "their glory is in their shame."

What is tragic and ironic about this is that One World Trade Center observes the thousands of lives lost on 9/11 at the twin towers of the World Trade Center. The National September 11 Memorial and Museum in New York City honors 11 expectant mothers and their unborn children among those who lost their lives in the 9/11 terrorist attacks. In a social media post that is attributed to Joni Eareckson Tada and taken from her book *When Is It Right to Die?*, we read, "And gradually, though no one remembers exactly how it happened, the unthinkable becomes tolerable. And then acceptable. And then legal. And then applaudable."

I could dedicate several pages to the ways that the last-days characteristics described in the New Testament are evident in the world today, but we all read and hear the news and can see for ourselves what is happening.

THE LAST HOUR

John refers to these last days as "the last hour" in 1 John 2:18: "Dear children, the last hour is here. You have heard that the Antichrist is coming, and already many such antichrists have appeared. From this we know that the last hour has come" (NLT). If John referred to the last days as "the last hour," then surely we must be in the last milliseconds of that hour before Christ's return, but because "no one knows the day or hour when these things will happen" (Matthew 24:36 NLT), no one can put a date on how long those milliseconds will last.

John said that "the Antichrist" is coming, setting this figure apart from others by using the definite article "the," thus pointing to the one and only Antichrist. Notice that he said many such antichrists have appeared, or false teachers who deceive others about the person of Christ (1 John 2:22; 4:2-3; Jude). It is the appearing of these antichrists (false teachers) on the scene that led John to write, "From this we know that the last hour has come" (NLT).

John becomes more specific about the "many such antichrists" in 1 John 2:19: "They went out from us, but they did not really belong to us. For if they had belonged to us, they would have remained with us; but their going showed that none of them belonged to us." John is writing to the church when he says, "They went out from us." People who had once been in church began to twist and pervert the Word of God, setting themselves up against Christ; in this sense they became antichrists. Pastor Jim Cymbala says,

> John says, "many antichrists, plural, have come." This is how we know it's the last hour. Notice that as he talks about these antichrists, that he identifies them as people who had once been in the church. How do we know who doesn't belong to the body of Christ? They don't stay. If they had belonged to us, they would have remained with us, but their going showed that none of them belonged to us.[5]

Paul warned the early believers that "fierce wolves will come in among you, not sparing the flock; and *from among your own selves* will arise men speaking twisted things, to draw away the disciples after them" (Acts 20:29-30 ESV).

In the days of the apostles, there were already many so-called believers who had "gone out" from the body of Christ, rejecting Him, and twisting and perverting His gospel of truth. How many more are there today?

The apostles knew they were living in the last days. They knew that things were looking up and they anticipated the return of their Savior. When Christ ascended to heaven, angels told the disciples that He would return just as He ascended, in the clouds (Acts 2:11). From that time onward, the disciples and the early church eagerly looked for and waited for Christ's return. Are we?

AN OUTLINE TO FOLLOW

The book of Revelation has a clear outline that we can follow. In chapter 1, Jesus tells John, "Write, therefore, what you have seen, what is now and what will take place later" (Revelation 1:19). He told John to write:

1. *"What you have seen"*—what John saw of Jesus in heaven—chapter 1. (I encourage you to ask the Spirit of God to help you as you read Revelation 1.)

2. *"What is now"*—the present time—Christ's letters to the seven churches of Asia Minor, chapters 2–3. (Again, ask God's Spirit to help as you read chapters 2 and 3.) These letters were delivered to each church at the time of their writing. In a moment, we'll see how these churches represent the church age.

3. *"What will take place later"*—the future—this includes the tribulation (chapters 4–19), the millennial reign of Christ for 1,000 years (chapter 20), and the new heavens and new earth (chapters 21–22). When time allows, ask for God's Spirit to lead and teach you as you read these remaining chapters.

WHERE IS THE CHURCH?

The word translated "church" is the Greek word *ekklesia*. Consider these facts about the uses of the word:

- used 19 times in Revelation chapters 1–3

- there is no appearance of the word "church" (*ekklesia*) in the next 15 chapters, during the time of the tribulation

- is mentioned again in Revelation's final chapter (22:16)

- the words "church" or "churches" are used 92 times in the New Testament

- no familiar references or appearance of the word "church" (*ekklesia*) after the church age (Revelation chapters 2–3)

The disappearance of the words "church" and "churches" in chapters 4 to 18 gives encouraging support that the church will not be on Earth during the tribulation. We do see the word "saints" used thirteen times in Revelation. There are Old Testament and church-age saints in the Bible, and in Revelation we see that there are tribulation-era saints, those who come to Christ during the tribulation period.

There is exciting evidence that we do see a picture of the church in heaven beginning in Revelation 4:4: "Surrounding the throne were twenty-four other thrones, and seated on them were twenty-four elders. They were dressed in white and had crowns of gold on their heads." Beginning with the formation of the church in Acts, we see the word translated "elder" take on a different meaning from someone who is of advanced age, or a member of the great council or Sanhedrin, to someone who presided over the churches.

Elders still preside over many churches today. The twenty-four elders in Revelation are seated on thrones, and Jesus tells us that those who are in Christ will have the right to "sit with me on my throne" (Revelation 3:21). The elders in Revelation 4:4 are dressed in white like the bride of Christ (Revelation 3:5, 18; 19:7-8) and they are wearing crowns (Greek, *stephanos*, which refers to a victor's crown, symbolic of award and honor). All those who are in Christ will receive crowns

(1 Corinthians 9:25; 2 Timothy 4:8; James 1:12; 1 Peter 5:4; Revelation 2:10; 3:11). In Scripture, angels are never represented as wearing crowns, and we see that they encircle the throne *and* the elders in heaven, distinguishing them from the elders themselves (Revelation 5:11; 7:11).

Concerning what the elders are wearing, David M. Levy says,

> The crowns and white raiment gives evidence that the elders have already been judged and rewarded by Christ. This is not applicable to angels or Old Testament believers...David divided the Levitical priesthood into 24 courses (1 Chronicles 24) to represent the complete priesthood. In like manner, the 24 elders stand for the completed church, which is identified in Scripture as "a royal priesthood" (1 Peter 2:9).[1]

The completed church represent those who became believers in Christ during the church age, which began on the Day of Pentecost in Acts 2, when the church was formed. We are still living in the church age. There will come a time when this church age will come to its conclusion, but for now, we are still in the "what is now" portion of Revelation's outline (chapters 2–3). There are seven churches addressed in Revelation 2–3, and in the Bible, the number seven is said to represent completion or perfection. These seven churches represent the various kinds of churches present on Earth during the entire church age, ending with the church at Laodicea, the lukewarm church.

Peter Marshall, one-time chaplain of the US Senate, said,

> Millions of people in America live in moral fogs. The issues are not clear to them. They cannot face the light that makes them black or white. They want grays and neutral tints. They move in a sort of spiritual twilight. Surely, the time has come, because the hour is late, when we must decide. And the choice before us is plain, Jehovah or Baal. Christ or chaos. Conviction or compromise. Discipline or disintegration.[2]

What's startling is that Marshall didn't say that twenty, thirty, or even fifty years ago. He said those words in 1944, and according to his assessment, the church had already been lukewarm for years.

THE END OF THE CHURCH AGE

The conclusion of the church age is at the end of Revelation chapter 3, in which the last of the seven letters is issued to the church at Laodicea. Now notice in the very first verse of chapter 4 that John is called up to heaven in his vision:

> After this I looked, and there before me was a door standing open in heaven. And the voice I had first heard speaking to me like a trumpet said, "*Come up here*, and I will show you what must take place after this" (Revelation 4:1).

A door is open in heaven and a voice like a trumpet says, "Come up here, and I will show you *what must take place after this*." After what? Again, in Revelation 2–3, we've been reading the, "what is now" part of the outline: the church age. John is called up to heaven *after* he documents what will happen during the church age so he can be shown *what must take place after this*.

So…

- the church age concludes at the end of Revelation 3
- a door to heaven opens in Revelation 4:1
- a voice says to John, "Come up here"

WHY IS JOHN CALLED TO HEAVEN AT THE CONCLUSION OF THE CHURCH AGE?

Second Thessalonians provides insight. The Thessalonian believers had received some false teaching along the way "concerning the coming of our Lord Jesus Christ and our being gathered to him" (2 Thessalonians 2:1-2). They were shaken and alarmed by this false teaching that had supposedly come from Paul (it hadn't), telling them that Christ had already come for His believers, which could only mean that they were living in the tribulation period. This would seem true to them because they were being persecuted. Paul calmed their spirits and urged them not to be deceived.

> Now, brethren, concerning the coming of our Lord Jesus Christ and our gathering together to Him, we ask you, not to be soon shaken in mind or troubled, either by spirit or by word or by letter, as if from us, as though the day of Christ had come. Let no one deceive you by any means; for that Day will not come unless the falling away comes first, and the man of sin is revealed, the son of perdition, who opposes and exalts himself above all that is called God or that is worshiped, so that he sits as God in the temple of God, showing himself that he is God (2 Thessalonians 2:1-4 NKJV).

He said, "For that Day [also referred to as the Day of the Lord and anticipated by the Old Testament prophets as a time when God would visit the earth to judge the wicked and to save His people—Ezekiel 30:3; Joel 2:31; Amos 5:20; Zechariah 14:1] *will not come unless the falling away comes first, and the man of sin is revealed*, the son of perdition" (NKJV). Paul assures the Thessalonian believers that the Day of the Lord had *not* come because certain things had to happen.

Paul then says,

> Do you not remember that when I was still with you I told you these things? And now you know what is restraining, that he may be revealed in his own time. For the mystery of lawlessness is already at work; only He who now restrains will do so until He is taken out of the way. And then the lawless one will be revealed, whom the Lord will consume with the breath of His mouth and destroy with the brightness of His coming (2 Thessalonians 2:5-10 NKJV).

Note what Paul asks in verse 5: "Do you not remember that when I was still with you I told you these things?" Like us, they probably did remember, but because of the false teaching they had heard, they were now confused. Paul tells the Thessalonians not to be deceived and lists *three things that must happen before* the Day of the Lord, or the tribulation.

The Timing of the Day of the Lord

The Day of the Lord will not come until…

1. *The falling away comes first* (verse 3). The Greek word *apostasia* is used here, meaning "defection, revolt, apostasy." David Jeremiah says, "The definite article '*the*' indicates that there will be a specific, unique walking away from the truth people once believed."[3] First Timothy 4:1 says, "The Spirit clearly says that in later times some will abandon *the* faith and follow deceiving spirits and things taught by demons." There's that definite article "the"—people will abandon "the" faith. Not "a" faith, or faith in general, but "the" faith. Paul wrote and spoke and preached about faith in Christ alone and the tenets of the gospel, and it is *this* faith, *the* faith in Christ, that many will abandon in the last days.

Second, Paul said…

2. *He who now restrains will do so until He is taken out of the way* (verses 6-7). It's the convicting work of the Holy Spirit within believers that exhorts them to stay away from sin, and it is the Holy Spirit who holds back or restrains the "man of sin," the "lawless one," "the man of lawlessness"—all of these are names for the Antichrist.

What the Holy Spirit Does

THE HOLY SPIRIT GUIDES AND HELPS US

> Walk by the Spirit, and you will not gratify the desires of the flesh. For the flesh desires what is contrary to the Spirit, and the Spirit what is contrary to the flesh. They are in conflict with each other, so that you are not to do whatever you want (Galatians 5:16-17).

THE HOLY SPIRIT DWELLS WITHIN EACH BELIEVER;
WE ARE HIS VEHICLE ON EARTH

- Jesus said in John 14:16-17, "I will ask the Father, and he will give you another advocate to help you and be with you forever—the Spirit of truth. The world cannot accept him, because it neither sees him nor knows him. But you know him, for *he lives with you and will be in you*."

- "He who is joined to the Lord *is one spirit with Him*" (1 Corinthians 6:17 NKJV).

- "Do you not know that *your body is the temple of the Holy Spirit who is in you,* whom you have from God?" (1 Corinthians 6:19 NKJV).

- "Don't you know that *you yourselves are God's temple* and that God's Spirit dwells in your midst?" (1 Corinthians 3:16).

THE HOLY SPIRIT REVEALS THE NEED FOR SALVATION IN OUR LIVES AND CONVICTS US OF SIN AND OF COMING JUDGMENT

It is believers, with the Holy Spirit dwelling inside of us, who share the gospel with people; it is we who reveal to unbelievers that sin separates people from God. In speaking of the Holy Spirit, Jesus told His apostles, "When he comes, he will prove the world to be in the wrong about sin and righteousness and judgment: about sin, because people do not believe in me; about righteousness, because I am going to the Father, where you can see me no longer; and about judgment, because the prince of this world now stands condemned" (John 16:8-11).

Life in the Spirit is an intimate, personal relationship, one that changes us from the inside out. As a result, we become salt and light in the world (Matthew 5:13-16). As salt, our presence in the world adds flavor to the earth. Our presence cleanses and preserves the earth by battling sin and evil, and our presence helps prevent decline and corruption in a decaying, dying world. The Holy Spirit's presence within those who are in Christ restrains the rise of complete lawlessness, but "He who now restrains" will one day be taken out of the way, when all those who are in Christ are removed, allowing the earth to fall subject to sin without restraint.

Pastor Jeff Kinley has said, "Wherever there are people, there are God's people and His Spirit working in and through them, impeding sin while advancing His kingdom. John's words still ring true: 'Greater is He who is in you than he who is in the world.'"[4]

WHO IS "HE WHO RESTRAINS"?

There have been many thoughts throughout the ages of the identity of "He who now restrains" in 2 Thessalonians 2:7 (NKJV). Mark Hitchcock provides four clues to the identity:

- The phrase "what is holding him back" uses a neuter verb, suggesting a principle.

- The phrase "the one who is holding him back" uses a masculine verb, suggesting a person.

- Whatever the restrainer is, he or it must be removable.

- Last, the restrainer must be powerful enough to hold back the outbreak of evil under the Antichrist.

These four clues permit only one satisfactory identification for the restrainer—God Himself. In this case, it is God the Holy Spirit who is the restrainer.[5] Again, where does the Holy Spirit dwell? Within us as believers, who experience the power of the Holy Spirit through our prayers, our actions, our influence in culture, and even our influence with God.

While it's true that "He who now restrains" will be removed, Scripture makes it clear that the Holy Spirit will still be at work on Earth during the tribulation, just as He worked in the Old Testament, and before Pentecost in the New Testament, because He is omnipresent. A void will most certainly be felt during the early days of the tribulation because the church's fighting against, holding back, and restraining of sin and rebellion will be removed. It's in the midst of this void that the 144,000 Jewish men will be sealed by Jesus and scattered throughout the world to preach the gospel by the power of the Holy Spirit.

So, before the Day of the Lord or the tribulation comes, there will first come a falling away from the faith, and the restrainer will be taken out of the way.

The third thing that must happen is…

3. The man of sin, the son of perdition (verse 3), the lawless one (verse 8), the Antichrist (1 John 2:18), will be revealed.

What is keeping the Antichrist from appearing on the world's stage? Donald Grey Barnhouse emphatically states,

> *You* are! You and every other member of the body of Christ on earth. True, it is the Holy Spirit who is the real restrainer. But as both First Corinthians 3:16 and 6:19 teach, the Holy Spirit indwells the believer. Put all believers together then, with the Holy Spirit indwelling each of us, and you have a formidable restraining force.[6]

We live in the church age, the age of grace, where because of the prayers and the actions of the church, sin is somewhat restrained. But the day is coming when lawlessness will overtake the earth, and before that day comes, *before* the man of lawlessness is revealed, those who are in Christ will be called to "come up here"—just as John was in Revelation 4:1.

While we are still in this age of grace and while things are increasingly looking up, will you pray for ways to sprinkle salt and shine light into your community? This could be the church's finest hour. Will you pray for boldness to reach out to someone with the gospel of Christ today?

THE BRIDE OF CHRIST

It's important to note that there is absolutely no prophecy that has to take place before this great snatching away or catching up (Greek, *harpazo*) of the bride of Christ occurs. The bride of Christ is a reference to the body of believers who follow Christ:

- "I am jealous for you with a godly jealousy. *I promised you to one husband, to Christ,* so that I might present you as a pure virgin to him" (2 Corinthians 11:2).

- "You yourselves can testify that I said, 'I am not the Messiah but am sent ahead of him.' *The bride belongs to the bridegroom.* The friend who attends the bridegroom waits and listens for him, and is full of joy when he hears the bridegroom's voice. That joy is mine, and it is now complete" (John 3:28-29). John the Baptist is speaking here about the Messiah, explaining that he is not Him; but rather, he's the bride belonging to the bridegroom, the Messiah, or Jesus.

- "'For this reason a man will leave his father and mother and be united to his wife, and the two will become one flesh.' This is a profound mystery—but *I am talking about Christ and the church*" (Ephesians 5:31-32).

243

- "The kingdom of heaven is like a king who prepared a wedding banquet for his son" (Matthew 22:2).
- "The wedding of the Lamb has come,
  and *his bride has made herself ready.*
  Fine linen, bright and clean,
  was given her to wear" (Revelation 19:7-8).

THE SEIZING OF THOSE "IN CHRIST" OR THE SECOND COMING?

The words above in Revelation 19:7-8 refer to the bride in heaven, who is ready to return with Christ to Earth at His second coming. Many confuse the seizing or catching up of those in Christ and assume it is the same event as the second coming, but there are significant differences between the two.

First Thessalonians 4:15-18 refers to the seizing, catching up, or snatching away of those who are in Christ:

> According to the Lord's word, we tell you that we who are still alive, who are left until the coming of the Lord, will certainly not precede those who have fallen asleep. For the Lord himself will come down from heaven, with a loud command, with the voice of the archangel and with the trumpet call of God, and the dead in Christ will rise first. After that, we who are still alive and are left will be caught up together with them in the clouds to meet the Lord in the air. And so we will be with the Lord forever. Therefore encourage one another with these words (1 Thessalonians 4:15-18).

Revelation 19:11-16 refers to the second coming of Christ:

> I saw heaven standing open and there before me was a white horse, whose rider is called Faithful and True. With justice he judges and wages war. His eyes are like blazing fire, and on his head are many crowns. He has a name written on him that no one knows but he himself. He is dressed in a robe dipped in blood, and his name is the Word of

God. The armies of heaven were following him, riding on white horses and dressed in fine linen, white and clean. Coming out of his mouth is a sharp sword with which to strike down the nations. "He will rule them with an iron scepter." He treads the winepress of the fury of the wrath of God Almighty. On his robe and on his thigh he has this name written: KING OF KINGS AND LORD OF LORDS (Revelation 19:11-16).

As we carefully compare these two passages, we notice significant differences:

The Seizing of Believers 1 Thessalonians 4	The Second Coming Revelation 19
Jesus steps into the air, not on Earth	Jesus returns to Earth
Comes as Deliverer	Returns as Warrior
Comes *for* His bride	Returns *with* His bride
Comes in love for His bride	Returns in wrath and judgment
Comes as a Bridegroom	Returns as King of kings and Lord of lords

Let's look closely at some more distinctions between the seizing/snatching away of believers and the second coming:

TWO SEPARATE PHASES

Soon we'll read more verses dealing with both the seizing or snatching away of those in Christ and the second coming, but based on what we have read so far, this is a good place to expand on the fact that there are two separate phases to Christ's return (or two separate events):

1. Christ coming *for* His bride when He seizes her/snatches her away (*harpazo*), and

2. Christ returning to Earth *with* His bride at the second coming

Many people fear Christ's return because they haven't been taught He will come in two phases. Instead, they think of Christ coming solely for judgment. When I was a little girl, I remember our pastor and visiting pastors saying things like, "Jesus is coming again," or "Christ will return." But as I mentioned in the Where in the Word? Introduction, I've heard very few similar statements since that time. As I talk with friends around the country, I know I'm not alone, and I don't think this is a recent trend. In 1917, William E. Blackstone wrote, "An elderly Methodist clergyman in Florida said that he had heard only five sermons on the Lord's coming, and he preached them all himself."[1] That was more than 100 years ago! It's not unusual for Christians to be in the dark about end-time events.

Look up at Revelation 19 again. The "armies of heaven" following Jesus out of heaven in verse 14 are identified as the bride in verses 7-8, who has been given "fine linen, bright and clean" to wear. (Angels are also part of this great army—see Matthew 25:31; 2 Thessalonians 1:7.) The bride will return with Christ, at His second coming, when He returns in judgment and wrath against sin and rebellion, at the end of the tribulation (Daniel 9:24-27). Revelation 19:8 clarifies what the bride's clothes represent: "Fine linen stands for the righteous acts of *God's holy people.*"

Other Scripture writers also prophesied about these holy people. In 1 Thessalonians 3:13, Paul says, "May he strengthen your hearts so that you will be blameless and holy in the presence of our God and Father when our Lord Jesus comes *with all his holy ones.*"

Noah's great-grandfather Enoch also prophesied about them: "Enoch, the seventh from Adam, prophesied about them: 'See, the Lord is coming with thousands upon thousands of his *holy ones*'" (Jude 1:4). Zechariah wrote, "Then the Lord my God will come, and *all the holy ones with him*" (Zechariah 14:5).

Now contrast what Revelation 19 says about Jesus on a white horse, followed by His holy ones out of heaven, with the passages that describe the snatching away of believers.

Regarding this snatching away/seizing up of believers, Paul says in 1 Corinthians 15:50-54 that it happens in an instant, a flash, "in the twinkling of an eye" (verse 52). The bride of Christ will be snatched away so quickly that no eye will detect what happens.

However, the second coming of Christ will be seen *by everyone*, people will mourn because they have not believed in Him, and angels and holy ones will be with Him:

> "Look, he is coming with the clouds,"
> and "*every eye will see him,*
> even those who pierced him";
> and *all peoples on earth "will mourn because of him."*
> So shall it be! Amen (Revelation 1:7).

> Then will appear the sign of the Son of Man in heaven. And then *all the peoples of the earth will mourn when they see the Son of Man coming on the clouds of heaven*, with power and great glory (Matthew 24:30).

> This will happen *when the Lord Jesus is revealed from heaven* with his mighty angels…(2 Thessalonians 1:7—see also Jude 4 and Zechariah 14:5).

Note that the people of Earth will mourn upon seeing Jesus at His second coming. This is in direct opposition to Paul's description of Christ's coming as our "blessed hope," as stated in Titus 2:13: "…while we wait for the blessed hope—the appearing of the glory of our great God and Savior, Jesus Christ."

Why do the peoples of the earth mourn when they see Jesus coming in the clouds? When they see Christ arriving, they will know that everything that the 144,000, the two witnesses, their mothers, fathers, brothers, sisters, neighbors, or even the proclaiming angel of Revelation 14:6 tried to tell them about Him was indeed true, and that time has run out. Jesus's visible return will cause grief and mourning like the world has never known. For them, there will be nothing blessed about that appearance.

The early church, however, never spoke of mourning the return of Jesus. These Christians knew that things were looking up and were anticipating the return of their *blessed hope* in the air, who would snatch them away before the wrath of God fell on the earth.

TWO GATHERINGS

Matthew 24:30-31, which describes Christ's second coming, says,

> Then will appear the sign of the Son of Man in heaven. And then all the peoples of the earth will mourn when they see the Son of Man coming on the clouds of heaven, with power and great glory. And he will send his angels with a loud trumpet call, and *they will gather his elect from the four winds*, from one end of the heavens to the other.

At the second coming, the angels will gather the elect, those who have believed and followed Jesus during the seven-year tribulation, and Christ Himself will separate these believers from the unbelievers in what is commonly known as "the sheep and goats judgment."

> When the Son of Man comes in his glory, and all the angels with him, he will sit on his glorious throne. All the nations will be gathered before him, and he will separate the people one from another as a shepherd separates the sheep from the goats. He will put the sheep on his right and the goats on his left. Then the King will say to those on his right, "Come, you who are blessed by my Father; take your inheritance, the kingdom prepared for you since the creation of the world."... Then he will say to those on his left, "Depart from me, you who are cursed, into the eternal fire prepared for the devil and his angels."...Then they will go away to eternal punishment, but the righteous to eternal life (Matthew 25:31-34, 41, 46).

Note the distinction here: At the snatching away/seizing up of believers, *it is Christ who gathers His followers to Him in the air* (1 Thessalonians 4:16-17; 2 Thessalonians 2:1). But at His second coming, *it's the angels who will do the gathering* (Matthew 24:31), and it's Jesus who will do the separating, sending believers into His kingdom and unbelievers to eternal punishment (Matthew 25:31-34, 41, 46).

TWO MEETING PLACES

When Jesus eagerly snatches away those who are in Him, believers will meet Him *in the air* (1 Thessalonians 4:17). At the second coming, those who have believed and followed Christ through the seven-year tribulation, will be gathered to Him *on the ground* as He stands on the Mount of Olives (Zechariah 14:2-9).

TWO REMOVALS

At the snatching away, Christ will remove His *followers* from the earth. At the second coming, angels will remove *unbelievers* from the earth.

There will be a clear dividing of believers from unbelievers, as evidenced by the verses that describe God's judgment. In Matthew 13:24-29, 36-43, it is the angels at the end of the age who throw the weeds (the wicked) into the blazing furnace, separating them from the wheat (believers).

In Matthew 24:37-41 and Luke 17:34-37, we read more about the dividing of people, distinguished now between those "taken" and those "left." Matthew 24:37-38 tells of the days of Noah and the flood, comparing those days to the return of Jesus. Matthew 24:40-41 says "one will be taken and the other left." The one taken is the believer, just like Noah and his family were taken into the safety of the ark. But concerning the unbeliever, the one who is "left," the Greek word translated "left" means "to send away, of a husband divorcing his wife." When the door of the ark closed, there were those who were left—the unbelievers, who met their end. At the second coming, angels will gather the believers, but those who are left, the unbelievers, will be sent away to their judgment and end.

TWO TIMES

When Jesus snatches away those who are in Him (His bride), He will do so prior to God's wrath being poured out on the earth. In Revelation 3:10, Jesus says to the church at Philadelphia, "Since you have kept my command to endure patiently, I will also *keep you from the hour of trial that is going to come on the whole world* to test the inhabitants of the earth."

Jesus is promising the Christians there that because of their faithfulness, they will be kept "from the hour of trial that is going to come on the whole world." Since that prophecy was declared, there has *never been a trial that has come upon the entire globe*. There have been many wars, but those have never truly encompassed all people everywhere. In Revelation 3:10, Jesus is precise in His language. This deliverance is *not only from the trial itself, but from the very period of time during which the trial takes place*—"the hour of trial." John Walvoord wrote, "If the expression had been simply 'deliverance from trial,' conceivably it could have meant only partial deliverance."[2]

But that's not what Jesus said. He promised that the church would be kept from "the" hour of trial, using the definite article *the* to set this apart from a general trial. Every major event has a starting time: when polls open for election, professional sporting events, church services, concerts, theater performances, movie show times, conferences, etc. Everyone knows the hour when a specific event will begin. Jesus promises that the church will be kept from the very hour, from the beginning of the "trial that is going to come on the whole world." Notice that He does not say He will keep the church "through" the hour of trial, but that He will keep the church "from" it.

In 1 Thessalonians 1:10, Paul says that Jesus "delivers us from *the* wrath to come" (NKJV). He will deliver us *from* it, not *through* it. Again, Paul uses the definite article *the* to set this wrath apart from the general wrath we experience in life. He's speaking specifically of the coming wrath of God.

So, there will be two times that Jesus will leave heaven. First, at the snatching away/seizing up of those in Christ, He will step into the air and call up His bride to be with Him "in the clouds" (1 Thessalonians 4:16-17), prior to the pouring out of God's wrath. At the second coming, Jesus will leave heaven with His bride and come back to Earth at the end of the tribulation (Matthew 24:29-31; Revelation 19:11-14).

As we look up in anticipation for Christ to call His bride up to the clouds, consider these words from William E. Blackstone, whose book *Jesus Is Coming* was first published in 1878.

> The High Priest went into the Holy of Holies alone, and the whole congregation waited in expectation outside

until he had made the offering and came out to bless them (Leviticus 16; Numbers 6:23-26; Luke 1:10). So has our High Priest entered once for all into the *true holy place,* and the church should look for Him in fervent expectation until He appears the second time not to bear sin, but to bring salvation. She must watch, dressed for service and with lamps burning, like men waiting for their Lord (Luke 12:35, 36). Yet we have the blessed assurance that every passing day brings our salvation nearer than when we first believed.[3]

What Needs to Happen Before the Snatching Away of Believers and the Second Coming?

What needs to happen before the seizing/catching up/snatching away of believers? In a word, nothing. This seizing of those who are in Christ is imminent, meaning that it could take place at any moment; *there are no signs that precede it.* According to Charles C. Ryrie, an imminent event is one that is "impending, hanging over one's head, ready to take place."[1] Concerning an imminent event, Renald Showers says, "It's literally hanging over your head, every moment of every day, and therefore, it will fall upon you at any time."[2] We need to understand that in this case, *imminent* doesn't mean "soon," but rather, that it's inevitable—it *will* happen.

While there are no signs before the snatching away event, there are years' worth of signs to be fulfilled before the second coming occurs.

Here are a few of the signs that will occur before the second coming of Christ:

- A confederation of ten nations will form and be led by the Antichrist (Daniel 7:7, 20, 24)

- The rise in power of the Antichrist (numerous scriptures describe him, including Daniel 8:23-24; 2 Thessalonians 2:3, 8)

- The Antichrist will confirm a covenant with Israel (Daniel 9:27)

- The rebuilding of the Jewish temple (Daniel 9:27; 11:31; 2 Thessalonians 2:4; Revelation 11:1)

- The emergence of the False Prophet (Revelation 13:11-12)

- The abomination of desolation set up inside the temple (Daniel 9:27; Matthew 24:15; Mark 13:14; 2 Thessalonians 2:4)

- The ministry of the two witnesses (Revelation 11:1-13)

- The gospel preached to the entire world (Matthew 24:14)

- The campaign of Armageddon (Revelation 16:16)

- Signs of the end as stated in Matthew 24, Mark 13, and Luke 21

THE SIGNS OF THE TIMES

Although we can't put a date on Christ's return, we can say that we're closer today than we were yesterday. If anyone says he knows when Jesus is returning, he's a false teacher and can't be trusted (there have been more than a few false date-setters through the years). Not even Jesus or the angels know that day, only God the Father (Matthew 24:36). While we are unable to determine the date of Christ's return, still, we are told to discern the signs of the times:

- In 1 Chronicles 12:32, we learn from the sons of Issachar that "all these men understood *the signs of the times* and knew the best course for Israel to take" (NLT).

- In Luke 12, Jesus chastises the religious leaders, saying, "When you see a cloud rising in the west, immediately you say, 'It's going to rain,' and it does. And when the south wind blows, you say, 'It's going to be hot,' and it is. Hypocrites! You know how to interpret the appearance of the earth and the sky. *How is it that you don't know how to interpret this present time?"* (Luke 12:54-56).

- In Matthew 16:3, Jesus says, "You know how to interpret the appearance of the sky, but *you cannot interpret the signs of the times."*

A sign always directs us to something, indicating what is ahead. Just as road signs get closer together as we approach our exit, so do the signs of the times get closer and closer together as we get nearer to our exit from Earth. As I mentioned in a previous chapter, 1 Timothy 4:1-2, 2 Timothy 3:1-5, and 2 Peter 3:3 mention characteristics (or signs) of the last days. If you haven't read these passages, I encourage you to read them so you can, as Jesus said, "interpret the signs of the times." Jesus gives us a heads-up regarding the signs as well.

IS MATTHEW 24 JUST ABOUT THE DESTRUCTION OF JERUSALEM?

In Matthew 24:1 we read that Jesus left the temple, and in verse 2 He says to His disciples, "Truly I tell you, not one stone here will be left on another; every one will be thrown down." This prompted the disciples to ask, "Tell us...when will this happen, and what will be the sign of your coming and of the end of the age?" (verses 2-3).

There are some who believe that Matthew 24 is solely about the destruction of Jerusalem in AD 70, while others believe the entirety of the chapter is about the end times. The *Holman New Testament Commentary* says, "The best solution should probably begin with the assumption that Jesus was looking ahead toward several acts of judgment, spread throughout history, and foretelling them as a conflated, composite unit. Some details of Jesus' prophecy have been and will be fulfilled at more than one point in history."[3] The commentary further states that "this judgment, in its prophetic entirety, would take centuries to complete."[4]

This prophecy "would take centuries to complete." Remember, prophecy unfolds over time. While speaking in a synagogue (Luke

4:18-19), Jesus read Isaiah 61:1-2 to His listeners: "He has sent me to bind up the brokenhearted, to proclaim freedom for the captives and release from darkness for the prisoners, to proclaim the year of the LORD's favor, and the day of vengeance of our God." Do you see how that verse ends? It says, "…and the day of vengeance of our God." Except when you read Luke 4, you see that Jesus didn't read "…and the day of vengeance of our God." He stopped reading at the comma, after the word "favor." Who stops reading at a comma? No one! But Jesus couldn't say "the day of vengeance of our God" because it wasn't time for that; at His first coming, He had not come in vengeance. That's His second coming. We're still waiting for that part of the prophecy to be fulfilled.

When we read Matthew 24:2-3, the disciples pose their inquiry as one question. To them, if the temple was to be destroyed, then surely that meant the end of the world had come because the temple was enormous! Their inquiry can be broken down into three separate questions:

- When will this (the throwing down of the temple) happen?

- What is the sign of your coming?

- How will we recognize the end of the age?

This prophecy has been unfolding for nearly two millennia. The destruction of Jerusalem came in AD 70, and just as Jesus said, not one stone was left upon another. That particular part of the prophecy was fulfilled. As I mentioned earlier, there are many who believe that every sign mentioned in Matthew 24 was fulfilled in AD 70, not just the destruction of Jerusalem. Although some of the signs mentioned in chapter 24 were evident in AD 70, not all of them were. The temple's destruction was only *one* of the judgments foretold by Jesus. He was also foretelling the signs of His coming and the end of the age. These signs are also mentioned in Mark 13 and Luke 21. Read through these chapters and take note of the signs that are *already* visible today:

- deception
- wars and uprisings

- famines and pestilence
- earthquakes
- fearful events
- roaring and tossing of the sea
- persecution and killings
- apostasy (turning from the faith)
- those who turn from the faith will betray and hate each other
- an increase of wickedness
- the growing cold of love
- great signs in the heavenlies
- the preaching of the gospel to every nation
- false prophets and messiahs show great signs and wonders
- great distress

The abomination of desolation in the temple is among the signs that must be fulfilled before Christ's second coming. This sign will happen during the tribulation, when the Antichrist sets up an image of himself inside the temple, which has yet to be built.

As we look around the world, we can see that...

—most of these signs are in existence *today*, increasing in frequency and intensity,

—getting us closer to the snatching away (Greek, *harpazo*) of those in Christ,

—which moves the world into the tribulation period, where the signs will only intensify

—and will usher in the second coming at the conclusion of the tribulation.

A CONVERGENCE OF SIGNS

Like no other time in history, there is a stunning convergence of signs taking place. Because there are way too many signs to cover in this book, let's look at just a few of them.

Deception

As Jesus responded to His disciples, His first words were, "Watch out that no one deceives you" (Matthew 24:4). Jesus was warning them that deception would be so prevalent in the world that even His closest followers could be deceived. He speaks of deception four more times in Matthew 24 (verses 5, 11, 23, 24), so we know that this problem will be widespread as we get closer to the end of the age.

In recent years, studies have concluded that the Christian share of the US population is declining, while the fastest-growing religious affiliation is the "nones"—those who do not affiliate or self-identify with any organized church or religion. The nones represent 26 percent of the population, ahead of evangelicals at 22.5 percent.[5] A Barna Group poll revealed that Generation Z (those born between 1999 and 2015) are the least-Christian generation in American history, with 35 percent calling themselves atheists, agnostics, or of no religious affiliation. Only 4 out of 100 teens hold a true biblical worldview.[6]

A gospel of "niceness" has left a void in the hearts of young people and in adults as well. For decades now, many pulpits have offered fare that has left the church spiritually malnourished. Sixty-seven percent of Millennials have no religious affiliation.[7] Among the reasons Millennials cite for not going to church is that they only learn morality there, and they already consider themselves to be moral people: They don't murder or steal, they help the poor and disenfranchised; what they learn at church they've already learned from self-help books and podcasts.

Another study reported that 56 percent of Americans say that God is not a prerequisite for good values and morality.[8] Most people in America today believe that they can be good without God, without the cross. More than half of the people in the United States say Jesus isn't necessary.

Deception of the Highest Order

Jesus said in Matthew 24:24, "False messiahs and false prophets will appear and perform great signs and wonders to deceive, if possible, even the elect." We like to think that false prophets or teachers will look like crazy-haired people shouting about Jesus on a street corner, but the reality is they often come in a beautiful or handsome package and say only "non-judgy" things. If we don't agree with the truth a pastor preaches, then we can find any number of pastors, ministers, authors, talk-show hosts, journalists, speakers, professors, and celebrities who will say exactly what we want to hear. It doesn't matter if it's not truth; our ears will receive it as truth because it's what we want to hear.

Terry James says,

> False christs and false prophets have been a part of human culture since the early days of history. Soothsayers of every sort have always been able to delude. The human mind, since the fall in Eden, has always seemed to gravitate toward false promises rather than toward truth.[9]

In 2 Timothy 4:3-4, Paul told Timothy,

> For the time will come when people will not put up with sound doctrine. Instead, to suit their own desires, they will gather around them a great number of teachers to say what their itching ears want to hear. They will turn their ears away from the truth and turn aside to myths.

Deception is slick and comfortable and makes us feel good. Paul told Timothy what would happen in the last days, saying that unbelievable things would be taking place and that deception would be rampant. After stating the warning in verses 3-4, Paul said to him, "But you, keep your head in all situations" (verse 5). The English Standard Version says, "As for you, always be sober minded."

Yes, "keep your head in all situations"; crazy and unbelievable things are happening, and will continue, reminding us again that things are looking up to Christ's return.

MANY WILL FALL AWAY

Jesus said in Matthew 24:10, "Many will fall away and betray one another and hate one another" (ESV). In place of the words "fall away," other translations use the words "turn away" or "shall…be offended" (KJV), and they all mean the same thing in the original Greek text: "to put a stumbling block or impediment in the way, upon which another may trip and fall, to offend, to entice to sin, to cause to fall away, to be offended in one, i.e. to see in another what I disapprove of and what hinders me from acknowledging his authority."[10]

The last part of that definition is particularly interesting. To many people, the truth of the Bible is offensive and they disapprove of it, which hinders them from acknowledging God's authority. It's common to hear people say, "I don't think that's what the Bible means," or "I don't think God would do that," or "I feel this is what God means," or "I don't agree with that."

But nowhere in Scripture does it say, "What do you think?" "How does that make you feel?" Or "Do you agree with that?" God's Word is about what He says, not what we think or feel or agree with, and there's the problem for many. Pastor Darren Tyler said, "If you say, I could never agree with or serve that God—the one I disagree with, the one I don't understand—I can only agree with a god who can't change, challenge, or transform me. I can only serve a god that agrees with me… what you're saying is that god is you."[11] For many today, even within the church, if the truth hurts, offends, or contradicts "their truth," if they disapprove of what God's Word says and don't like or agree with what they read in Scripture, they won't acknowledge God's authority in those areas, leaving them open to anything but truth.

Pastor Allen Jackson said,

> We've been a little stubborn with regard to the Word of God. We've approached it a bit arrogantly. We've been reluctant to give God's thoughts room in our thoughts. We've determined that our thoughts are higher than His… When truth is rejected by the people of God, demonic influence steps into the void.[12]

In a word, deception. According to Barna Group research, 3,500 people leave the church every day. It is estimated that between 6,000 and 10,000 churches close their doors each year.[13]

Decades ago, the Western church decided it needed a makeover; surely there was a way to make the gospel less offensive. In "What Happened to My Church?," an article from Olive Tree Ministries, Jan Markell writes,

> Someone made a conscious decision that we should have a "new way of doing church," although many members and attendees agreed *there was nothing wrong with old ways of doing church.* Terms began being used like "purpose-driven," "seeker-sensitive," "church-growth movement," "postmodernism," "Emergent," and more. People started to hear about love, unity and tolerance. We must be known for what we agree on, not what we disagree on. Everything and everyone must be accepted. Aberrations must be accepted. Sin must be accepted. People loved having their ears tickled. They would be encouraged to "feel good" and have their self-esteem built up. Sound doctrine was being set aside...*sound doctrine will separate and divide so we must tread lightly in that area...* It seemed like an "eleventh commandment" came into the church: *Thou shalt not offend.*[14]

When the truth isn't spoken or taught, deception creeps in, making the truth intolerable to bear. Jeremiah called out the prophets and priests of his day for not speaking the truth saying, "An appalling and horrible thing has happened in the land: the prophets prophesy falsely, and the priests rule at their direction; my people love to have it so, but what will you do when the end comes?" (Jeremiah 5:30 ESV).

False teachers hadn't gone away in the New Testament era, and according to Jude, they often slipped in unnoticed (verse 4). They are similarly unnoticed in many churches today. Many have huge platforms on the Internet and in social media, where they are retweeted, reposted, and shared to thousands upon thousands of people. Jackie Hill Perry said of these false teachers, "They hide well because we've made liars our heroes."[15]

The power of these false teachers can't be underestimated or trivialized; they cause great confusion and because of this, when the truth is finally spoken, even when it's spoken in love, believers can also be easily "offended" and turn or fall away from the faith. Many false teachers present "their truth" with bits of God's truth thrown in. In this way they twist and pervert the truth.

Again, for many people, the truth is offensive. When Pilate asked Jesus in John 18:38, "What is truth?," he didn't let Jesus answer. Scripture says he turned around and went out again to the Jews. People today are fighting, arguing, and bickering over the truth, but if the truth comes from Jesus, they don't want to hear it. They find it offensive.

In December 2017, Google released its "Year in Search 2017" list of most popular searches for the year. The Bible and God were not listed in the top 100. There was absolutely nothing religious in the top 100 searches, but pornographic content was listed several times. Google processes more than 63,000 searches every second; that's 5.6 billion searches a day.[16] Now let this sink in: God was nowhere to be found in the top 100 searches. Jesus said, "I…came into the world to testify to the truth" (NLT). But very few people want to Google that.

Earthquakes

The link between the earth's rotation and seismic activity was highlighted in a paper by Roger Bilham of the University of Colorado in Boulder, and Rebecca Bendick of the University of Montana in Missoula, for a meeting of the Geological Society of America. "The correlation between Earth's rotation and earthquake activity is strong and suggests there is going to be an increase in numbers of intense earthquakes next year," Bilham said.

In their study, the scientists looked at earthquakes of magnitude 7.0 and greater since 1900. "Major earthquakes have been well recorded for more than a century and that gives us a good record to study," said Bilham. The researchers discovered that when the earth's rotation decreased this would be followed by periods of increased numbers of intense earthquakes. The earth's rotation began one of its periodic slowdowns more than four years before their research became available. "It is straightforward," Bilham said. "The inference is clear." In speaking of severe earthquakes, he said, "We could easily have 20 a year starting in

2018."[17] Their research proved close. According to World Earthquakes Live, 2018 was marked by 18 earthquakes that were 7.0 or greater in magnitude.[18]

The United States Geological Survey reported that a record 70 earthquakes had occurred in a 48-hour period, including a magnitude 6.2 earthquake off the coast of Oregon and a magnitude 6.3 earthquake in Alaska. (Three months later, a magnitude 7.1 earthquake struck in Alaska.)[19] This caused scientists to speculate on the "increased seismic activity" along the Ring of Fire, where about 90 percent of the world's earthquakes occur.

Wars and Rumors of War

According to warsintheworld.com, there are 69 countries involved in active conflicts globally at the time of this writing. In Africa, 265 ongoing conflicts are being waged, 181 in Asia, 82 throughout Europe, 260 in the Middle East, and 30 in the Americas (many of these waged against drug cartels).[20] Right now, there are 824 active conflicts being waged around the world. Remember, Jesus called wars and rumors of war part of "the beginning of birth pains."

Nation Rising Against Nation and Persecutions and Killings

In Matthew 24:7 Jesus said that "nation will rise against nation." The Greek word translated "nation" means "a people." A people group will rise against another people group. The Center for the Study of Global Christianity, an academic research center, monitors worldwide demographic trends in Christianity. In a ten-year period, it is estimated that more than 900,000 Christians were martyred, or an average of 90,000 Christians each year. [21]

Christian persecution is worse now than any time in history.[22] More than 70 million Christians have been killed since Jesus walked the earth.[23] According to TRT World, a Turkish international news channel, in a 15-year period, the Christian population in the country of Iraq alone has plunged from 1.5 million to 250,000 today.[24] The Open Doors USA World Watch List reported that in the top 50 countries globally where persecution takes place, an average of 11 Christians are killed every day for their faith.[25] We are told 215 million Christians faced persecution this year, with a projected 14 percent increase next year that represents 30 million more people abused for their faith. This means that 1 in 9 Christians experience high levels of persecution worldwide.[26]

Open Door USA also reports that millions of Christians have been persecuted in Africa and the Middle East, forcing them to flee their homes for refugee camps. In a seven-month period, more than 6,000 Christians, mostly women and children, were killed in Nigeria. Many of the people in these regions have turned against the Christians among them just because of their differing beliefs, and the Christians are killed in horrific acts of genocide. There are too many stories to document them all here, but just as Jesus said, believers will be persecuted, and "nation will rise against nation" as people groups continue to slaughter one another.

Famine

At the time of this writing there are more than 20.7 million people who are starving or at the risk of starving in Yemen, Somalia, South Sudan, and northeastern Nigeria. According to the Center for Strategic and International Studies, "A famine diagnosis means that at least one in five households faces an extreme lack of food, that more than 30 percent of the population is suffering from acute malnutrition, and that at least two people out of every 10,000 are dying each day."[27] According to the World Food Programme, The Global Report on Food Crises provides the latest estimates of severe hunger in the world. "An estimated 124 million people in 51 countries are currently facing Crisis food insecurity or worse."[28] This is an 11 percent rise from the previous year.

The Gospel Being Preached to the Whole World

In a YouTube video message from Israel entitled "Expecting to See Jesus," Bible teacher and author Anne Graham Lotz talked about the preaching of the gospel to the whole world (Matthew 24:14). She said,

> The gospel of Jesus Christ, right now, is being preached
> to the whole world for the first time in history. He (Jesus)

didn't say that everybody in the world would hear it, but that it would be preached to the whole world. Everyone in the world can hear the gospel.

And in an interview with CBN News, Lotz said, "It may not be in their first language, but may be in a second language, or third language…it might not be a live presentation but could be in printed material, through the Internet, the media, ham radio, or even tweeting the gospel; the gospel is going out to the whole world."[29]

CONVERGENCE OF SIGNS

These are just a few of the signs that are all converging at once. Can you sense how things are looking up? When I was a child, I would hear about a natural disaster or fearful event on the news, and then months would go by before I heard of another. My mother, who's in her eighties, has commented frequently that in her lifetime she's never seen so many major things happening all at once. Deception, false prophets, wars and uprisings, earthquakes, nation rising against nation, kingdom against kingdom, and famines are all just the *beginning* of the birth pains signaling the nearness of the end times. I could go on and on, but take a moment to read Matthew 24, Mark 13, and Luke 21, and take note how many of the signs mentioned in these chapters are converging today.

There are people who say that the world has always had floods, wars, hurricanes, persecution, famine, violence, earthquakes, and fearful events. Yes, that's true, but Jesus's words in Matthew 24:33 serve as a trumpet call for anyone with ears to hear, and a great sign for anyone with eyes to see: "*When you see all these things*, you know that he is near, at the very gates" (ESV). As never before in history (with the exception of the still-future abomination of desolation that will occur in the Holy Place, as stated in Matthew 24:15), *all of these signs are now converging*. We are the generation that is seeing these things take place more frequently and with increasing intensity. The tribulation period is casting a long shadow on the remaining days of the church age.

It's easy to become discouraged and overwhelmed by all that is taking place, but according to Jesus, things are looking up: "Now when these things begin to happen, look up and lift up your heads, because your redemption draws near" (Luke 21:28 NKJV). As Jan Markell has said, "Things aren't falling apart. They're falling into place." Remember, God knew the end from the beginning and has a plan!

THE SUPERSIGN

Have you ever wondered why the tiny nation of Israel is always in the news? There isn't space in this book to cover Israel's significance in the end times (we'll dig deeper into that in the books that follow), but many Bible scholars agree that the number one sign, what they refer to as the supersign, that we are ever closer to the return of Christ is the existence of the modern nation of Israel.

Isaiah 66:8 says,

> Who has ever heard of such things?
> Who has ever seen things like this?
> Can a country be born in a day
> or a nation be brought forth in a moment?

Ezekiel prophesied about the dry bones of Israel coming to life, with flesh again, in Ezekiel 37. He saw a valley of dry bones, which represent death. In AD 70, Jerusalem was burned and destroyed by the Romans and the Jews were driven away. The land did not thrive or flourish. It became a wasteland; it was dead, just as Ezekiel and other prophets prophesied.

After nearly 2,000 years of being scattered around the world, beginning in the late nineteenth century the Jewish people began to move back to their homeland in large numbers. This continued for the next few decades, and then it happened. Just as Isaiah prophesied, Israel was "born in a day." On May 14, 1948, Israel became a nation recognized by the UN. The regathering and restoring of the Jewish nation are prophesied in several places in Scripture (Isaiah 43:5-6; Ezekiel 34:11-13; 36:34; 37:1-14; Jeremiah 30:3; Romans 11:25-27), and this fulfillment continues to take place today as even more Jews go back to their land.

Throughout God's Word we learn that He will make the Jews a

nation; He will do the scattering and regathering of them; He will rebuild them; He will cleanse them; and despite their rejection of Him (and despite what many churches teach today about the Jews), God will never reject them. As the apostle Paul said, "God has not rejected His people, has He? May it never be!" (Romans 11:1 NASB). He will do all these things according to His Word; as He says in Ezekiel 36:36, "I the LORD have spoken, and I will do it." Take a moment and read Ezekiel 36, taking note of how many times God said, "I will." God's love for Israel isn't based on the Jews' faithfulness, but on His!

Never in the history of the world has a nation been reborn. There is no ancient civilization that, after being cast out of its land, has ever been regathered and restored to that land to become a nation again. Never. Ever. This was a historic, unprecedented event. The fulfillment of the prophecy in Isaiah 66:8 is absolutely remarkable!

Many people in the world believe the core problem with Israel has been who should control the land, but British journalist, author, and broadcaster Melanie Phillips calls this "historical illiteracy of high order." She states that the Jewish people are "the only people for whom the land of Israel was ever their national kingdom in history. Unfortunately, many in the West who are ignorant of Judaism, of the Bible, of history, and of the Middle East have bought into this [historical illiteracy] in large measure, and they believe it."[30]

WHY IS ISRAEL THE SUPERSIGN?

The reason that the Jewish people's return to their ancient homeland is the supersign is because many end-time prophecies can't be fulfilled without Israel's existence. The people had to be back in their land and become a nation in order for many prophecies to be fulfilled. For example:

- The Antichrist will confirm a seven-year covenant with Israel (Daniel 9:27)

- The Jewish temple will be rebuilt; the first two temples were destroyed and there is currently no Jewish temple in

Israel, but a future one is mentioned in the Bible in Daniel 9:27, Matthew 24:15, 2 Thessalonians 2:3-4, and Revelation 11:1-2

- The Antichrist will invade Israel and desecrate the temple (Daniel 11:40-41; Matthew 24:15-20)

- All the nations will turn against Israel, invading her land (Zechariah 12:1-9; 14:1-2)

Bible scholar John Walvoord says that "few events can claim equal significance as far as Bible prophecy is concerned with that of the return of Israel to their land. It constitutes a preparation for the end of the age, the setting for the coming of the Lord for His church, and the fulfillment of Israel's prophetic destiny."[31]

Walvoord once said that when we see decorations and advertisements for Thanksgiving show up, then we know that Christmas is right around the corner. With all the visible end-time signs converging in the world today we can also anticipate what's around the corner, but it will be better than any Christmas we've ever known! When we see that Christmas is near, we shop, we decorate, we bake, we put special events on the calendar, and we do whatever else must be done to prepare for Christmas Day.

As you see so many end-time signs converging, are you preparing for Christ's return?

DIFFERENT LIVES

In review, our "blessed hope" (Titus 2:13) is Christ coming in the air (the snatching away or rapture) for His bride, the church. It is comforting and encouraging to know that Christ will first raise the dead who are in Him, then He will remove His bride before God's wrath falls against evil.

Look again at 1 Thessalonians 4:16: "The Lord himself will come down from heaven with a loud command, with the voice of the archangel, and with the trumpet call of God. And those who have died believing *in Christ* will rise first" (NCV).

"IN CHRIST"

Why do I keep emphasizing *in Christ*?

A Key Distinction

First, this resurrection of the dead will not include all the dead believers from throughout the centuries, but only those who died during the church age, those who became believers after the Day of Pentecost, when the church was born (see Acts 2). The church didn't exist prior to that.

Old Testament believers did not put their faith in Christ because He hadn't died on the cross yet. They believed on the basis of God's promises to them. Now, those who become believers during the tribulation will put their faith in Christ *after* the catching up of those who are in Christ, so this group will be resurrected at the end of the great tribulation (Daniel 12:1-2; Revelation 20:4). David Reagan explains,

> Some people are startled by the thought that the Old Tes-
> tament saints will not be resurrected until the end of the
> Tribulation. But keep in mind that the rapture (Greek: *har-
> pazo*, emphasis mine) is a promise to the Church, and the
> Church only. Also, the book of Daniel makes it clear that
> the Old Testament saints will be resurrected at the end of
> the "time of distress" (Daniel 12:1-2).[1]

Even Demons Believe

Second, I keep emphasizing *in Christ* because the resurrection of the dead and the great snatching away of believers is not just for any believer, but for those who are in Christ. Many people around the world believe in other gods, many believe in God and might also believe that Jesus is the Son of God, but that doesn't mean that those people are in Christ. That only happens when they place their faith and trust in Christ alone as Lord and Savior.

Jesus says in John 14:6, "I am the way and the truth and the life. No one comes to the Father except through me." We don't make the rules. Jesus said that there is only one way to the Father. Either we believe that Jesus is that only way or we don't, and either Jesus said those words because He is in fact the only way, or because He was insane. We also know that there is more to being in Christ than mere belief. The Bible tells us that even the demons believe:

- "You believe that there is one God. Good! Even the demons believe that—and shudder" (James 2:19).

- "Whenever the unclean spirits saw him, they fell down before him and cried out, 'You are the Son of God'" (Mark 3:11).

Even the demons knew who Jesus was. They had enough knowledge of God to shudder at His power. How many of us shudder and are in awe of His power?

By definition, our culture's "gospel of accommodation" doesn't allow for shudder or awe. Paul pointed out that "if anyone is *in Christ*, the new creation has come: The old has gone, the new is here!" (2 Corinthians 5:17). On his Facebook page, pastor and author Alistair Begg said, "A man or woman should not profess to be a follower of Jesus unless their life is changed by Jesus."

Author Jaquelle Crowe was just a teenager when she wrote,

> Jesus followers don't live like they did before following Him. We don't talk about the same things or read the same books. We no longer dress or act or think the same way. Jesus makes people one hundred percent new. He takes the spiritually dead and makes us thrillingly, beautifully, and abundantly alive. But this is where we encounter a problem. There are people all across our world—from magazine cover celebrities to the soccer mom down the street to perhaps that person who occupies the locker next to yours—who claim to follow Jesus but actually don't. While saying they have hearts devoted to a passionate pursuit of God, they live unchanged lives. Indifferent lives. Lives that blend in, conform to, and meld with the world. Jesus changed nothing in their lives.[2]

This change means that we are to no longer indulge what our flesh desires ("do not use your freedom to indulge the flesh"—Galatians 5:13). If we are truly in Christ, then the Holy Spirit is living inside of us, in constant battle with our flesh. Galatians 5:16-18 says,

> Walk by the Spirit, and you will not gratify the desires of the flesh. For the flesh desires what is contrary to the Spirit, and the Spirit what is contrary to the flesh. They are in conflict with each other, so that you are not to do whatever you want. But if you are led by the Spirit, you are not under the law.

THE SPIRIT AND THE FLESH

This battle between the lusts of the flesh and the Holy Spirit results in one of two things:

- We will no longer practice our sin because we can no longer tolerate it in our lives.

Or

- We quench the leading of the Holy Spirit, our actions telling Him to get out of our lives.

In case there is any confusion, Paul lists the works of the flesh in verses 19-21 of Galatians 5:

> The acts of the flesh are obvious: sexual immorality, impurity and debauchery [debauchery is excessive indulgence of the appetites: lust, drunkenness, sensuality, drug use, sexual immorality]; idolatry and witchcraft [the word translated witchcraft, in the Greek, is *pharmakeia*: "spells and potions, drugs"]; hatred, discord, jealousy, fits of rage, selfish ambition, dissensions, factions and envy; drunkenness, orgies, and the like. I warn you, as I did before, that those who live like this will not inherit the kingdom of God.

Did you read that last verse? Paul doesn't advise us or offer us a tip. He *warns* us, saying that *those who practice these sins will not enter the kingdom of God* (see also 1 Corinthians 6:9-10; Revelation 22:15). If Jesus really lives in us, then we are guided by the Holy Spirit. We want to be more like Jesus and less like ourselves. We want to be drawn closer to Him and away from the sins that entice us and hold us in bondage.

When it comes to the practice of sin, Jim Cymbala said, "If you love God and have been born again, you can't live in that. It's contrary to the Word of God. Those who belong to Christ have crucified the flesh with its passions and desires."[3] Pastor Cymbala referenced Galatians 5:24 when he said those words, and I'll add Galatians 2:20, which says, "I have been *crucified with Christ and I no longer live, but Christ lives in me.* The life I now live in the body, I live by faith in the Son of God, who loved me and gave himself for me."

If we are in Christ, we can no longer live to gratify our flesh. We surrender our fleshly desires. Do we sin? Of course! Even the apostle Paul, in Romans 7, wrote of his own struggles with sin:

> What I want to do I do not do…Although I want to do good, evil is right there with me. For in my inner being I delight in God's law; but I see another law at work in me, waging war against the law of my mind and making me a prisoner of the law of sin at work within me (verses 14, 21-23).

For this reason, Paul says, "Count yourselves dead to sin but alive to God in Christ Jesus. Therefore do not let sin reign in your mortal body…Do not offer any part of yourself to sin" (Romans 6:11-13). We all sin, but there's a difference between a person who turns to God in genuine repentance and desires to avoid sin and a person who actively engages in sin without repentance.

DIFFERENT LIVES

Jesus Himself described what it means to be in Christ:

> I am the vine; you are the branches. If you remain in me and I in you, you will bear much fruit; apart from me you can do nothing. If you do not remain in me, you are like a branch that is thrown away and withers; such branches are picked up, thrown into the fire and burned (John 15:5-6).

If we are in Christ, our lives are different from the world; we deny ourselves the sins that please our flesh as we follow Christ, living surrendered and fruit-bearing lives. If we don't remain in Him, we aren't in Christ, and the chains of enslavement get heavier around our necks as we practice sin. When we don't remain in Christ, we are just like a branch that is pruned and has fallen to the ground, where it withers and dies, and is thrown into the fire. We are nothing more than kindling that goes up in flames.

Hebrews 10:26-27 warns of the consequence of the intentional, habitual practice of sin: "*If we deliberately keep on sinning* after we have received the knowledge of the truth, no sacrifice for sins is left, but only a fearful expectation of judgment and of raging fire that will consume the enemies of God." How can we say that we are in Christ if we keep deliberately sinning without shame? According to Scripture, those who do this aren't God's children but the devil's children (1 John 3:9-10).

If we wrestle with sin, if it plagues us and causes us shame while we're sinning, that's a good thing, because that means the Spirit of God within us is wrestling with our flesh. But if we do not find ourselves wrestling with sin, we're in a dangerous place, and God will give us over to a depraved mind (Romans 1:28), meaning He won't hold us back from what we want. When we persistently rebel against God, He lifts His hedge of protection from around us.

WORTHY TO ESCAPE

Regarding the end of the age, Jesus said in Luke 21:36, "Watch ye therefore, and pray always, that ye may be accounted *worthy to escape* all these things that *shall come to pass*, and to stand before the Son of man" (KJV). Here, Jesus speaks of escaping what is to come. The Greek word translated escape is *ekpheugo*, meaning "to flee out of, to escape."

This same word is used in 1 Thessalonians 5:3: "When people are saying, 'Peace and safety,' destruction will come on them suddenly, as labor pains on a pregnant woman, and they will not *escape*." That is, they won't escape God's judgment. Only believers will be "accounted worthy to escape," as Luke 21:36 says. The word "escape" is used in Acts 16:27 and 19:16 (take a moment and read those verses), but in those instances the Greek translation of escape means "a covering of safety and protection in flight." Do you see the amazing difference? Jesus didn't say that we would have a "covering of safety and protection" during all these things that will come to pass (the New Living Translation says "escape these coming horrors"); He spoke of escaping/fleeing out of what is to come.

Jesus will return, and according to His own words, there is a *worthiness* attached to escaping the things that will come to pass. When He spoke to His disciples about the kingdom of heaven in Matthew 22, He said,

The kingdom of heaven is like a king who prepared a wedding banquet for his son...[The king] said to his servants, "The wedding banquet is ready, but those I invited did not deserve to come. So go to the street corners and invite to the banquet anyone you find." So the servants went out into the streets and gathered all the people they could find, the bad as well as the good, and the wedding hall was filled with guests. But when the king came in to see the guests, he noticed a man there who was not wearing wedding clothes. He asked, "How did you get in here without wedding clothes, friend?" The man was speechless. Then the king told the attendants, "Tie him hand and foot, and throw him outside, into the darkness, where there will be weeping and gnashing of teeth." *For many are invited, but few are chosen* (verses 2, 8-14).

All have been invited into the kingdom, but not all have accepted the King's invitation. Only the worthy, those who are in Christ and wearing wedding clothes, are permitted to stay. Not everyone who claims to be a Christian truly is one. In Matthew 7, Jesus said,

Not everyone who says to Me, "Lord, Lord," will enter the kingdom of heaven, but he who does the will of My Father who is in heaven will enter. Many will say to Me on that day, "Lord, Lord, did we not prophesy in Your name, cast out demons, and in Your name perform many miracles?" And then I will declare to them, "I never knew you; depart from Me, you who practice lawlessness" (verses 21-23 NASB).

Again, there's more to entering the kingdom of God than merely believing in Jesus. That's easy. We must *be in* and remain *in Christ*. That's the mark of a true believer, one who walks a life of surrender. All those who are in Christ will escape the hour of trial that will come upon the whole world and stand before Him in His kingdom.

When Jesus steps into the clouds to snatch up His followers, will He find you *in Christ*?

After Jesus Gathers His Bride

A friend once said that he wasn't making a commitment to Christ now because he felt he could be a leader during the tribulation period and point others to Christ then. But if he isn't willing to live and make a commitment to Christ before the tribulation, then there's little chance he will choose to follow Christ during "the hour of trial that is going to come on the whole world" (Revelation 3:10).

Again, the tribulation will begin when the Antichrist confirms a peace covenant with Israel (Daniel 9:27). He will break that covenant with Israel three-and-a-half years into the seven-year treaty—as Daniel says, "in the middle of the seven," or three-and-a-half years into that time frame. At this time the Antichrist will desecrate the temple in Jerusalem and declare himself to be God (2 Thessalonians 2:4), and this will thrust the world into the final three-and-a-half years of the tribulation, which is known as the *great tribulation*. When Jesus spoke of the abomination of desolation that would take place at the temple, He said, "For then there will be *great tribulation*, such as has not been from the beginning of the world until now, no, and never will be" (Matthew 24:21 esv).

Among the terms used in Scripture to speak of the tribulation are "the time of Jacob's trouble" (Jeremiah 30:7 NKJV), "Daniel's seventieth week" (see Daniel 9:27), "a time of trouble" (Daniel 12:1 NKJV), "the hour of his judgment" (Revelation 14:7), "a day of wrath" (Zephaniah 1:15), "the great tribulation" (Revelation 7:14), "the hour of trial" (Revelation 3:10), and "the day of the Lord" (Revelation 5:2).

WHAT IS THE DAY OF THE LORD?

Concerning the Day of the Lord in Scripture, Mark Hitchcock says, "The Day of the Lord is anytime God intervenes directly and dramatically in history either to judge or to bless."[1]

WHEN IS THE DAY OF THE LORD?

The Day of the Lord isn't one day, but a period of time beginning with the snatching away of all those in Christ and continuing to Christ's second coming, His millennial kingdom on Earth, and the creation of the new heavens and Earth. So the term *the Day of the Lord* doesn't speak of just one particular day, but rather *a period of time, or a season*. It's somewhat like saying, "I remember the day when an ice cream cone was a dime," or "Back in my day…"

Earlier, we looked at 1 Thessalonians 4:13-18, where Paul spoke to the Thessalonians about the snatching away of both dead and living believers in Christ. Then in 1 Thessalonians 5 he talked to them about the Day of the Lord. Keep in mind that this comes *after* the teaching in 1 Thessalonians 4. In chapter 5, Paul referred to two sets of people: believers and unbelievers. You can see this as you read along:

> Now, brothers and sisters, about times and dates we do not need to write to *you*, for *you* know very well that the day of the Lord will come like a thief in the night. While *people* are saying, "Peace and safety," destruction will come on *them* suddenly, as labor pains on a pregnant woman, and *they* will not escape. But *you, brothers and sisters*, are not in darkness so that this day should surprise *you* like a thief. *You* are all children of the light and children of the day. *We* do not belong to the night or to the darkness (1 Thessalonians 5:1-5).

A CLOSER LOOK

Many misunderstand 1 Thessalonians 5:1-5 to mean we can't know the general season of Christ's return because He will come "like a thief in the night" (verse 2). But two verses later we read, "You, brothers and sisters, are not in darkness so that this day should surprise you like a thief. You are all children of the light and children of the day" (verses 4-5). That day won't surprise the believer, the person who is in Christ. Notice how Paul changes personal pronouns from *we* and *you* (representing believers) to *them, they,* and *people* (representing unbelievers).

- When Paul speaks of "them" and "they," he's referring to the sudden destruction that will come on these "people." "They" will not escape the Day of the Lord (verse 3).

- There will be "people" who will talk about "peace and safety" because "they" are in darkness (verse 3).

- The other group—"you" and "we"—know that the Day of the Lord will come as a thief in the night (verse 2).

- Paul says that "you" are "children of light and day" (verse 5).

- "We" don't belong to the night as "they" do (verse 5).

- Others are asleep, not like us, who are awake and sober.

- "You" and "we" are "brothers and sisters" and "children of the light and children of the day" (verses 1, 5).

Two Different Groups of People

First Thessalonians 5 speaks of two different groups of people when it comes to the Day of the Lord:

1. those doomed for sudden destruction who won't escape the tribulation, and

2. the children of light and day, brothers and sisters who don't belong to the night or the darkness

The second group will be ready for Christ's coming. They will have known that things are looking up and would have been waiting, watching, and preparing, and they will be snatched away prior to the pouring out of God's wrath during the tribulation (remember, God hands the scroll to Jesus, and He is the one who opens the seal judgments beginning in Revelation 6:1, beginning the fall of God's wrath).

Not Just Any Wrath

In 1 Thessalonians 5, Paul confirms that believers are not destined for the tribulation when he goes on to say, "For *God did not appoint us to suffer wrath but* to receive salvation through our Lord Jesus Christ... Therefore encourage one another and build each other up, just as in fact you are doing" (verses 9, 11).

And remember Christ's words in Revelation 3:10: "I will also keep you from the hour of trial that is going to come on the whole world to test the inhabitants of the earth." This is good news! Jesus promises to keep His faithful ones, all those who are truly in Christ, from the time of trial that will come upon the entire globe.

In 1 Thessalonians 1:10, Paul encourages us to "wait for His Son from heaven, whom He raised from the dead, even *Jesus who delivers us from the wrath to come*." In the Greek text, the word translated "delivers" means "to draw or snatch out to oneself, to rescue, to save, to preserve." Wow! Before God pours out His wrath in judgment of sin on the earth, He will send Jesus to rescue, save, snatch us away to Himself. Greek scholar Marvin Vincent, the author of *Word Studies in the New Testament*, says the word "deliver" literally means "to draw to one's self" and refers to deliverance from some evil or danger or enemy.[2]

Paul also uses the definite article "the" in 1 Thessalonians 1:10 to indicate that he wasn't speaking in general about God's wrath, but "*the* wrath to come." He was speaking of a specific time of judgment.

ENCOURAGING NEWS

Look at and compare these two scriptures:

> ...the dead in Christ will rise first. After that, we who are
> still alive and are left will be caught up together with them

in the clouds to meet the Lord in the air. And so we will be with the Lord forever. Therefore encourage one another with these words (1 Thessalonians 4:16-18).

He died for us so that, whether we are awake or asleep, we may live together with him. Therefore encourage one another and build each other up, just as in fact you are doing (1 Thessalonians 5:10-11).

1 Thessalonians 4:16-18	1 Thessalonians 5:10-11
The dead in Christ	Asleep
We who are still alive	Awake
Encourage one another with these words	Encourage one another and build each other up

Someday, there is coming a generation of believers who will never walk through the valley of the shadow of death. They will be hard at work, eating dinner, laying in a hospital bed, running drills on a basketball court or football field, shopping for groceries, sitting in a classroom, fishing from a boat, painting their house, laughing with friends, returning books to the library, and simply walking through life when their mortal bodies will be snatched from Earth and made immortal in an instant. This isn't doom-and-gloom or wring-your-hands-together news. It is awesome and encouraging news! Things are looking up with the soon return of Christ, and we must encourage one another with these words.

How Will Believers Be Gathered Up to Jesus?

As a reminder, this snatching up of all those who are in Christ is mentioned in John 14:1-3, 1 Corinthians 15:51-55, and 1 Thessalonians 4:13-18. So that we can better understand how this will happen, let's take a closer look at the 1 Thessalonians 4 passage:

> Brothers and sisters, we do not want you to be uninformed about those who sleep in death…For we believe that Jesus died and rose again, and so we believe that God will bring with Jesus those who have fallen asleep in him. According to the Lord's word, we tell you that we who are still alive, who are left until the coming of the Lord, will certainly not precede those who have fallen asleep. For the Lord himself will come down from heaven, with a loud command, with the voice of the archangel and with the trumpet call of God, and the dead in Christ will rise first. After that, we who are still alive and are left will be caught up together with them in the clouds to meet the Lord in the air. And so we will be with the Lord forever. Therefore encourage one another with these words (verses 13-18).

Here, Paul is addressing the Thessalonian believers who are concerned about their deceased loved ones. In an earlier visit to the Christians in Thessalonica, Paul had taught about the Lord's return. This time around, they have questions as to what would happen to those who had already died. Would they miss out on the Lord's return? Paul didn't want them to be "uninformed" (verse 13), so he explains the Lord's return in steps.

PAUL'S BREAKDOWN OF WHAT WILL HAPPEN

Paul said that if we are alive on Earth at the time of Christ's coming in the air, that "according to the Lord's word," this is what will take place:

1. Jesus Will Step Out of Heaven into the Air

- *With a loud command (verse 16):* Only Christ's sheep will hear that command. Jesus said in John 10:27, "My sheep listen to my voice; I know them, and they follow me." In John 18:37, He said, "Everyone who is of the truth hears My voice" (ESV). Second Timothy 2:19 says, "The Lord knows those who are his." Only Jesus's followers know and believe that what He said in John 14:6 is true: "I am the way and the truth and the life. No one comes to the Father except through me."

- *With the voice of the archangel (verse 16):* Michael is the only archangel specifically named in the Bible (Jude 9), but there appear to be others (Daniel 10:13). At the rapture, the voice of an archangel will be heard.

- *With the trumpet call of God (verse 16):* This is the same trumpet sounded in 1 Corinthians 15:52, when believers will be removed from the earth.

2. Then the Dead in Christ Will Rise

First Thessalonians 4:16 tells us that "the dead *in Christ* will rise first." The spirits and souls of those who have been in heaven will be reunited with their bodies at that very moment.

The phrase "in Christ" lets us know that not just any dead will rise, but only those who had put their faith and trust in Jesus. As mentioned earlier, Old Testament believers will be raised later—they lived before Christ. At the rapture, no matter what condition a corpse is in—whether a grave, an urn, sprinkled remains, or at the bottom of the sea—every person in Christ will be resurrected.

It's hard to wrap our minds around the idea of corpses bursting out of graves, but God has already proven Himself able to raise the dead:

- In John 11:17-44 Jesus called Lazarus from the tomb where he had been laid four days earlier. The Lord was very specific and called out only the name of Lazarus. Otherwise, all the dead inside that tomb would have come racing out of it! Similarly, Jesus will call only those who are *in Him* out of their graves when He steps out of heaven and into the air on that coming day.

- When Jesus died on the cross, the veil in the temple was torn in two from top to bottom, tombs broke open, and "the bodies of many holy people who had died were raised to life." These resurrected people then went strolling through the holy city, appearing to many (Matthew 27:51-53).

- After three days, God raised His own Son from the tomb.

Opening graves and bringing people to life may seem impossible for some to believe, but it's a nonissue for God. The empty graves following the catching up of those in Christ will be a deep, gaping testimony of the true Word of God and the power of Christ.

3. Then Those Who Are Alive Will Be Caught Up

- After that, we who are still alive...will be "caught up" (Greek, *harpazo*) together with them (the dead in Christ who have already been raised) in the clouds (verse 17)

- To meet the Lord in the air (verse 17)
- Then we will be with the Lord forever (verse 17)
- We must encourage one another with these words (verse 18)

Christ's coming for His own isn't a dark and depressing event of which to be terrified. With regard to Jesus's return, Paul said that we must "encourage one another with these words." How could we comfort or encourage each other if this event is horrific and petrifying?

Jesus said in John 14:1, "Do not let your hearts be troubled." He was saying, "If you are one of Mine, you shouldn't be dreading this day or frightened of it." In this topsy-turvy world, it's tempting for us to walk through the day afraid of what's going to happen next. But that's not how those who are in Christ are to live. Jesus said in Luke 21:28, "When these things begin to take place, stand up and lift up your heads, because your redemption is drawing near."

All around us we see the signs of the times taking place, yet we're not supposed to crumple and fold. We're to stand up. We're to lift up our heads. We're to encourage one another. We're to tell people the gospel message because things are looking up; our redemption is drawing near!

WHAT'S NEXT?

The happenings in chapter 41 of this book will be explained in the next book, and I look forward to joining you again so that we can see how God's great plan for the future will unfold, according to Scripture.

WHAT NOW?

I'm so honored you took the time to read *The Time of Jacob's Trouble*. My prayer is that this book has encouraged your faith, answered some nagging questions, or piqued your desire to know more about Christ so you can walk in a personal relationship with Him. If you don't know Him, you can, and upon receiving Him as your Savior and Lord, He will guide and lead you for the rest of your life.

The Bible says,

> If you declare with your mouth, "Jesus is Lord," and believe in your heart that God raised him from the dead, you will be saved. For it is with your heart that you believe and are justified, and it is with your mouth that you profess your faith and are saved. As Scripture says, "Anyone who believes in him will never be put to shame." For there is no difference between Jew and Gentile—the same Lord is Lord of all and richly blesses all who call on him, for,

"Everyone who calls on the name of the Lord will be saved"
(Romans 10:9-13).

God knows our hearts and whether we're truly repentant; He knows when we are honestly seeking Him. If you want to know Him, tell Him that. Tell Him that you believe that He raised Jesus from the dead and proclaim with your mouth that Jesus is Lord, and you will be saved.

St. Augustine said that God gives where He finds empty hands. Would you open your hands today and surrender to Him the sin that has separated you from Him so that He can fill your hands with His good gifts, including the gift of salvation? Would you ask Him to guide and lead your life?

The Time of Jacob's Trouble covers the snatching away by Jesus of all those who are in Him and the days immediately after. We'll explore more of the end times in the next two books. Until then, may God bless you and keep you and make His face shine on you, being gracious to you. May the Lord turn His face toward you and give you peace—in Jesus's name.

THE DAY OF EZEKIEL'S HOPE

The ground shakes beneath the enemy armies; there is no time for them to attack as planned. The earth emits a powerful, ear-splitting moan as mountains are overthrown and cliffs topple, the Wailing Wall crumbles to the ground in Jerusalem and the armies cry out in terror. The quaking grows violent and fissures split the ground open, swallowing thousands of mortified troops into canyon-deep crevices. Smoke, dust, and ash rise as the trembling continues, blinding the troops who remained on the ground. They shout and scream in their many languages, throwing each other into greater confusion. Panic sets in among the throngs of soldiers and they turn their weapons against one another, masses perishing at the hands of their allies. An outbreak of boils covers the once-healthy skin of each soldier and their shouts and violence intensify. Piercing screams of fighter pilots inside their cockpits penetrate the war rooms in Syria and Russia when the painful boils erupt on their skin, curdling the blood of all who are listening. The flesh of every person in the war rooms oozes with ulcers, wrapping their eyes with the raw sores and sealing them shut.

Zerah's heart pounds against his ribs as he watches the heavens open, flooding the skies over Israel's enemies, drowning them in a torrential deluge and beating them with hailstones. As the rain falls, fire pours down on enemy aircraft, surrounding every plane in a massive ball of flame. The entire sky over Israel glows orange and red, the infernos falling and lapping up the enemy armies.

An additional excerpt from Donna's
upcoming 2021 title *The Day of Ezekiel's Hope*
is available at
www.DonnaVanLiere.com/EzekielsHope

NOTES

WHERE IN THE WORD? INTRODUCTION

1. Tom Hughes, "Five Reasons Pastors Don't Teach Bible Prophecy," *Hope for Our Times* (July 10, 2018), https://hopeforourtimes.com/five-reasons-pastors-dont-teach-bible-prophecy-by-tom-hughes/.

2. J.D. Farag in "Before the Wrath: Why There Must Be a Rapture," Olive Tree Ministries, October 19, 2019, https://olivetreeviews.org/radio-archives/before-the-wrath-why-there-must-be-a-rapture/.

3. Renald Showers on *The John Ankerberg Show*, April 17, 2017.

4. Showers, *The John Ankerberg Show*.

5. C.S. Lewis, *Mere Christianity*, Lewis Signature Series, pp. 226-227.

WHERE IN THE WORD? AMAZING FACTS

1. David Reagan, Lamb and Lion Ministries, *Christ in Prophecy TV*, "The Importance of Bible Prophecy," July 5, 2009.

2. Michael Brown, "Have Millions of Christians Been Misled About the Second Coming of Jesus?," *Charisma News* (March 20, 2019), https://www.charismanews.com/opinion/in-the-line-of-fire/75624-have-millions-of-christians-been-misled-about-the-second-coming-of-jesus.

3. Mark Hitchcock, *The End* (Carol Stream, IL: Tyndale House, 2012), p. 9.

4. Hitchcock, *The End*, p. 21.

5. Ron Rhodes on *Understanding the Times* with Jan Markell, April 22, 2017.

6. David Jeremiah, *Agents of the Apocalypse* (Carol Stream, IL: Tyndale House, 2014), pp. 11-12.

7. Ed Hindson on *The John Ankerberg Show*, "The Glorified Jesus Reveals the Future," June 17, 2017.

WHERE IN THE WORD? AMERICA IN THE END TIMES

1. Kathleen Sutcliffe, "The Growing Nuclear Club," *Council on Foreign Relations* (November 17, 2006), https://www.cfr.org/backgrounder/growing-nuclear-club.

2. Mark Hitchcock, *101 Answers to the Most Asked Questions About the End Times* (Sisters, OR: Multnomah, 2001), p. 33.

3. John Walvoord, *The Nations in Prophecy* (Grand Rapids: Zondervan, 1978), p. 175.

4. PBS Newshour, February 16, 2019.

5. Sam Kiley, "No medicines, records or equipment: Haiti hospital struggles during protests," *CNN* (February, 17, 2019), https://www.cnn.com/2019/02/17/americas/haiti-protests-state-university-hospital-intl/index.html.

6. Samuel Smith, "120 people killed, 140 homes destroyed by Nigeria Fulani since February," *The Christian Post* (March 15, 2019), https://www.christianpost.com/news/120-people-killed-140-homes-destroyed-by-nigeria-fulani-since-february.html.

7. "Suspect in New Zealand mosque shootings was prepared 'to continue his attack,' PM says," *CNN* (March 16, 2019), https://www.cnn.com/2019/03/15/asia/christchurch-mosque-shooting-intl/index.html.

8. Joseph A. Seiss, *The Apocalypse: Lectures on the Book of Revelation* (Grand Rapids: Kregel Classics, 2000), p. 161.

9. John Walvoord, *Revelation* (Chicago: Moody Publishers, 2011), p. 141.

10. Robert Jeffress, *Perfect Ending: Why Your Eternal Future Matters Today* (Brentwood, TN: Worthy, 2014), p. 116.

11. David Jeremiah, *Agents of the Apocalypse* (Carol Stream, IL: Tyndale House, 2014), p. 72.

WHERE IN THE WORD? THE END OF THE AGE

1. Ronnie Floyd, "This is the No. 1. cause of death in the world—and it's (almost) 100 percent preventable," *The Christian Post* (January 24, 2019), https://www.christianpost.com/voice/no-1-cause-death-world-100-percent-preventable.html.

2. Melissa Barnhart, "7 states already allow abortion up to birth—not just New York," *The Christian Post* (January 30, 2019), https://www.christianpost.com/news/7-states-already-allow-abortion-up-to-birth-not-just-new-york.html.

3. "'Dark day': Illinois governor signs abortion bill far worse than New York's," *Live Action* (June 12, 2019), https://www.liveaction.org/news/illinois-house-passes-abortion-worse-new-york/.

4. Jessica Chasmar, "One World Trade Center lit pink in celebration of New York abortion law," *The Washington Times* (January 23, 2019), https://www.washingtontimes.com/news/2019/jan/23/one-world-trade-center-lit-pink-celebration-new-yo/.

5. Jim Cymbala, The Brooklyn Tabernacle, "The Anointing," message given October 17, 2017.

WHERE IN THE WORD? AN OUTLINE TO FOLLOW

1. David M. Levy, *Revelation: Hearing the Last Word* (Bellmawr, NJ: The Friends of Israel Gospel Ministry, Inc., 1999), p. 72.

2. Peter Marshall, "Trial by Fire," a sermon preached at the St. Charles Presbyterian Church in New Orleans, Louisiana on March 11, 1944.

3. David Jeremiah, *Jeremiah Study Bible*, NKJV (Franklin, TN: Worthy Books, 2013), p. 1693.

4. Jeff Kinley, *As It Was in the Days of Noah* (Eugene, OR: Harvest House, 2014), p. 77.

5. Mark Hitchcock, *The End* (Carol Stream, IL: Tyndale House, 2012), p. 164.

6. Donald Grey Barnhouse, *Thessalonians: An Expository Commentary* (Grand Rapids: Zondervan, 1977), pp. 99-100.

WHERE IN THE WORD? THE BRIDE OF CHRIST

1. William E. Blackstone, *Jesus Is Coming*, updated edition (Grand Rapids: Kregel, 1989), p. 235.

2. John Walvoord, *Revelation* (Chicago: Moody, 2011), p. 84.

3. Blackstone, *Jesus Is Coming*, p. 22.

WHERE IN THE WORD? WHAT NEEDS TO HAPPEN BEFORE THE SNATCHING AWAY OF BELIEVERS AND THE SECOND COMING?

1. Charles C. Ryrie, *Come Quickly, Lord Jesus* (Eugene, OR: Harvest House, 1996), p. 22.

2. Renald Showers on *The John Ankerberg Show*, April 19, 2017.

3. Stu Weber and Max Anders, *Holman New Testament Commentary: Matthew* (Nashville, TN: Holman Reference, 2000), p. 392.

4. Weber and Anders, *Holman New Testament Commentary: Matthew*, p. 393.

5. "In U.S., Decline of Christianity Continues at Rapid Pace," Pew Research Center, October 17, 2019, https://www.pewforum.org/2019/10/17/in-u-s-decline-of-christianity-continues-at-rapid-pace/.

6. Samuel Smith, "Gen Z Is the Least Christian Generation in American History, Barna Finds," *The Christian Post* (January 24, 2018), https://www.christianpost.com/news/gen-z-is-the-least-christian-generation-in-american-history-barna-finds.html.

7. Michael Lipka, "Millennials increasingly are driving growth of 'nones,'" *Pew Research Center* (May 12, 2015), https://www.pewresearch.org/fact-tank/2015/05/12/millennials-increasingly-are-driving-growth-of-nones/.

8. Gregory A. Smith, "A growing share of Americans say it's not necessary to believe in God to be moral," *Pew Research Center* (October 16, 2017), https://www.pewresearch.org/fact-tank/2017/10/16/a-growing-share-of-americans-say-its-not-necessary-to-believe-in-god-to-be-moral/.

9. Terry James, "End-Times Deceivers," *Rapture Ready*, https://www.raptureready.com/2018/04/22/end-times-deceivers-terry-james/.

10. "Skandalizo," *Blue Letter Bible*, https://www.blueletterbible.org/lang/lexicon/lexicon.cfm?Strongs=G4624&t=kjv.

11. Darren Tyler, "Restoring Your Identity," message given February 17, 2019, Conduit Church, Franklin, TN.

12. Allen Jackson, "God Bless America," message given October 14, 2018, World Outreach Church, Murfreesboro, TN.

13. Jonathan Merritt, "America's Epidemic of Empty Churches," *The Atlantic* (November 25, 2018), https://www.theatlantic.com/ideas/archive/2018/11/what-should-america-do-its-empty-church-buildings/576592/.

14. Jan Markell, "What Happened to My Church?," *Rapture Ready*, https://www.raptureready.com/2018/09/05/happened-church-jan-markell/.

15. From an Instagram post by Jackie Hill Perry in March 2019.

16. "63 Fascinating Google Search Statistics," *Seotribunal.com* (September 26, 2018), https://seotribunal.com/blog/google-stats-and-facts/.

17. "Upsurge in big earthquakes predicted for 2018 as Earth rotation slows," *The Guardian*, https://www.theguardian.com/world/2017/nov/18/2018-set-to-be-year-of-big-earthquakes.

18. "Significant Earthquakes—2019," *USGS*, https://earthquake.usgs.gov/earthquakes/browse/significant.php.

19. "Significant Earthquakes—2018," *USGS*, https://earthquake.usgs.gov/earthquakes/browse/significant.php?year=2018.

20. "List of ongoing conflicts," *Wars in the World*, https://www.warsintheworld.com/?page=static1258254223.

21. "Nearly 1 million Christians reportedly martyred for their faith in last decade," *Fox News* (last update, July 6, 2017), https://www.foxnews.com/world/nearly-1-million-christians-reportedly-martyred-for-their-faith-in-last-decade.

22. Cristina Maza, "Christian Persecution and Genocide Is Worse Now Than 'Any Time in History,' Report Says," *Newsweek* (January 4, 2018), https://www.newsweek.com/christian-persecution-genocide-worse-ever-770462.

23. "70 million Christians martyred for their faith since Jesus walked the earth," https://www.christiantoday.com/article/70-million-christians-martyred-faith-since-jesus-walked-earth/38403.htm.

24. Ash Gallagher, "Christians in Iraq dwindle and struggle to survive," *trtworld* (August 27, 2018), https://www.trtworld.com/opinion/christians-in-iraq-dwindle-and-struggle-to-survive-19772.

25. "World Watch List 2019," *Open Doors USA*, https://www.opendoorsusa.org/wp-content/uploads/2019/01/WWL2019_FullBooklet.pdf.

26. Raymond Ibrahim, "11 Christians Killed Every Day for Their Faith," *Gatestone Institute* (March 3, 2019), https://www.gatestoneinstitute.org/13813/christians-persecuted-killed.

27. Kimberly Flowers, "The Four Famines: The Alarm Bells Are Ringing, but Who Is Listening?," *Center for Strategic & International Studies* (September 6, 2017), https://www.csis.org/analysis/four-famines-alarm-bells-are-ringing-who-listening.

28. "2018 Global Report on Food Crises," *World Food Programme*, https://www1.wfp.org/publications/global-report-food-crises-2018.

29. Mark Martin, "Anne Graham Lotz: I Believe I Will Live to See the Return of Jesus," *CBN News* (April 21, 2016), https://www1.cbn.com/cbnnews/us/2016/april/anne-graham-lotz-i-believe-i-will-live-to-see-the-return-of-jesus.

30. Melanie Phillips on *Understanding the Times* with Jan Markell, May 17, 2017.

31. John Walvoord, *Israel in Prophecy* (Grand Rapids: Zondervan, 1967), p. 26.

WHERE IN THE WORD? DIFFERENT LIVES

1. David Reagan, Lamb and Lion Ministries, *Christ in Prophecy TV*.

2. Jaquelle Crowe, *This Changes Everything: How the Gospel Transforms the Teen Years* (Wheaton, IL: Crossway, 2017), p. 18.

3. Jim Cymbala, "Only Love Conquers All," message given at The Brooklyn Tabernacle, July 30, 2017.

WHERE IN THE WORD? AFTER JESUS GATHERS HIS BRIDE

1. Mark Hitchcock, *The End* (Carol Stream, IL: Tyndale House, 2012), p. 100.

2. As stated in Ron Rhodes, *The End Times in Chronological Order* (Eugene, OR: Harvest House, 2012), p. 43.

ACKNOWLEDGMENTS

I write a book working alone in a room, but a book is never finished alone. It takes a team. *The Time of Jacob's Trouble* would not have been finished and in your hands without the help of…

Our longtime friend Mark Maxwell, who was persistent in contacting publishers, always kind to everyone he talked with, and encouraging to me throughout the wait. This book would not exist without your belief and great efforts, Mark, and I'm grateful for you. Big hug to Carol!

My editor Steve Miller, who is absolutely the best editor for this series. He caught the things I missed, questioned me on things that weren't clear, and was an invaluable source of direction and knowledge. He is steady, wise, gracious, and kind, and *The Time of Jacob's Trouble* could not have been published without his guidance and expertise. Thank you, Steve!

My publisher Bob Hawkins Jr., who has been a champion encourager from day one. This series wouldn't have a home without him and his team's belief. Thank you for looking up, Bob. Your hope is contagious!

Terry Glaspey, who was the first to believe in the manuscript at Harvest House and get it into Steve's hands. Terry, I'm so glad you took Mark's phone call many months ago!

The entire Harvest House team, who have worked with excellence on every aspect of the book, and my friend Barbara McGee, who was a volunteer reader, helping to catch things I missed. Your work isn't overlooked, and I appreciate all of you!

These are just some of my heroes of the faith, who are or have been a voice like John the Baptist, proclaiming Truth in the wilderness and preparing the way for Messiah. Thank you, Oswald Chambers, Francis Chan, Carter Conlon, Jim Cymbala, J.D. Farag, Jack Hibbs, Mark Hitchcock, Thomas J. Hughes, Allen Jackson, David Jeremiah, Carmen LaBerge, C.S. Lewis, Anne Graham Lotz, Jan Markell, Leonard Ravenhill, David Reagan, Ron Rhodes, A.W. Tozer, Amir Tsarfati, Darren Tyler, and David Wilkerson for your books, messages, radio programs, or podcasts that have pointed to the Truth that can only be found in Christ.

Enormous thanks to my family, who make me want to be a better mom, wife, daughter, and friend.

And I love and am grateful for eternity to the One for whom I'm looking up and saying, "Come, Lord Jesus!"

Does Bible prophecy often leave you confused and frightened? You're not alone. There are some strange and mystifying Bible passages that have bewildered generations of Christ-followers. Many aspects of Bible prophecy could never be understood by our parents and grandparents simply because the signs of the end times had not yet become apparent.

But did you know that the meanings of many of these same Bible verses are being revealed before our very eyes? It is our generation that is seeing end-time prophecies being fulfilled.

Join Donna VanLiere and listen to her free podcast *Things Are Looking Up*, in which she shares significant and specific prophecies that only our generation has been able to understand, and discusses the very real connection between Bible prophecy and our world today.

www.DonnaVanLiere.com/LookingUp

To learn more about Harvest House books and
to read sample chapters, visit our website:

www.harvesthousepublishers.com

HARVEST HOUSE PUBLISHERS
EUGENE, OREGON